STORM OF STARS

PRIDE OF PRAXIS DUET
BOOK 2

NIKKI ROBB

CONTENT WARNINGS

Storm of Stars is an adult dystopian MMFFM why-choose novel, that includes and alludes to sensitive topics such as governmental corruption, blood, death, including death of elderly and children, family member with a degenerative illness, deadly competition, loss of limbs (in secondary characters), fire, burns, surgery, blood transfusions, gun violence, mention of death by suicide (not on page) murder, kidnapping, graphic sexual descriptions, and torture.

ISBN: Paperback: 978-1-964036-14-4

ISBN: Hardback: 978-1-964036-16-8

This novel is a work of fiction. Any similarities to real people and events are entirely coincidental.

Cover and Interior design by Nikki Robb

Cover Background Attribution: a href="https://www.vecteezy.com/free-photos/gold-marble">Gold Marble Stock photos by Vecteezy</a

To the readers who want some feminine rage and overthrowing corrupt governments, with a healthy dose of smut.

PART ONE

THE REBELS

PROLOGUE

BEX

THE DOWNSIDE to a memory like mine is that I often relive the worst moments of my life in bright, vivid clarity. In the middle of the night, sometimes instead of dreams, my mind will cycle through the greatest hits of my darkest moments.

My mother's death.

My brother's illness.

Ava's family's devastation.

It doesn't come gently.

It rushes in sharp and sudden, stuck in a loop. Her face. His hands. Their cries. The sound of someone screaming... me, probably. I don't always remember that part right away.

And when it hits, it feels like I'm back there again. Like no time has passed at all.

People think memory is a gift. But it isn't. Not always. Not when it's this sharp. Not when it cuts both ways.

Because when you remember everything, you don't get to move on from anything. You just carry it forward.

All of it.

And I do.

I carry those moments like a wound that never scabs over. Like pain that no one can see.

But maybe that's why I've never felt comfortable in the skin Praxis forced me to wear. Maybe it's because no matter how many glittering veils they drape over their violence, no matter how many smiles they stretched across hollow faces, I could still see it. I can't unsee it. The death. The destruction. The devastation. The names of every person who'd ever lost their life in the Reclamation Run.

I remember what they tried to bury. I remember what they want scrubbed from history. I remember that for every gleaming gift Praxis offers, they take something greater in return.

Maybe, at first, all I felt was sorrow. Grief. Regret. A mourning for the world I thought I knew.

But it's different now.

Now, I've seen the truth with my own eyes. I've watched the light leave someone's face. I've laid awake, night after night, replaying it. The blood. The silence. The blind adoration.

They cheer for our deaths like it's a game. They celebrate loss and call it entertainment. They hold resources over our heads and call it reclamation. They call us heroes and send us to die.

And somewhere inside me, something broke. Something small at first. A crack. A shift.

A whisper of rage threading through the sadness. Now it's more than sorrow. Now, it's fire.

There's a darker anger rising in me. Something that doesn't tremble or apologize.

A spark of something dangerous. And for the first time in my life...

I think I'm ready to let it burn.

CHAPTER ONE

ZAFFIR

AFTER THORNE'S potentially treasonous declaration, we'd all gathered in the living room, the air thick with tension. Thorne and Briar claimed the chairs across from the couch where Brexlyn and I sat, and Ezra lingered in the back, a storm barely contained, leaning against the doorframe like it was the only thing keeping him from tearing the walls down.

They were shocked when they saw the state of me. I didn't blame them. I would be too. Even Briar, who was not my biggest fan, seemed to vibrate with worry and anger for me.

That was a pleasant shift. Not that I blamed her for her wariness toward me, considering who I was and where I was from.

I sat in front of them, my ribs still aching, voice raw from hours of pain and screams I wouldn't give voice to now. Brexlyn was tucked into my side, her hand gripping mine like she thought I might disappear again if she let go. The weight of her pressed against me sparked a sting where my body was still tender, but it soothed something deeper, filling spaces in my soul no pain could ever reach. Thorne's arms were crossed, but his eyes were soft. Briar leaned forward on the edge of the couch, a crease between her brows. Ezra stood across the room, like if he got any closer he'd lose every ounce of restraint.

"What happened, Zaffir?" Briar asked.

I nodded slowly and forced a breath into my lungs. "The interview ended and I went to go upload my footage to the server. I slipped into the production office, but it had been cleared out."

"And that's when they took you?" Thorne asked, voice low.

"Yeah," I said. "Guards were waiting. They grabbed me before I even saw them coming. Dragged me straight to Veritas."

I tried to keep my voice even, measured. "She said a lot of things about me not being motivated enough to do my job right. Said she'd have to try harder to inspire me."

Brexlyn turned in closer, her free hand resting lightly on my chest now. "What did she do to you?"

I hesitated.

"She—" My voice snagged. "She made sure I knew what it would cost if I defied her."

There was a beat of silence, the air sharp with it.

"Zaffir," Brexlyn whispered, her voice so soft it ached. "Please. Tell us."

Her eyes met mine, wide, glassy, and terrified. I felt her pulse in her fingers. I felt the tremble in her body she tried to hide. And I knew, if I told her everything, every detail etched into my skin and memory, *she* would carry it longer than I ever would.

She'd file it away, just like she had everything else.

So I shook my head, slowly. "No. Not to you."

"Why?" she whispered.

I touched her cheek gently, brushing away a tear she hadn't realized had fallen. "Because you'll see it every time you look at me. And I need you to remember me like *this*. Alive, holding you. Not like that."

Her lip trembled, but she didn't argue. She just curled into me tighter.

She never directly told me about her memory. But I've spent a lot of time watching people. And after scrubbing through every second of her trial footage, I started to notice it. The way her eyes tracked things, how she hesitated just a beat before speaking, like she was flipping through a mental filing cabinet.

It wasn't obvious at first. But the more I watched, the more I realized—her brain worked differently. Sharper. Faster. That's why I took the gamble and showed her that image of the filtration system. I didn't know if she'd be able to memorize it. I just had a gut feeling. And it worked. She locked it in like it was nothing. Like she'd seen it a hundred times. That's when I knew. So no, I wasn't going to recount my torture in any more detail than needed, because I don't want that image to be glued to her mind whenever she thought of me.

I pressed a kiss to the top of her head, breathing her in. "I'm okay," I said softly. "I'm here now."

Ezra hadn't spoken once. But I could feel him watching me like I was a grenade about to go off. His jaw was locked tight, one muscle twitching. His hands were fists at his sides, knuckles white.

When I finally went quiet, when there was nothing left to say without splintering, he turned without a word and stalked down the hall.

Brexlyn stirred against me, lifting her head. "I'll go," she whispered, already starting to push herself up.

But I stopped her, pressing a hand to her shoulder. "Let me," I murmured.

She gave a small nod, settling back as I forced myself to my feet, every bruise and cracked rib a fresh reminder of the night before. I followed him down the hall.

When I pushed open the door, Ezra was pacing, a caged animal barely holding it together. His eyes, when they landed on me, were molten.

"It's okay, Ezra," I whispered.

"They almost killed you," he ground out, his voice low, scraped raw by fury.

I swallowed hard, wincing as the split in my lip tugged. "They didn't."

"But they will," he spat, raking a hand through his hair. "They're coming for you, and they're coming for Bex. And you're just sitting there acting like it's nothing."

I closed the door behind me. "It's not nothing."

"Then why the hell are you acting like it is?"

"Because we can't afford to fall apart right now."

Ezra's fist lashed out, slamming into the wall. The crack of it split the air, plaster splintering under his knuckles. His face was so close to mine now that I could see the wild glint in his eyes, the flicker of something raw and wounded beneath the rage.

"Bullshit," he hissed. "They laid hands on you. Veritas..." His voice broke around her name. "I should've been there. I swear to God, Zaf, I'll burn Praxis to the ground for what they've done."

And damn me, some twisted part of me wanted that. Wanted to watch him tear the world apart in my name.

"I want that too," I whispered, my voice frayed and small. "But not yet, Ez."

His brow knit, his fury colliding with confusion. "Why not? What are we waiting for? Just say the word."

And God, he meant it. I could feel it in every fiber of him, in the space between us. That bone-deep promise.

I reached out, fingers wrapping around his wrist before he could pull away. His hand was bleeding, knuckles split, skin hot under mine. I let my thumb trace the sharp line of bone, and watched his breath catch.

"Because Bex needs you standing," I said, voice barely a breath. "Not broken. Not reckless. Not dead." I breathed. "We both do."

His gaze dropped to where my hand held his, his other fist slowly uncurled at his side.

"I can't lose anymore family," he murmured, the words catching in his throat.

For a long, aching moment, I didn't speak. Then something between us shifted, softened. He leaned in, and our foreheads touched, the lightest, ghosting brush of skin.

"You're not going to," I whispered. A quiet, desperate vow that reached inside and wrapped around something in me I hadn't even realized was bleeding.

I closed my eyes, let myself have that second of peace. The warmth of him. The weight of the moment. The fragile, fierce thing blooming between us that neither of us dared name yet.

When he finally pulled back, the rage in his eyes had cooled, tempered into something sharper. Protective.

When Ezra and I returned to the living room, we came shoulder to shoulder, an unspoken solidarity settled between us. I dropped carefully back into my spot on the couch, ribs screaming with every movement, my skin a patchwork of bruises, but it didn't matter. Not now.

Brexlyn looked up the moment I sat down, her eyes finding mine. She gave me a soft, knowing smile, the kind that didn't need words. Like she saw what I couldn't quite say out loud yet, like she'd always known that Ezra was more than just another Challenger to me. That he meant something.

Ezra settled onto the couch beside me, his thigh brushing against mine, and for the first time since the nightmare of last night, it felt like the room had steadied. Brexlyn curled against my other side, her head tucking gently against my shoulder. Between them, I could finally breathe, even if it hurt like hell.

THORNE

THE QUIET STRETCHED, thick and suffocating, pressing in on all sides like the walls themselves were leaning closer to hear. No one moved, no one breathed too loud.

Then I cleared my throat, and it sounded too loud in the tense stillness. I glanced around at the people in front of me, shoulders tight, a fire burning in my chest that hadn't dimmed since my childhood.

"So…" Zaffir started, my voice cutting through the heaviness. "Should we talk about what you said, Thorne?"

I swallowed heavily.

"What did you say?" Briar asked, turning to me.

I breathed in, trying to find the courage to speak the words that had come so easily just a few minutes ago. "I said we should fight back against Praxis," I said finally.

Briar let out a sharp, bitter breath, like the words physically pained her. She dragged both hands down her face, her jaw working, and when she spoke, it was with a sharpness meant to wound. "People don't rebel against Praxis, Thorne.

Not without paying for it in blood. I mean, look at Zaffir."
Her gaze cut to the redheaded cameraman for a brief, weighted
second, then back to me. Like she was begging me to
remember something. Like she was willing me to recall the
pain, I would never forget. "You *know* what happens to
anyone who so much as whispers the wrong thing. They
disappear. They get erased." She turned in a slow circle,
gesturing to the rest of the room. "And you wanna invite that
kind of hell on everyone in this room? On yourself?"

The room fell silent again, the unspoken things pressing
in.

"Someone needs to do it," I said, voice low but unflinching. "If not us, then who? The people out there waiting for
Praxis to deem them worthy of basic needs? Another Collective too scared to use their voice? How long are we supposed
to survive like this before surviving isn't worth it anymore?"

"You think we've got what it takes to do what nobody else
has ever been able to accomplish? What people have died for
even suggesting?" Briar snapped, her composure cracking as
she stepped closer, eyes flashing.

"Because we do!" I replied.

"You think we're different because we've got a couple of
wins under our belts and a handful of fans? Praxis doesn't care
about your fame, Thorne. Or your support. Or your goddamn
sense of justice. They will break you just like they broke
everyone else."

"Why are you so afraid?" I fired back.

Briar's jaw clenched, her hands balling into fists at her
sides. "Because everything you're saying right now," she bit
out, voice tight and cracking at the edges, "is exactly what got
Ma killed!"

The words hit like a slap. The room shifted, air growing
heavier, every pair of eyes locking onto the two of us like the
rest of the world had disappeared. Brexlyn inhaled sharply. She

looked like she was desperate to come to us, but she knew this was a conversation we needed to hash out on our own.

Briar swallowed hard, her shoulders rising with a ragged breath. Her voice dropped, rough and raw. "Did you forget, Thorne? Did you forget how fast they came for her after she spoke out. How they stormed into our home, and tore it apart. How they dragged her from us like she was nothing." Her voice broke on the last word. "Because I'll never forget it."

My breath hitched, and grief flickered through the defiance in my soul, but I didn't step back. Didn't back down. "Of course, I remember, Bry," I said softly, and there was a pain in my chest that made my throat tighten. "I remember every goddamn second. I remember the screams. I remember the blood. I remember what they did to her body after, to make sure everyone else stayed afraid."

I didn't need Brexlyn's magic memory to pull that image to the forefront of my mind. It haunted me every moment.

"You think I haven't carried that with me every day since?" I stepped closer, close enough that I could almost see my reflection in her eyes. Like two halves of the same storm. "But I also remember what she said before they took her. That it wasn't enough to survive. That we had to live for something." My voice hardened, and my gaze locked with Briar's.

Briar shook her head, blinking back tears she refused to let fall. "And you think she wanted you to die too? You think she wanted both of us to follow her down like martyrs? Because that's what this is, Thorne. It's suicide."

"I don't care," I growled, closing the last bit of space between us. "I'd rather die for something than keep breathing for nothing."

The air in the room cracked with the weight of it, the ghost of our mother's fate lingering like a curse and a promise.

"I didn't forget what happened to her, Briar," I said, softer now, voice thick. "I just refuse to let her sacrifice mean nothing."

And no one else said a word. Because what could you even say to that?

The air was thick with grief and fury, years of pain compressed into this one moment. Briar's lip quivered, her eyes burning, a storm trapped behind them. "People die when they defy Praxis. You will die. We all will."

I didn't flinch.

"She left us something," I said, his voice low but certain, then glanced over at the battered and bruised cameraman. "Zaffir... can I use your computer?"

He nodded without hesitation, wincing as he reached for his bag beside the couch. The weight of it clearly tugged at his battered ribs, but he ignored the pain and slid the laptop free, passing it to me.

Brexlyn's brow furrowed as I booted it up, the faint blue glow of the screen painting my face in ghostly light. "What are you talking about?" she asked quietly.

I didn't answer at first, as my fingers moved with sharp, practiced precision as I navigated through tabs and files. I'd cracked this code dozens of times, but it was designed to require complete focus. That's how it remained so hidden.

When I finally found my way in, I turned the screen toward the others. "This," I began, "is an encrypted thread. A resistance. They call themselves the Runaways. They're fighting for the disbandment of the Reclamation Run. They want to tear down Praxis."

Ezra's brows lifted, his scowl breaking just enough for a flicker of cautious hope to shine through. "I didn't even know something like this existed."

"I think that's the point," I said with a smile.

Brexlyn leaned forward, her curiosity blooming across her

face. She scrolled through the message board, eyes skimming over post after post. "There's... hundreds of messages here."

"Thousands," I corrected softly. "People from every Collective with the technology to support it. And there's in-person Runaway chapters in every Collective, technology or not. Even a good number from within the gates of Praxis itself. People who've lost family, who've watched their friends dragged into the Run and never come back. People who are angry. People who are done being afraid."

Ezra let out a low whistle, dragging a hand through his hair. "And no one knows about them?"

"Neither did I," I admitted, a crooked, bitter smile tugging at my mouth. There was no humor in it, only old pain and sharper memories. "Not until after they took Ma."

Briar sucked in a breath.

"When they stormed the house, tearing everything apart, she slipped me this card." My voice hitched just a little. "Told me it was the key to a new Nexum. Said to keep it close. Told me that not every story needed to have a bad ending."

Slowly, I reached into my pocket, pulling out a small, battered piece of plastic. It was the size of an old ID card, the edges worn soft by years of handling. The ink was faded, barely clinging to the surface like it was holding onto its last breath.

I held it between two fingers, my thumb brushing over a worn symbol in the corner. My mind was flashing to the moment she handed it to me. And everything that came after. "There was a coded message on the back," he went on, his voice quieter now. "It didn't make a damn bit of sense at first. Took me a few weeks... once the grief stopped swallowing me whole. But when I cracked it, when the pattern clicked, it led me here."

Briar was quiet, but her gaze stayed fixed on the screen,

lingering like a woman who desperately wanted to believe but didn't know how.

Ezra's arms were crossed, his jaw tight as he spoke. "Okay... but what's this got to do with us actually fighting back? People complain and argue in secret corners all the time. Doesn't mean they're willing to put action to their words in the light of day."

I didn't flinch at the challenge. Instead, I clicked through the screen, my jaw tight, until I landed on a single image.

A photo. Of the Wildguard.

A name that Zaffir helped coin to draw up support.

The four of us, bloodied and broken, standing side by side at the end of the Transportation Trial. Our faces streaked with sweat, dirt, and blood, eyes burning with something raw. Like fury or defiance. They all stared at the photo. Above us, someone had added the words, *For the will of the people. We survive.*

Beneath the image, a flood of comments. Thousands upon thousands of messages from anonymous profiles.

They're the rebels we need to finally take Praxis down.

If anyone can stop the Run, it's Wildguard.

We need them to stand up and fight.

They have the power to rally the people.

I should have known the Grey twins would be a part of the movement.

I'd been watching from the sidelines for years, quiet, cautious, never brave enough to actually join in. But I saw things. Little patterns that started to stand out once you knew what to look for.

There was one symbol that kept showing up all over the site. It was in the margins of long, frantic posts. Hidden in usernames and message tags. Even in the corners of blurry, shadowed photos. A single moth.

It was their mark, the sign of the Runaways. Of the rebellion nobody dared to speak of out loud. People talked about slipping it into conversations like a secret code. Leaving it behind like a trail for the desperate and the defiant. Scratched into walls, painted behind loose bricks, scribbled on scraps of paper passed from hand to hand.

The moth symbolizes change, transformation...growth. It means overcoming the darkness and finding the light.

Brexlyn's fingers hesitated over the trackpad, her voice a soft thread of sound in the still room. "If this is real... if we're not alone in this..."

"We're not," I said, steady and sharp. "Not even close."

The room felt different then. Like maybe, just maybe, the walls Praxis had built around us weren't as unbreakable as we thought.

But then, Zaffir spoke up. "Ezra is right though, there's a difference between hiding behind an anonymous profile and standing in the street with your head held high. If you lead... how can we be sure that they'll follow?"

Brexlyn looked up at us, something fierce in her gaze now. "Maybe we need to get them to trust us. Prove to them that we're willing to take the risk, and then maybe they will be too."

"How?" Ezra asked, his voice sharp, wary but needing an answer.

Brexlyn scrolled through the threads, her eyes taking in the thousands of messages that all spoke to a better life.

"We use their code," she said quietly, and we all turned to look at her. "This entire message board is full of coded messages. Symbols and phrases... So, let's use it. Let them know we see them. That we're one of them. We build momentum, build the following. Show them we're ready."

"And then," I added, a grim smile tugging at my lips, "when the time is right..."

"We strike," Brexlyn finished, her voice sure and steady.

I nodded, the unspoken words heavy between us.

"Ma was a part of this?" Briar's voice cracked around the question, her eyes flicking over the screen, skimming the messages, the rallying cries in the comments.

"Yeah" I said quietly, reaching for the computer. I scrolled through the thread until I found the post I'd saved. The post I found a few years ago, and haven't been able to go a few days without looking at since. The post that changed everything for me. "But she didn't just join it... she started it."

I turned the screen toward them, and there she was, a woman with features so unmistakably familiar, yet so distant, it punched the air right out of my lungs. The same sharp cheekbones as Briar, the same dark, defiant eyes as me. In a sea of anonymous profiles, there she was, clear as day. In the photo, she stood on a cracked, sun-bleached road, one fist raised high above her head, her face a storm of fury and unwavering resolve.

Beneath the image was a message. A post. The beginning of it all.

Briar's voice trembled as she read it aloud.

"Today I watched as yet another child was killed in the pursuit of resources that should be basic human needs. Today is also the day I start fighting back. For me. For my children. For the future I believe in. Maybe there's ten other people who feel the same, or maybe there's millions. But today I stop letting Praxis get away with it without opposition. I am a Runaway."

Her voice faltered, catching on the weight of the words.

I picked up where she left off, my voice low but steady, like it was something I'd recited a hundred times in my head. Because it was.

"Join me... and may the stars shine on us again."

The room was heavy with silence for a long, aching beat.

Then Briar let out a shuddering breath, her hand coming up to wipe at the tears streaming down her cheeks.

"She started it," she whispered, a tremor in her voice. "Ma started the resistance."

I nodded, my anger softening with a mixture of pride and grief. "She knew what she was risking. Knew Praxis would kill her if they found out. But she did it anyway. Because someone had to."

Briar let out a quiet, broken laugh, brushing away another tear. "She always did tell us to stop waiting for someone else to fix things."

"She believed in a better world," I said, closing the laptop gently. "And so do I."

Bex reached out and squeezed Briar's hand and they shared a silent but intimate moment.

"So," I said, my voice breaking the thick quiet of the room as I glanced at Briar, "can we do this?"

The air felt heavier then, like it pressed in around us, waiting for someone to flinch, to back out. We glanced at each other, each of us weighing what we stood to lose against what we might win.

I looked at Brexlyn.

"It's a risk," Briar said. "A huge one." Her voice dropped to a rough whisper. "One that might keep us from ever making it home to the people waiting for us." Her meaning was clear as she glanced at Brexlyn.

Jax.

I saw it in the way her brow tightened, the flicker of grief and fire in her eyes as she turned to look at him. The kind of grief that doesn't fade, only buries itself deep enough you can pretend it isn't there until a moment like this.

"My brother is dying. He has been for a long time. If I win the medical trials," Brexlyn said, her voice low but sharp-edged, "Jax will probably survive another year. Maybe two, if we're lucky. But then Praxis will tear the medicine out of our hands again, drag the doctors away, and make me watch him fall apart all over again... just in time for the next poor bastard to be forced into this archaic ritual."

She swallowed hard, and there was no fear in her eyes now, only fury. Only certainty.

"Winning the trials won't save him. It'll only delay his death. The only way my brother lives... is if Praxis dies."

The words settled over us like a war drum's beat.

"Bry, please." I gripped my sister's hands in mine. "Let's finish what Ma started."

After a few achingly long moments, Briar pulled me into an embrace and the room collectively took a breath.

A sharp ache bloomed in my chest as I whispered, "By the will of the people."

Briar met my gaze, voice sure and steady. "We survive."

CHAPTER
THREE

BEX

THE REBELLION STARTED SLOWLY, as I think most rebellions do.

In those early mental trials, we each tried to sneak in one or two of the phrases we'd found while scouring the encrypted pages of the Runaways' hidden site late at night. Words and phrases that would seem meaningless to anyone who wasn't looking for them. Little signals to prove you were paying attention, that you were one of them.

We agreed to fold them into casual conversation, careful to keep them light, to brush past them quickly so no one who wasn't listening would notice. It was dangerous, every word we spoke could lead to our execution if just one person who understood the meaning let Praxis know. But we did it anyway.

During the tools and materials mental trial they stuck us in a half-collapsed building, dust clogging the air, and set us loose to solve math problems and number puzzles scrawled on walls, old blueprints, and crumbling ledgers. Each solution unlocked one of the battered lockers scattered through the building. The right combination of tools inside was supposed to defuse a live bomb they'd wired into the floorboards.

Thorne made it look easy, his mind sharp, practiced, faster than anyone I'd ever seen. He solved those equations like they were child's riddles and walked out of there with first place so fast it left the rest of us scrambling. Briar managed to hang on, placing in the top five. Ezra and I both finished in time to stop our bombs from going off, thank God, but didn't place high enough for resources.

When Zaffir interviewed Thorne after, all grins and shining teeth for the cameras, he asked how it felt to take the win. And Thorne, never missing a beat, leaned on the railing, flashed a crooked grin and said, "You know, math's always been a bit of a natural thing for me. Me and numbers, we're like this." He intertwined his index and middle finger for the camera. "Like a moth to a flame, ya know?"

It sounded harmless enough. A clever turn of phrase for the cameras. But those of us who knew, who were watching, listening, we knew what he'd meant. The moth. The Runaways had claimed it as their token.

After that trial, the secret message boards had run wild with theories that we were in on the rebellion. But there were still some doubts.

The electricity trial was a nightmare. A sprawling power grid puzzle, with a single legend posted at the entrance of the plant. A map of the proper connections and sequences. Once you crossed that threshold, though, it was gone. No second chances to study it. No helpful reminders.

Easy enough for me. So I was able to lead my team through it quickly and easily. Devrin was locked in too, laser-focused, his brow furrowed in determination. I remembered Briar mentioning this was the one he'd been gunning for. Said it was the trial that mattered most to him, the one he wouldn't let himself lose.

For a moment, I considered beating him so soundly in this trial he'd carry the sting of it for years. Just to remind him how it felt to lose. To be helpless. To be trapped. Like I had been, back in those flooded canals. But then, just as fast, I let it go. Because no matter how stupid, reckless, or selfish Devrin could be, he wasn't the one who'd sent me into the canals in the first place.

And he sure as hell wasn't my real enemy.

So when I saw him reaching for the wrong coupling, a connection that would've lit him up like a goddamn torch, I called out. "Left one," I said, voice sharp but even.

His eyes snapped to mine, wary, distrustful. "Why the hell should I trust you?" he spat. "You're probably hoping I fry."

I shook my head. "Not all stories need bad endings," I told him, the words soft but pointed, a phrase from the boards, a message the Runaways had used. What Thorne's mother had said to him as she was dragged from their home. It was a reminder that we didn't have to let Praxis write the last chapter.

His expression twisted, caught somewhere between suspicion and something heavier. He looked like he wanted to fight me on it. Then, slowly, he switched to the coupling I'd pointed out. The grid whirred to life, a clean, perfect connection.

He shot me a tight, wordless nod before moving on.

Devrin won the trial. And we let him, much to my crew's irritation. Briar and Thorne looked like they could chew glass. Ezra was already mentally preparing his revenge. But I shot them a look to remind them what really mattered.

The week continued on at that relentless pace. Two trials a day, every day. No breaks, no mercy. Weapons. Solar. Air Filtration. Technology. Agriculture. Sanitation. Education.

Each one was designed to test us, to whittle us down, to see who cracked under pressure, who faltered, who the crowd would mourn and who they'd forget by the time the next challenge began.

The more mentally focused trials didn't stack bodies the way the physical ones did, but death still came, quieter, crueler, and often avoidable if Praxis had cared to make it so. By the end of the week, three more names had been crossed off the board.

The Horizon Collective's elected, a wiry kid named Callen, died during the electricity trial. One wrong connection, one misread coupling, and the surge hit him hard enough to drop him where he stood. The room smelled of scorched cloth and copper after they pulled him out.

Stormwatch's chosen succumbed next from the aftermath of the solar trial. The prolonged exposure to solar energy left her blistered and delirious as she couldn't create the shield quick enough. By morning, she was gone.

And Nellie Fulton from Oasis was killed during the sanitation trial. Tasked with creating a working sanitizer formula from scattered, unlabeled supplies, she picked the wrong combination. It wasn't an instant death. The formula spread contamination instead of neutralizing it, and within hours, infection took hold.

Nobody died during the education trial, thank God. For once, it was nothing more than a written exam, no traps, no sabotage, no sudden-death. Just a simple little test on the history of Praxis and the so-called 'Reclamation' of Nexum. Except it didn't feel like history. It felt like propaganda disguised as education.

Questions like, *"Why was Praxis forced to take control of Nexum and its resources?"* and *"How long has Praxis been generously caring for the Collectives?"* littered the page, each one more nauseating than the last. It was indoctrination.

Once I swallowed the bile rising in my throat, I forced my hand to move, giving them exactly the answers they wanted. Lies dressed up as history. Stories written by the victors.

In the end, my compliance earned me third place.

Not that it mattered much. I wasn't sure any of us were going to survive the end of this Run, or what would be left of Nexum when it was over. But if our rebellion didn't catch fire the way we hoped, if we failed here at the heart of everything, at least our Collective would have a year of education secured.

Although, what kind of education would they really be getting? A watered-down curriculum, scrubbed clean of the real truth, the brutal, bloody history of our country rewritten into a neat little fable. A glossy package where Praxis stood tall as the righteous, benevolent savior, while the death, the blood, the staggering loss they caused was buried beneath layers of lies.

Maybe an education curated by an overreaching government was worse than no education at all.

Now, only nine of us were left. More than half the contestants in this brutal, twisted game were gone, some with resources won for their collectives, others with nothing but blood and silence to mark their exit.

And with every name crossed off the roster, the balance shifted. My team... we were still standing. Stronger than most. It meant that we nearly outnumbered the remaining Challengers now.

We could feel it in every glance, every tense silence. I saw them watching us carefully, like they were studying our every move. Maybe they didn't trust us. Didn't like us. We'd become the threat lurking in the room, the alliance to watch, to fear, to despise. I found myself often wondering how close they were to open sabotage. Of banding together, not because they believed in each other, but because taking us down felt like their only shot at surviving what came next.

Zaffir hadn't heard from the Archon since the night he was taken. None of us had. And even though we kept a brave face for the cameras, for the others, and for ourselves, there was a thread of unease wound tight through every one of us.

We were careful. So careful. Zaffir and I. Not a glance too long, not a brush of fingers, not a single word exchanged outside the house unless it was part of the Run or the necessary interviews. Even at home, we kept our distance when Nova came by, which was unfortunately very frequently. She'd stay past her welcome, rattling off what we needed to know about upcoming trial schedules. Every night she was there, eyes sharp and grinning all teeth, and every night I pretended not to ache for him.

And I did ache. I was starting to miss him in a way that was bigger than the walls we'd built between us. Not just the feel of his hand in mine or the warmth of his body close to mine in those stolen moments we used to allow ourselves. I missed the way his eyes met mine like we were always in on the same secret, even when no one else could see it.

I had my other Wildguard, and they were there for me offering touches, soft words, stolen moments of warmth I clung to like a lifeline. I let them comfort me, let their affection ease the weight on my chest. But no matter how tightly I held on, it felt... incomplete. Hollow. Because as long as there was distance between me and Zaffir, something in me remained restless. Like a piece of my soul was missing from this little circle we'd built. And no matter how much I wanted to sink into the comfort of the others, it didn't feel right when I couldn't have all of them. When I couldn't have him.

So when we finally dragged ourselves home after the final trial of the week-long gauntlet and were at the start of a rare break on the schedule before whatever new hell Praxis had planned... I didn't think twice.

Zaffir disappeared into the shower without a word,

muscles tight with exhaustion and tension he wouldn't name. Ezra was the first to tilt his head, encouraging me to go after him. He knew, maybe as intimately as I did, how desperate I was for Zaffir's touch. Because I think he was too. I saw the way they gravitated toward each other. I would make sure they got their time soon.

I caught Briar's knowing smirk and Thorne's quiet nod as I passed, and I gave them both the most thankful smile I could manage. Then, without fanfare, I slipped into the bathroom after him.

The steam was thick, curling around me like it wanted to swallow the outside world whole. He hadn't locked the door. And when I stepped inside the look on his face, surprise first, then something softer, nearly undid me.

My gaze traced over him, drinking in every perfect line of his body. Pale, and smooth like something carved from marble. Water slid down his shoulders, racing along the planes of his chest and over the sharp cut of his hips. I bit my bottom lip, hunger curling low in my belly as I took in the sight of him.

"Brexlyn," he rasped, a raw edge in his voice, like it physically hurt him to stay still.

I met his eyes which were stormy and desperate, and without a single word, I began to strip. One piece at a time, slow enough to torture us both. Each discarded scrap of clothing earned a fresh groan, a sharp inhale, a barely-there clench of his jaw that made me ache to touch him.

When I was bare before him, I stepped forward. His gaze swept over me, dark and possessive, and I swore I could feel the heat of it lick across my skin, leaving goosebumps in its wake. My pulse thundered, my body tight and aching, my thighs clenching with a need so sharp it nearly brought me to my knees.

"I missed you," I said, voice low, barely audible over the rush of water.

For a moment, neither of us moved. The distance we'd forced between ourselves clinging like a second skin. And then he reached for me, not desperate, not reckless, but like someone finally allowing themselves to breathe again. I stepped into the stream of water and the warmth was nothing compared to the heat in his gaze.

"You're not supposed to be in here," he murmured, a smile ghosting at the corner of his mouth as his fingers brushed my wrist. "What if Nova comes by again?"

"I've never been very good at following rules," I breathed back, pressing a kiss against his lips.

He moaned into the kiss, his slick arms wrapping around my waist and holding me in place. My breasts slid against his chest and I felt his cock hardening against my pelvis. His kiss was devouring, making up for lost time, and I let my hands trail across every inch of his body that I could reach. I'd been keeping my distance for so long, but right now, I didn't want an inch between us.

My hand dipped between us, and when I wrapped my fingers around the base of him, he groaned. "Brexlyn," he sighed.

"I've missed you," I kissed his lips. "I've missed this," I said, stroking a long languid hand up and down his length. His hips bucked forward almost involuntarily. "I've missed your dirty mouth."

His eyes snapped open with burning intensity. "My dirty mouth, huh?" he asked, his voice rough and lust laden.

"Yes," I replied.

"Does my girl want me to tell her what to do? And to praise her when she does it well?" he asked, his fingers digging into my back as he held me. I shivered with excitement.

"Yes," I said again.

"You know, only good girls get praise," he teased darkly, falling perfectly into his role. "Are you a good girl?"

I nodded, my breath coming in ragged spurts.

"Then get on your knees and show me how good you are, Brexlyn," he demanded and I felt pleasure jolt through my core. I wanted to please him, the desperation nearly knocked me off my feet as I lowered myself before him. My hand continued its gentle stroking of his cock, and I licked my lips at the sight. The water poured over us, and the sinful image was almost too much for me.

He wanted me to show him how good I could be, and I wanted to be perfect for him. I darted my tongue out, gently teasing the head of his cock, tasting that precious bead of precum. We both let out a soft moan as the sensation enveloped us. Then I took the head into my mouth, swirling my tongue around him as my hand moved.

"Is that as far as you can take me, Brexlyn?" he challenged, and when I glanced up at him, he had one hand cupping my jaw, and one bracing against the tiles of the shower. He knew I hadn't even gotten started yet. I sank onto him, opening my throat to take him all the way to the base. My nose pressed against his stomach and he let out a dark and sinful sound.

"Holy fuck," he cursed. "That's it. God, your mouth is perfect for my cock, isn't it baby?" I bobbed on his length to show him just how perfect I could be, and he let out a string of low curses, his hand gathering my hair in his grip as he directed my movements.

"Touch yourself for me," he demanded and I didn't have to be told twice. My body was desperate for release. After a few rough brushes of my fingertips against my swollen bundle of nerves, I came. My cries were muffled around his cock and I felt my body jolt with the waves of unexpected pleasure.

"Fucking gorgeous," Zaffir praised, and when I opened my eyes, he was staring down at me like I was a goddess at his feet. Like he was the one worshipping me not the other way around.

I let my tongue dance along the underside of his length and he groaned, then pulled me off of him. I whimpered, already missing the feeling of him stretching my throat.

But when he pulled me off the shower floor, hitched one of my legs over his hips and lined his cock up with my entrance, all disappointment was gone and replaced with pure unbridled lust.

"Take me, Zaffir. Please... I'm yours," I begged, my fingers clutching at his shoulders as I tried to sink down and claim him, desperate for the connection. But he held me there, a breath away, refusing to give me what we both craved just yet.

His honeyed eyes locked on mine, fierce and unrelenting. "Let's get one thing straight baby," he rasped, his voice a promise and a vow all at once. "You don't belong to me. I belong to you."

Then he drove into me, claiming every part of me like it was the only thing that mattered. A broken, desperate cry tore from my throat, the sensation too much, too perfect, too needed. He pinned me against the cool tile, his thrusts relentless, fueled by the kind of desperate hunger you only feel when you know tomorrow might never come.

Our eyes locked as he drove into me, each relentless thrust was a silent conversation neither of us dared to voice aloud. There was love in it. Trust. Reckless, dangerous risk. A promise sealed in sweat and skin and the knowledge that tomorrow might rip us apart. This wasn't allowed, not here, not now, not between us. But it was mine. Ours. And it was goddamn beautiful. I couldn't be as open with him as I was with the others, couldn't reach for his hand in front of Nova or steal a kiss before the trials. But that didn't mean I didn't ache for him just the same. And here, in this stolen, sacred moment, as he pushed me to the edge of bliss, I knew without question, he burned for me too.

I buried my head in the crook of his neck and whispered,

"I love you, Zaffir." Suddenly, his thrusts slowed to a calmer, more languid pace.

"Say that again," he demanded. I pulled my head back and met his searching gaze. "Say it again, please."

"I." I kissed his cheek. "Love." Then the other. "You." Then his lips. He drank up the kiss, pistoning his hips faster, chasing the release we both felt building in our cores. Our breath mixed, our groans of pleasure dueting into a symphony of sinful music as he sent me tumbling over the edge into an oblivion of passion. His body shook beneath mine, and I felt his cock twitch within me as my walls clenched around him.

We didn't move for a long time, we simply stood there, breathing each other in, letting the water rain down on us as we soaked up each other's touch. The touch we'd both been starving for.

"I love you too, Brexlyn," he whispered against my skin, the words sinking deep, rooting in the hollow places I hadn't realized were still empty. And something inside me shifted, like the last jagged piece of a puzzle was finally snapping into place.

The ache of distance, of ignored glances and careful silences, had been necessary... but cruel. It had hollowed me out in ways I couldn't name. But here, with my arms wrapped around him, his body still joined with mine, the world outside faded. And suddenly, I felt whole. Like the scattered pieces of my family, they all fit here, in the heat of this moment, in the space between us.

I just hoped I could hold onto it for as long as fate would allow. We were risking everything, playing a dangerous, reckless game. And while every one of us had chosen this fight, I couldn't shake the terror that my Wildguard might not survive it. The thought of losing them now, right when I'd finally found where I belonged, was a pain I didn't ever want to feel.

THORNE

THE TECHNOLOGY TRIAL was nothing like the others. No sprawling arenas, no physical challenges, and no teamwork. Just a locked, suffocating room with a single flickering computer terminal and the grim promise that no one else was coming to save you. It made my stomach twist.

Briar and I had grown up in Darkbranch, where we'd managed to win our fair share of technology trials. Even if we preferred to be out in the trees, chasing the wind and climbing crumbling towers, at least we knew what a terminal was. How to navigate a screen. What code looked like when it scrolled like a living thing across the glass.

But Bex and Ezra? Canyon barely had enough power to broadcast the Reclamation Run on cracked public screens, let alone put a terminal in anyone's home. Ezra once admitted he hadn't touched a computer in his life until Zaffir taught him how to turn one on. The thought of him locked alone in a room like this made my chest ache.

The cell they shoved me into was claustrophobic and

windowless, lit by the pulse of dim, blood-red emergency lights. An alarm blared overhead, a high-pitched, shrieking sound that cut like a knife through the thick air. The only thing in the room besides me was a rusted computer terminal, the old keys grimy beneath my fingers as I slid into the chair.

The screen flared to life in front of me, strings of code rolling like a tide. It wasn't a language I fully understood, but I could spot the patterns. The loops, the false ends, the triggers buried inside lines of commands. Annalese had told us the rules before locking us in, eight winners, one loser. The first eight to complete the task would be released. The last?

The last would die here.

Not like a public execution. Just a quiet, unnoticed death behind sealed bars. Left to rot in the dark until nature took them or Praxis decided to speed things up.

My stomach churned as I flexed my fingers and got to work. I could feel the clock ticking in my bones, though no timer counted down. Every second was a second closer to someone's life ending. My life. Ezra's. Bex's. I couldn't help them here. Couldn't shout through the walls or trade a glance that meant, 'I've got you'.

The thought of one of them not making it through this was a weight that sat heavy in my chest, making it hard to breathe.

Losing more people to Praxis would hurt me in ways I wasn't sure I'd ever be able to recover from.

My mother's eyes were the same deep, warm shade as ours. Like rich, melted chocolate. But that night, they shimmered with something else entirely. Fear barely concealed behind the mask she wore when she didn't want to scare us. The sounds outside were getting louder. Angry voices. Heavy boots crunching against gravel.

She didn't flinch. Not when a bottle shattered against the wall outside and smoke started climbing inside, not when the distant roar of a small army of guards rolled toward our doorstep like a tidal wave. Instead, she turned to me and gripped my shoulders so tightly it almost hurt. I could feel the tremble in her hands, even though she tried to hide it.

"Listen to me, honey," she said, her voice low and thick with urgency, the kind of voice you use when you know you don't have much time left. "I don't want you to ever think I regret what I said, or what I've fought for."

I nodded, though my chest felt tight, my throat too thick to speak.

"There are so many of us out there," she whispered, her gaze darting to the window where the angry glow of torches was beginning to flicker against the night. "But we're in the dark right now. And we need someone, someone brave, to shine a light on it."

"I don't... I don't understand, Ma," I stammered, the weight of the night settling heavy in my bones.

"I know, baby," she whispered, her voice cracking in a way it never did. "I know you don't. But you will." She pulled something from the pocket of her worn, patched coat, a small, slick card. She pressed it into my palm, her fingers wrapping around mine, firm and unyielding.

"Hide this," she breathed. "Don't let them see it. No matter what happens, no matter what they say, this... this is the beginning of a new chance. A key to a new Nexum. For all of us."

I glanced down at it, confused and scared and desperate for this to be some awful dream. "Ma... you're not making any sense."

"It won't. Not for a while," she said, tears glinting in her dark eyes. "But one day... one day the stars will shine on us again." She spoke it like a vow, like an old promise passed down through bloodlines and desperate prayers.

A crash came from outside, followed by a shout, and my heart lurched into my throat.

"Briar, honey," she called out, barely loud enough to be heard over the chaos. And then she was there, thundering down the stairs, face pale, eyes wide.

"Ma, there's people out there," she panted, fear making her voice crack in a way that made my stomach twist.

"I know, sweetheart," she said softly, brushing the hair from her forehead with a tenderness that made my eyes sting. "And I need you both to listen to me very carefully now."

She knelt, one hand on each of us, her fingers warm and rough and real. "Do exactly what they say. Don't fight them. Don't look them in the eye. Don't talk back. Don't give them a reason." Her voice broke then, just a little. "Your fight... your fight is not today. Do you hear me?"

"What do they want?" Briar asked.

"They're upset at the things I've said. The injustices I've shed light on," she replied, nodding reverently.

"Tell them you didn't mean it. Take it back!" Briar cried, but she was already shaking her head.

"No, honey. Because I did mean it. I meant every word," she said, and there was something so beautiful about the strength she carried, even to the end.

"No, Ma," Briar started, voice thick with defiance. "We can help you—"

"No," she snapped, then softened immediately, her eyes pleading. "I need you to promise me, Briar. Both of you. Promise me you'll be smart. Promise me you'll survive this. To fight another day."

Her words wrapped around us like a threadbare shield, a last-ditch protection against a world that didn't care if we made it out alive. She leaned in closer, pressing her forehead to ours.

"Promise me."

The words hung in the air, sharp and heavy.

"We promise," Briar and I whispered together, though the words tasted bitter in my mouth.

She embraced us both then, fierce and trembling and so heartbreakingly human. I buried my face in the worn fabric of her coat, breathing in the scent of her, rosemary, woodsmoke, something wild and untamable.

"It's not enough to just survive, my loves. You need to live for something."

Then the door flew open with a violent crack, light and noise spilling inside like a tidal wave. And my mother stood, squaring her shoulders, facing them down like a warrior made of fire and shadows.

And she didn't look back.

I bit my lip to force the memories back and let my fingers fly, stringing together commands, bypassing dead ends, watching as the screen flickered when I hit the correct sequence. Faster. Faster. I pushed down the rising panic, the sound of the alarm like nails dragging down my spine.

I hit the final key.

For one agonizing heartbeat... nothing.

Then the red lights in my cell flickered, stuttered, and snapped to stark, sterile white. The bars in front of me groaned and slid open.

I didn't celebrate. Didn't even smile. I just bolted. Sprinting out into the circular chamber beyond where the other contestants still worked in their cells, faces illuminated by the sickly glow of their terminals. Eight cells. Eight Challengers. And only seven spots beside me left.

I didn't care about the victory. Didn't care that I'd made it through. My eyes weren't on the scoreboard. They were on the faces of the people I loved.

Because if Bex or Ezra didn't make it, if Praxis took one of them here, I wasn't sure any of us could crawl our way back from that.

I felt Zaffir beside me, the quiet hum of his camera whirring as its lens stayed locked on me. I flicked him a look, sharp and fleeting, the kind of glance no one else would ever catch but us. A message in a fraction of a second.

Then the clang of a cell door snapping open cut through the thick air.

Another Challenger. Then another.

I didn't need to look to know which Collectives they were from. Shocker, they'd all be from ones that'd won the tech trial in the last decade.

My stomach twisted as my gaze snapped toward the still-closed cells where Ezra and Bex worked. I could see them through the bars, both hunched over their terminals. Ezra's brow furrowed, his lips moving with each string of code, fingers stumbling now and then. Bex's face was tighter, her jaw set like stone, but panic flickered in her eyes. The kind she couldn't hide.

Fuck.

Another heavy clang, and Briar burst from her cell, her dark hair damp with sweat, eyes wild as they darted across the room. I knew she'd be able to do it, but relief hit me nonetheless as I reached for her hand and squeezed once.

"How do you think they're doing?" she asked, breath ragged, her voice low but sharp.

Ezra slammed his fist down on the desk in his cell and let out a guttural sound of frustration.

I swallowed hard. "Not good."

Another door slid open.

Five now. Five of us safe. All of them from Collectives with the luxury of screens in their homes. If I wasn't so goddamn terrified for the people I loved, I'd be shouting about the injustice, the impossible weight stacked against them. Praxis didn't even bother pretending this was fair.

My eyes snapped back to Bex and Ezra. Their fingers moved fast, but I could see the strain, the desperation in the way their shoulders tensed, in the way their eyes scanned the screens as if willing the code to make sense. If Bex had ever seen code like this before, she'd have it memorized, and would've been able to recite it perfectly. But brilliance meant nothing when the language was foreign.

Another heavy groan of metal. Six.

Only two spots left. With three of them still in there.

My pulse pounded so hard it was all I could hear.

"Fenly Nots, Stormwatch," Briar whispered, leaning closer to me, her voice just a breath against the roar in my ears. "They haven't won a tech trial in years. He's in the same boat as Bex and Ezra. It's not over."

I nodded, but the movement felt distant, like it belonged to someone else. I wasn't in my body anymore. I was floating somewhere outside it, caught between hope and horror.

Then...

Clang.

Bex's cell door flew open.

Relief slammed into me so hard my knees nearly buckled. I was already moving before I registered it, sprinting across the floor as she stumbled from the cell, her face pale, her chest heaving. She embraced Briar first, and my sister pressed a gentle kiss to her lips, whispering words meant for only her. And then, Bex turned and she was in my arms, colliding against me with a force that rattled every bone I had.

Her heart pounded against mine. Or maybe it was mine pounding against hers. I buried my face in her hair, breathed in the scent of her sweat and adrenaline. My arms tightened around her like I could anchor both of us with sheer will alone.

"Thank God," I whispered, voice breaking as I pressed my lips to hers.

She kissed me back, fierce and trembling, like neither of us were sure this moment wasn't a dream that would splinter apart. I held on anyway.

But even as the relief swelled in my chest, a jagged, brutal fear still lingered.

Because Ezra was still inside.

And there was only one spot left.

"Ezra," Bex whispered, her voice barely more than a breath against my chest. She twisted in my arms, her eyes darting to his cell across the room. I followed her gaze. Ezra was still at his terminal, his shoulders hunched, his jaw clenched so tight it looked like it might shatter. His whole body was a coil of tension, the kind of pressure that could crush a person if it lasted a second too long.

"He's still got a chance, love," I murmured against her hair, holding her tighter, like maybe if I kept her close enough, my words would become true.

Briar sidled up beside us, her voice low, almost ashamed. "Fenly looks just as lost," she said, motioning subtly toward the last remaining Challenger, Fenly Nots, sweat beading on his brow. "Same boat as Ezra and Bex were. He's scrambling."

I hated how Praxis had turned me into this, someone silently hoping for another person to fail, for a life to be condemned just so the people I loved could crawl one step closer to survival. How easily these trials twisted us into their monsters.

"Come on, Ezra," I whispered under my breath.

"That was nearly impossible," Bex choked out. Her fingers clung to the fabric of my shirt like a lifeline. "I think I... I just got lucky. I caught a pattern in the code, but barely. And if he can't..." her voice cracked, and she bit down hard on the words like maybe if she didn't say them, they wouldn't come true. "What if he can't do it?"

She started trembling, a ripple running through her body. I tightened my hold.

Then a metallic *clang* echoed through the room.

Another cell door slid open.

Bex screamed. A raw, gut-wrenching sound that tore through the chamber like a blade. The sound of a heart breaking open in real time.

Fenly Nots stepped from his cell, pale and shaking... but free.

And just like that, Ezra was the last one left.

Bex broke from my grasp, sprinting forward before I could catch her. She collided with the bars of Ezra's cell, gripping them so tightly her knuckles went bloodless. Ezra was already there, meeting her at the divide, the two of them just inches apart but impossibly far.

"No, no, no, they can't... they can't do this!" Bex sobbed, trying to reach through the bars, desperate to touch him.

"Shh, baby," Ezra murmured, his voice so gentle, so steady it made my chest ache. He cupped her face through the bars, his thumb tracing the wetness on her cheeks. "It's okay."

"I can't lose you," she cried, her voice shattering around the words. Her legs buckled beneath her, and she crumpled to the floor, clutching at the bars like she could tear them down with sheer grief.

Ezra dropped down with her, mirroring her posture, refusing to let her fall alone. The anger that had lived in him through the trial was gone now, in its place, something quieter, heavier. Acceptance, maybe. Or the last, thin veneer of bravery.

"You'll never lose me," Ezra promised, voice rough. "I'm yours, Bex. My soul, my body... all of it. It's yours. And no matter what happens to me, you get to keep it."

Bex sobbed harder, banging her fists against the bars like if she hit them enough, they'd bend for her. Ezra caught her hands in his, holding them tight.

"Look at me, baby," he begged, voice breaking. "I'm so sorry. We had so much left. You and I... God, we were just getting started."

He lifted her hands to his lips, kissed them. His gaze flicked, for a fraction of a second, to where Zaffir stood off to the side, camera still rolling, as if his words were meant for him too. Zaffir's jaw twitched, his face straining to stay neutral, but I saw the sheen in his eyes, the tremble he was fighting. But there were eyes everywhere, and he couldn't show them how much he cared. Not unless he wanted another trip to Archon's torture chamber.

"I love you, I love you," Bex whispered, over and over like a desperate prayer she could use to barter with.

"God, Bex. I love you too," Ezra breathed, a tear slipping down his cheek. "But you're gonna go out there, and you're gonna win this."

We all knew he wasn't talking about the Reclamation Run anymore. The war was already moving in the background, gathering like a storm on the horizon. And Ezra, even now, was still making sure Bex would be part of it.

"I can't," she sobbed, shaking her head.

"You can," he vowed, pressing her hands to his heart. "And you won't do it alone. You've got them." He motioned to me, to Briar, even broadly toward Zaffir. "Let them help you, baby. Please."

Bex nodded, barely.

Ezra leaned forward, pressing a kiss to her lips through the cold, unyielding bars. Both of them were crying now, and I felt the burn of my own tears sliding down my face, unstoppable.

A piece of me that had begun to heal these last weeks was being torn open again, raw and bleeding.

Bex finally collapsed fully, sliding to the floor. I moved fast, dropping beside her, pulling her into my arms as she clung to me like the world might tear her away next.

"Keep her safe," Ezra told me, his voice steady but his eyes betraying everything.

I nodded. "You know I will," I said. And I meant it.

Briar crouched, reaching for our girl, and Bex shifted toward her, letting herself fall into Briar's open arms.

I stood, pacing a few steps away because the walls felt too close, the air too thin. My lungs couldn't find enough to fill them. I ran a hand through my hair, trying to pull myself together before I shattered too.

"I'm so sorry," a voice said, soft and hesitant.

I turned. Fenly Nots. His face was blotchy, eyes rimmed with red. I felt a sharp burst of rage, white-hot, an instinct to lash out at the easy target. But I swallowed it down.

It wasn't his fault. He didn't set the rules. Praxis did.

I took a breath, forced my voice steady. "Yeah," I said quietly. "So am I."

Fenly's gaze drifted, his eyes distant, fixed on the display across the room where Bex clung to Ezra in their tear-soaked goodbye. Cameras circled them like vultures, every eye in the chamber drawn to the heartbreak on full display. His voice came so softly it barely reached me.

"I didn't know it was him," Fenly murmured.

I turned, watching him. His face didn't move, but I could feel his mind working, his thoughts roaring. His eyes stayed locked on the scene, as if by looking away it might make the weight of what he'd done real.

"I didn't want to separate your team."

The words lodged in my chest. There was so much I wanted to say, or scream, but even though the cameras might not have been on us, I didn't want to chance my ire being broadcast.

"You didn't," I said quietly, though the words tasted bitter. I bit my tongue before I added anything else. As furious as I was, as much as my heart ached knowing we were one down and might never get them back, I couldn't risk what was left of our goal.

I watched him carefully. There was something so...

contemplative about the haunted tilt of Fenly's shoulders, the way his fingers toyed with the edge of his sleeve like a man stalling before his last move.

He finally turned to me, and for the first time, I really met his eyes. There was something there I recognized. A quiet finality. The same look my mother had worn the night she pressed a card into my hand and told me my fight hadn't started yet.

"Yeah," Fenly said, his voice low, almost a sigh. "It was them."

A flicker of shock crossed my face before I could stop it, the breath stalling in my lungs. Something unspoken passed between us, a wordless understanding only people marked by their anger could ever truly share.

"You've all done a lot of good for us," Fenly murmured after a moment. "You're brave. Braver than most I've seen in years." He smiled faintly, but it didn't reach his eyes. "You've given a lot of people out there something to hold onto."

I opened my mouth to thank him, but he wasn't finished.

"That kind of hope doesn't stay quiet forever," he said, leaning in slightly. "It's the kind that ignites what's been simmering... you know."

I swallowed hard, my pulse pounding in my ears. He reached out and gripped my hand, firm, steady, resolute.

And then, barely louder than a breath, he whispered, "I always believed that one day the stars would shine on us again."

The world tilted. My stomach dropped. My jaw parted on instinct, words scrambling up my throat, questions, demands, pleas. It was a line only Runaways used, a promise buried in whispers and rebellion. My mother's words.

"And I think you all might be our stars," he whispered, glancing back at the others. Ezra, Bex, Briar and even Zaffir, though his participation was a carefully guarded secret.

But before I could ask him anything, before I could so much as tighten my grip, Fenly was already moving, sauntering toward the cameras like a man heading to the gallows on his own terms.

"I can't accept this victory," he called out, loud enough to bring the entire room to a stunned halt. His hands lifted in surrender. "I cheated. I didn't complete this trial fairly."

Every head turned. The guards stiffened. Murmurs rippled through the crowd like a crackle of wildfire. Someone barked into a comm. Another raised a camera. Faces twisted in confusion. Nobody understood what he was doing.

Except me.

I felt it like a pulse in my chest.

Praxis guards closed in around him, their hands clamping down on his shoulders, but he didn't resist. No fight, no struggle. He simply let them lead him away, a strange calm settling over him like a man who'd made peace with his fate. The heavy bars of his once opened cell slammed shut behind him.

And a second later, Ezra's opened.

He spilled out, the shock and disbelief on his face melting instantly as Bex flew into his arms. He held her so tightly I thought she might break. He whispered something unintelligible as he kissed her face, her hair, his hands running along her arms as if he was trying to memorize her touch.

But I couldn't look away from the cell that Fenly now inhabited. Couldn't shake the truth in his gaze. The belief. The sacrifice. He'd given himself up so we could stay whole. So we could finish what we started.

And somewhere deep in my chest, the old words stirred again.

One day, the stars will shine on us again.

CHAPTER
FIVE

BEX

I'D SPENT the entire day curled up against Ezra's side, my fingers constantly brushing over his skin, his hair, gripping his hand as though sheer touch alone could anchor him here, could convince both of us that he was still breathing. Still alive. Still mine to hold. I couldn't believe how close we'd come to losing him. If Fenly hadn't admitted to cheating, something I still couldn't quite believe, he would've been gone.

And it rattled me.

I'd let myself grow comfortable. I didn't mean to, but it happened anyway. I let the familiarity of my team, the way we moved together, trusted each other, looked out for one another, lull me into a false sense of security. A dangerous mistake in a place like this. In the Run, safety wasn't real. I'd forgotten that for a moment. Ezra's near-death reminded me.

And I couldn't ignore what it meant for us in the eyes of the world. The only thing audiences loved more than a champion to cheer for... was a favorite to tear down. And we were making ourselves far too easy to watch.

Ezra was asleep, his chest rose and fell in steady, careful breaths. I laid beside him, one hand resting on his ribs, feeling the soft warmth of him beneath my palm. My heart ached in ways I didn't have words for. A hollow, scraping kind of ache that came from almost losing something vital. If he'd gone...I didn't know what would've been left of me. I couldn't imagine a life without any of my Wildguard. They'd found their way into the deepest parts of my heart and took root there.

I stayed there longer than I should've, watching him in the low light of the room, the way his lashes lay against his cheeks, the small crease between his brows even in sleep. Eventually, my stomach's low growl pulled me from my vigil. I slipped from his bed, pressing a final touch to his hand before leaving the room, careful not to wake Zaffir who was asleep in the bed beside us. The cabin was quiet, still wrapped in the hush of late night. The moon hung high, silver light spilling through the windows and pooling on the wooden floorboards like liquid glass.

I padded barefoot to the kitchen, only half-aware of my surroundings. Hunger gnawed at my stomach, but my mind was elsewhere, on Ezra's pained face behind bars, on the cameras always watching, on the quiet, creeping fear curling up inside me.

I didn't notice the figure at first. Not until the fridge's pale light caught movement, and a silhouette shifted, a glint of metal in their hand. My heart slammed against my ribs, a startled sound catching in my throat as I staggered back a step.

A voice, low and warm, cut through my panic.

"Easy, love."

Thorne.

I let out a breath, pressing a hand to my chest. "You scared me."

He turned toward me with a crooked grin, setting the knife down beside a jar of something on the counter. The dim light softened his sharp features, and made his eyes look darker. His hair was slightly mussed, and he smelled faintly of rain and earth, like fresh air after a storm.

"Sorry," he said, rounding the kitchen island to pull me into a hug without hesitation. His arms circled me, grounding me in that moment. I let myself lean into it, wrapping my arms around his waist, breathing him in like something clean and steady.

"How's Ezra?" he asked softly, stepping back, though his hand lingered on my arm a moment longer than necessary.

"He's sleeping," I said, sliding onto a stool at the counter. "Though I think he's more pissed at himself than anything. Kept saying he should've made Zaffir teach him how to work the 'damn machine' before we got in there." I attempted a passable impression of Ezra's grumbled frustration.

Thorne laughed, grabbing sandwich fixings from the counter. "Sounds about right."

He gestured to the knife. "Can I interest you in a midnight sandwich? It's not bobcat stew, but I promise it's edible."

I smiled, feeling the tension in my chest ease. "An exclusive meal at *Restaurante de la Grey*? How could I possibly say no?"

His grin tugged at something in my chest, and I watched his hands as he moved. Steady, capable, thoughtful. It struck me how often he'd taken point on cooking for us in the Wilds. Even when everything was unpredictable and terrifying, Thorne always found a way to feed us.

"Do you like to cook?" I asked, resting my chin in my hand as I watched him layer ingredients on the bread.

He shrugged with a small, wistful smile. "If you think putting some mayonnaise on a piece of bread is cooking, I have a lot to teach you." he teased, pointing the knife in my direction.

I laughed.

"But yeah. Ma tried to teach us both. Briar wasn't into it. Too restless, always climbing trees or eavesdropping on the neighbors. But I kind of liked it. There's a rhythm to it, you know? A small thing you can control."

I hesitated, then asked, "Did you know... about your mom being part of the Runaways? While she was alive, I mean."

His hands stilled, a shadow passing through his expression. "I knew more than Briar did," he admitted. "But Ma never said it outright. Not until she gave me the card."

"I thought Briar was really good at reading people, how did she miss that?"

"I think she was too close to it. You know? Like you only see what you want to see when it comes to those you love?"

I nodded.

He drew in a breath, slicing through the bread carefully. "Briar knew that she spoke up a lot. Not always about Praxis directly, but about the Collectives, about the injustice of the Run. Enough to get her noticed. Not enough for them to kill her... until it was." His voice cracked faintly, and I felt the ache of it in my own chest.

"When I figured out what she'd been a part of, what she created, it wasn't a surprise. She hated what the Reclamation Run did to people. To families. To us."

I swallowed, tracing a crack in the counter with my finger. "Why did Briar want to be elected?" I asked quietly.

He met my eyes then, a sad, knowing kind of smile ghosting across his face. "That's a story she should tell you herself." He slid a plate toward me and came around to sit beside me.

I picked up the sandwich, its warmth and weight oddly comforting. "So... how is it?" he asked, raising a brow.

I took a bite, pretending to chew thoughtfully. "You know, I think I actually miss the bobcat," I teased.

He snorted and bumped his shoulder against mine, a real laugh breaking through this time. "Careful, love. Insult the chef again and I'll have to punish you."

I smiled, the ache in my chest easing as heat took its place.

I took another bite, and for a few minutes we ate in a comfortable, easy silence. But my mind wouldn't settle. It drifted, spiraling back to the same thought it had all day when the quiet stretched too long.

"What's on your mind?" Thorne asked, bumping his shoulder against mine, pulling me back from the edge I hadn't realized I was teetering on.

I sighed. "Fenly," I admitted, the name tasting heavy on my tongue. Between worrying over Ezra and trying to hold the pieces of our team together, Fenly Nots hadn't left my thoughts for a second.

A flicker of something, recognition, regret, grief, crossed Thorne's face. His expression tightened, and he ran a hand through his hair as he stood, collecting his empty plate and walking it to the sink. I watched the way his shoulders tensed, the way his whole frame looked wound tight, like a storm ready to snap.

I stood too, carrying my plate with me. When I reached him, I slid it into the sink and slipped my arms around his waist from behind, resting my cheek against the solid line of his back. His body softened, just a little, at the contact but the tension was still there, humming beneath his skin.

"What is it?" I asked quietly.

He exhaled a shaky breath. "Fenly sacrificed himself for Ezra," Thorne whispered, his voice rough, like it scraped against something sharp on the way out. "He didn't cheat. He lied. Lied to save him."

I jerked back, the shock hitting me like a punch to the

chest. I stepped away until my back met the counter. Thorne turned to face me, his eyes shadowed and weary.

"What are you talking about?" I asked, my voice barely above a whisper.

"Fenly lied to get Ezra out of there."

"Why would he do something like that?"

Thorne hesitated, then said softly, "Right after the trial, Fenly told me something. He said... one day, the stars will shine on us again." Thorne's voice cracked a little on the words, and a cold rush of recognition swept through me.

"He thinks we might be the stars Nexum's been waiting for," Thorne continued.

My heart stuttered. "He knew about the Runaways?"

Thorne nodded once, gravely. "I think he *was* a Runaway, love," he said, stepping closer, his hands finding my arms, grounding me.

I swallowed hard. "And he... he sacrificed himself so our team could stay together? I don't understand. Why?"

Thorne's expression was pained as he nodded again. "He believes in us. In what we can do together. Just like I do." His fingers lifted to gently grip my chin, tilting my face up until our eyes locked. "I believe in us, Bex. In the five of us. That we can finish what my Ma started. That maybe, for the first time in a long time, we can change how this story ends."

A wave of emotions crashed over me, hope, regret, pain, and I wasn't sure which one would drown me first.

"What if it wasn't worth it? What if I can't do what he sacrificed himself for?" I whispered.

"You don't even realize how incredible you are, love," he whispered, his voice rough with honesty. "You don't see what the rest of us see. This fierce, unyielding woman with a heart too big for a world like this, and a soul that aches for peace, the same way my Ma's did." His gaze held mine, unflinching.

"The rebellion's a powder keg, Bex... and you? You're the fucking spark."

Thorne leaned in, pressing his lips softly to mine, a kiss that started tender and unhurried, a promise in the darkness. His tongue brushed along the seam of my lips, and I parted for him, wanting to lose myself in the heat, the quiet desperation of it. My arms wound around his neck, pulling him closer until there wasn't a sliver of space left between us, the kiss turning fiercer, hungrier.

He hooked his hands beneath my thighs, lifting me effortlessly. I wrapped my legs around his waist, our bodies pressed together so tightly, but it still felt like too much space lingered between us.

His mouth claimed mine with a hunger that left me breathless as he carried me forward. I barely registered where we were headed until my back hit the couch and he hovered over me, arms braced on either side, caging me in. His body pressed against mine, a solid, unrelenting heat. He broke the kiss, his eyes scorching as they roamed my face, then down the length of me. My chest rose and fell, desperate for air, desperate for him. I needed to feel his skin against mine. I reached for the hem of my nightdress, arching my back as I tugged it over my head in one swift motion. His gaze darkened, his breath hitching as he took me in.

"You're a fucking work of art, love," he whispered, leaning his head down to take one of my peaked nipples into his eager mouth. I arched into him as his other hand trailed deliberate lines along my lower stomach. Close enough to my desperate core to drive me frantic with need, but far enough to have me whimpering under his fingertips. "There's stardust in your skin. I swear, I can feel the universe when I touch you."

"Then touch me, Thorne," I begged as he dragged his tongue between the valley of my breasts until he could claim the other nipple.

"I want to worship this body," he whispered against my sensitive, goosebump-covered skin. "I want to taste every inch of you. Mark you with my fingers, my mouth, my cock." I cried out as his fingers brushed across my clit, barely and featherlight. A tease.

"Please," I begged.

"I want you to remember the exact moment I make you mine, love. I want you to memorize the look on my face, the tremble in your body. I want you to be able to recall exactly how I made you come apart when you're lying alone at night." He kissed my collarbone, then my neck, as his hands got to work, sliding his silk boxers down his legs, exposing his long cock to me. He was longer than both Zaffir and Ezra, but with less girth. I couldn't wait to feel the depths he could reach.

"I will," I promised, wrapping my legs around his waist again and trying to pull him into me.

He reached between us, gripping his cock and then gently pressed the head of it against my clit. We both sighed at the contact. My body was so sensitive and desperate for him that my blood was nearly boiling under my skin. He directed the tip through my wetness, sliding through my slit, gliding easily against my opening. We both groaned a guttural, satisfied sound. He continued that taunting, teasing move for a while, and I could feel my body tensing, thrashing with need beneath his simple but sinful touch. His cock slid along my clit, over and over and I felt the telltale signs of an orgasm creeping up on me.

"I'm going to come," I cried out, bucking my hips to chase the feeling. His eyes burned as he watched me, keeping his relentless, perfect pace against my clit. My fingers and toes tingled as the climax built and built, until it exploded through me.

The minute my orgasm crested, he slammed his cock into my heat, reaching a deep part of me that no one else had. I almost screamed, but his mouth pressed against mine to silence me. He fucked me, hard and fast through my first orgasm.

"Holy shit, you're squeezing me," he whispered against my lips.

I couldn't even form words, because my body was one continuous cycle of sensation and ecstasy. I simply tightened my legs around him and forced my hips up to meet him thrust for thrust.

His mouth trailed down my chin, then to my throat, and finally back to my nipples which he licked, and kissed, and bit down on gently, only making my core tighten more around him. I wasn't even sure if my orgasm ended, or if he was prolonging it by not giving my body a break. I was mindless, feral. I clawed at his shoulders as he slammed into me like a man desperate for what only I could give him.

"I'm going to need you to come one more time for me, love," he said, through gritted teeth. "I need to feel your body clamping down on me before I paint your pussy with my release."

I groaned at his filthy words, and sure enough, I felt the crest begin to rise again. His mouth on my breasts, his cock pounding into me, I couldn't stand it. I was sensation and lust. I was ecstasy.

I climaxed again, and I felt my muscles tighten around him, drawing out his own release. He slowed his thrusts as he shuddered and emptied himself.

He lowered himself onto me, his weight a welcome comfort against my chest as we both fought to steady our breathing. I ran my hand slowly down the length of his spine, feeling the tension still lingering beneath his skin, tracing each dip and curve with gentle care.

In the hush of the dark, his eyes found mine, fierce, tender, and unguarded.

"I was wrong," he murmured, voice rough and reverent. "The stars have nothing on you."

I giggled, kissing his shoulder playfully. He circled his hips, his cock still buried deep within me, and I gasped at the sensation. Despite feeling drained and exhausted my body jolted to life at the motion. I squeezed my muscles around him which earned me a groan.

"Is my girl ready for round two?" he asked, his eyes dark and sinful with promise.

I nodded, biting my bottom lip.

"Prove it," he challenged. And I intended to do just that.

CHAPTER SIX

BRIAR

ONLY FOUR MORE TRIALS STOOD BETWEEN us and the end of the Run. The final two, the medical trials, were the ones Hollis had her sights set on. And because of that, so did I. Even with our little secret rebellious secondary mission, we wanted to accomplish what we could while tearing them down from the inside. It surprised me, if I'm honest, how quickly my priorities had shifted since meeting her. It was like she'd taken one look at the road I was walking, ripped up the map, and redrawn it entirely. I still wanted what I came here for. The reasons that drove me into the Run hadn't vanished. But now I wanted so much more. I wanted liberation. I wanted to finish my Ma's work. But above that all...

I wanted Brexlyn Hollis.

I'd done my best to keep my distance, to give her room. I wasn't blind to the way she'd fallen for the others in the house, for Thorne, for Ezra, for Zaffir. And it didn't bother me. Hell, I'd told her once I was good at sharing, and I meant it. She wasn't the first woman to end up tangled in sheets with both

Thorne and me... at different times, of course. But Brexlyn wasn't like anyone else. She wasn't a passing comfort or a distraction in the middle of all this madness. She was lightning in my veins, a storm I'd gladly drown in.

I'd kissed her several times now. Each one hotter, deeper, more perfect than the last. And with every touch of her mouth on mine, every soft sigh against my skin, I wanted more. So much more. But I held myself back, careful not to push, not to make her feel boxed in by the fact that I was here, under the same roof as the men she was already falling for. The last thing I wanted was for her to feel like she owed me anything. I desired her, yes. But she had so much on her plate.

And truth be told, so did I.

I was still reeling from the weight of what I'd learned about my mother. That she was the spark that lit this rebellion, the one who'd started it all... and she'd never told me. Not once. She carried that secret until the day they dragged her away, and the only person she confided in at the end was Thorne. Not me.

I hated how jealous I was of that. Of him. Of their connection. She was our mother, but I guess I never really saw her for who she was. And maybe she never really saw me, either. I've always been good at reading people. Could peel back their walls, get them to bleed truth if I wanted it badly enough. But somehow, I'd missed the biggest truth of all when it came to her.

And it was eating me alive.

Thorne had always been her little boy. And I guess, for as long as I had him, I had Pa. He was my anchor, my best friend, my mentor, the one person who understood me without needing me to say a word. Even more than Thorne ever did. When he passed a few years before they took Ma, it shattered me in ways I still can't fully explain. Losing him felt like losing the only person who really saw me. And when Ma was taken, it was like the last thread holding my world together snapped. The grief of losing them both... it was unbearable. Some days, it still is.

So yeah, I had plenty to focus on. Hollis might've rerouted my priorities, but the ghosts of the past had their claws in me too. And the closer we got to those final trials, the more it felt like everything I believed about who I was, why I was here, and what I wanted was coming undone.

But maybe that wasn't such a bad thing.

Nova, the Canyon's Praxis liaison, stopped by this morning to inform us about the next trial. Even though I knew it was coming, hearing it aloud still made my stomach tighten with nerves.

The Entertainment Trial was always similar, most years it involved some form of artistic expression, whether it was a performance, writing, painting, or something along those lines. This year, the task was simple. We'd have to put together a performance. We'd be paraded across the stage in front of thousands of Praxis citizens, with the screaming masses in the stands and even more watching from home and forced to perform for them. Even though we'd already been performing for them in a way the entire Run so far.

I loved music. I loved telling a story through words and melody, the way a song could speak to the soul. But I'd only ever sung for my family, the forest, and, I guess, Brexlyn too, now.

But this was why I was here. This trial. I needed to win. Or at the very least, place high enough to get what I needed. But now, I wasn't sure how our little rebellious plans factored into all of this. Would we ever return to our Collectives? Did we even want to? If we managed to convince the Runaways to fight back, would we ever see the fruits of the labor we've put in here? Would we unlock all the resources for everyone, or lose everything in the process? Would we face the same fate Ma did? I didn't know. But I did know that when I arrived here, I wanted one thing.

So, when Nova asked what we needed for our performance so she could procure it for us, my response came without hesitation.

"A guitar."

I sat on the edge of my bed, guitar in hand, and for the first time in over a decade, I felt whole again. The smooth wood beneath my fingers, the familiar weight, the strings ready to be strummed, it was like finding a part of myself I thought I'd lost forever.

The door creaked open, and I glanced up at Bex, feeling the familiar flutter of warmth in my chest as she entered, a soft smile on her lips. She gently closed the door behind her.

"Hope I'm not interrupting," she said with that smile that had become my anchor, walking toward me before settling down on the bed beside me. Her presence was a balm to the anxious knots twisting in my stomach. I gave her a gentle smile in return.

"Just trying to remember how to do this," I said, motioning to the guitar in my hands, feeling the weight of it again after so long. "It's been a while since I've played."

"I've never even seen one of these up close," she murmured, her eyes studying the instrument with a curiosity that tugged at me. Her fingers traced delicately along the frets, and the motion stirred something in me. Something raw. I swallowed hard, wondering how it would feel if those fingers explored me instead, but pushed the thought away.

"We haven't had them in Darkbranch in a long time either," I confessed, feeling the weight of those words settle between us. Her gaze shifted to me, her eyes intense, as though she could see right through me.

"What's on your mind?" she asked, her voice soft and full of care.

I sighed, letting my fingers hover over the strings before strumming a single, gentle chord. The sound was quiet, almost tentative. "My Pa taught me how to play the guitar. How to sing too," I replied, my voice quieter now, as if the memories were still fresh enough to sting. She didn't interrupt, just sat there, her attention unwavering, giving me space to breathe.

"Music was kind of our thing," I continued, the words flowing now, each one easier than the last. "He worked for an entire year to save up enough to buy me my very own guitar." My gaze drifted to the instrument in my hands, fingers brushing over the worn wood. I wished it was the one he gave me. But I knew that guitar was long gone, reduced to ash and dust by now.

I tried to play another chord, but my fingers were stiff and unpracticed, and the sound that came out was harsh, dissonant. I winced, feeling the familiar frustration rise in my chest.

"The year after he died, we lost the Entertainment Trial... well, I guess 'lost' would imply we still had someone in the race, which we didn't. Our Challenger was long dead by then," I said, my voice tinged with bitterness. "They came in the middle of the day. The guards. It was like any other day, except this time, they were there to take it all from us." My hands tightened around the guitar neck, my thoughts drifting back to that moment. "They tore through our houses, the community buildings... everything we had left to lose. They ripped it all away. Medicine, technology, supplies, things we'd grown accustomed to because our Challengers tended to perform well."

I closed my eyes for a moment, trying to breathe through the weight of it. "They took the guitar right out of my hands. I cried, I screamed, I almost fought back, but Ma... Ma held me close. Whispered that it was going to be okay." I could still feel her arms around me, her voice a soft lullaby against the chaos. "I know it's silly, when you really think about it. Frivolous. Darkbranch lost so much that day, and with the medicine and the life-saving resources at stake, my little guitar didn't seem like much." I swallowed, the lump in my throat thickening. "But it meant everything to me. They stole music from me that day. And then, a few years later, they stole my Ma."

I swallowed hard, trying to hold the tears at bay, but one slipped down my cheek. Without a word, she reached up, gently brushing it away with her thumb. Her touch was soft, tender, as if she knew that in this moment, it wasn't just about the guitar. It was everything.

"You want your music back," she whispered, not a question, but a quiet affirmation. "Because it'll feel like you have him back. Even for a second."

I nodded, my throat tight. "I'm not used to people seeing me that clearly. That's usually my job. Am I that easy to read?"

She smiled, but it was gentle, understanding. "Just to me," she said, pressing her hand to my cheek. I leaned into her touch, feeling the warmth of her palm spread through me, grounding me in the present.

"You might be the only one of us with a chance of actually placing in this trial," she said lightly, a teasing edge to her voice that didn't quite mask the admiration behind it.

I snorted, my mouth curling up into a half-smile. "Not if I don't remember how to play."

She shook her head softly, her hand brushing against mine, sending a jolt of heat straight through me. "Music is a part of you, Briar. Anyone who watches you can tell that." She smiled softly. "You know you hum when you're thinking."

"I do?" I asked.

She nodded. "Your eyes sort of glaze over and you look off into nothingness, and you hum. Or if I'm lucky, you'll sing a little." She closed her eyes and sighed. "It's peaceful."

"It used to come so easily," I replied softly, looking longingly at the guitar in my hands.

"It'll come back to you."

Her hand was warm against mine, and I let my fingers curl around hers instinctively. My pulse quickened, and I found myself leaning into her presence, even if only for a moment, before the reality of the trial came crashing back into my thoughts.

"What are the others planning to do for the show?" I asked, trying to steer the conversation away from the sudden tension rising between us. I could still hear the muffled voices of the others in the living room, plotting their next moves for the performance.

Bex let out a soft laugh, her eyes dancing with amusement. "Well, Thorne's going to recite a poem he wrote. One he swore wasn't explicit or about me."

I raised an eyebrow. "But it totally is, right?"

She let out a huff of laughter. "He rhymed 'your deep hole' with 'my large pole,'" she said flatly, and I couldn't help but burst into laughter.

"That definitely sounds like Thorne," I said, still chuckling.

"Ezra says his talent is putting up with Thorne," Bex added with a smirk. I nodded in agreement.

"That does take a certain level of skill," I said with a grin.

"But really, I think he's a little less focused on planning anything," Bex continued, rolling her eyes in mock exasperation.

I tilted my head, watching her as she spoke, feeling a pull in my chest that I didn't want to name. "What about you?" I asked, already knowing the answer, but wanting to hear her say it.

She shrugged nonchalantly. "I don't really have any talents."

I couldn't resist teasing her. "I dunno about that. We all heard Zaffir in the shower the other day. It sounds like you have at least one talent."

Her skin flushed, the pink spreading across her cheeks in an instant, and I felt a surge of satisfaction from the effect I had on her. A temptation, raw and unfiltered, rose within me, but I reined it in.

She sighed, rubbing her temples. "Let me rephrase, I have no talents I can show on a stage in front of cameras and a live audience." We both laughed then.

I fell silent for a moment, watching her carefully, my thoughts spinning. The idea of her voice joining mine in song had lodged itself in my mind, and it wouldn't leave. "Sing with me," I said finally, the words tumbling out before I could stop them.

She blinked, clearly taken aback. "What?" she asked, her brow furrowing.

"Sing a duet with me," I repeated, my heart pounding at the thought. "I'll teach you the song Pa used to sing to me. We can sing it together. Or we could write something else. I think it's... something we could do. For the trial."

I could feel her eyes on me, searching my face, trying to read the sincerity behind my request. The thought of our voices intertwined in harmony, of sharing something so vulnerable and real, made my chest tighten with longing.

Her gaze dropped to her hands, fingers nervously picking at the edge of her sleeve. She sighed, and my heart stuttered in my chest. "I can't."

"Why not?" I asked, my voice softer now, coaxing.

"I don't know how to sing," she whispered, her voice barely audible.

I blinked, the shock of her words sending a ripple of confusion through me. "You don't know how?"

She shook her head. "I've never tried."

The weight of her confession settled heavily on me, and I felt a sting of regret, like I'd failed to notice something so important about her until now. "Not once?" I asked, my voice almost a whisper.

She shook her head, the vulnerability in her expression pulling me closer to her than I had been before.

"Then let me teach you," I offered, my voice soft yet full of intent.

"The trial is tonight, we don't have time," she said, shaking her head, but there was a flicker of hesitation in her eyes.

I set the guitar aside, then slowly sank to my knees in front of her. Her gaze followed every movement, her breath catching in her chest as I moved closer.

"Briar, what are you doing?" she asked, her voice a mix of uncertainty and something else I couldn't quite place.

I met her eyes, my heart pounding in my chest as my fingers hooked in her waistband and pulled her pants down her legs until she was bare to me.

"Maybe you just need a little incentive," I whispered, my eyes catching on her glistening center. She was already so wet for me. I pressed forward, tossing her legs over my shoulders. She fell back onto the bed, her elbows holding her up.

My breath dusted over her core, but despite how badly I wanted a taste, I didn't move. "Sing for me, Hollis," I demanded quietly.

She sighed. "I...can't..." she replied.

"You can if you want me to taste you," I challenged tracing a light touch along her inner thighs. She groaned, as her whole body reacted to my touch.

"Briar-" she begged.

"Sing it," I commanded.

I felt her struggle between her desire, and her uncertainty.

"It's just us, Hollis. Open your mouth, and sing."

She began with a soft hum, gentle and cautious, like

testing the waters. Then, barely above a whisper, she breathed out a few words, so quiet I almost couldn't hear them over the frantic beat of my heart. I froze, the sound sinking in as I recognized the melody. It was the song I sang in the Wilds. She had remembered it. Her voice, light and ethereal, wasn't perfectly controlled, but there was a raw beauty in it that made my chest tighten.

I listened to her sing, breathlessly, as her core pulsed before me. "That's it, baby," I praised before pressing my tongue against her clit, then her opening, swirling my tongue around her center like I was playing her body like an instrument. She gasped, her song giving way to soft moans. Her taste exploded on my tongue and it was divine. I wanted all of her, but we had a lesson to finish. I pulled back, leaving her gasping beneath me.

"Keep singing," I demanded.

She groaned. "Briar-"

I slid a finger into her tight core and she bucked against me with a loud gasp. When I pressed a thumb against her clit she arched off the bed, pressing her core into my hand. It took all my willpower to keep from moving my hand, from pulling her pleasure from her body.

She knew what I was doing, knew that I wasn't going to move until she gave me what I wanted. Finally, broken between soft moans, and desperate wimpers, she sang. The words of my song on her tongue as her body sang on mine.

She continued the song, softly and broken, as my fingers and my tongue worked in tandem to bring this beautiful perfect girl to the edge of desire. Her body thrashed under my hold as her climax neared. I pressed my hand against the lower part of her stomach as my mouth ravaged her core. When her song stopped, and a desperate scream of pleasure ripped from her throat, I tasted her release on my tongue. A taste so uniquely and perfectly her, I never wanted to forget it.

"That is my new favorite song," I whispered against her skin.

I languidly drank up her release, not willing to waste a drop of it, and she gripped my hair, trying to pull me off her sensitive core.

She slid off the side of the bed, kneeling in front of me, her eyes locked onto mine with a raw intensity. Like she couldn't hold back any longer, she cupped my face in her hands and kissed me with a hunger that felt desperate and untamed. A soft moan escaped her as she tasted herself on my tongue, and her body pressed into mine, urgent and electric.

Her hands ripped at my clothing, in a storm of mindless desire, until we were both kneeling naked before each other. Her fingers danced along my skin, and I felt my blood sing beneath her touch. She trailed a finger down my stomach until she brushed along my clit. Briefly, teasingly. I moaned, pulling her lips to mine again.

She continued to drink from my lips as her fingers slid through my slick center. When she finally slid her fingers into my wet heat, I cried out into her mouth. My body was hers to play.

"Your turn to sing for me," she whispered against my lips. Her fingers pressed into me as her thumb circled my clit, drawing euphoric passion from every part of me.

She pressed her hands against my shoulders and I let her lead me to the ground until I was laying on my back on the hardwood floor. The chill of the panelling was a cooling balm to the heat of the moment. She continued pressing her fingers into me as she hovered above me, my every nerve ending was thrumming in harmony with her. When she withdrew her fingers and slid them into her mouth, I groaned, a guttural, ferocious sound.

She moved reverently, slowly, keeping her eyes on mine as she lifted my left leg and slid hers beneath it. Gently sliding her body closer to mine until our bare centers pressed against each other. My head fell back at the first slide of her pussy against mine.

"Hollis-" Her name, almost like a vow, fell from my tongue as my mouth fell open.

I gripped her legs tightly, pulling her body tightly to mine as we moved our hips against each other in sinful dance. Our cries of pleasure spilled from our mouths in a dark delicious harmony, creating my new favorite song.

I met her eyes, as she circled her hips against mine. Her clit pressed and slid against mine and I hoped she saw the truth of how I felt about her in my gaze. It was a slow, languid dance, one that felt real, honest, and raw.

When our breaths started coming more rapidly, and our bodies heated as we chased release, I kept my eyes locked on hers. She was everything I hadn't even known I was missing, a force that filled the empty spaces I'd grown accustomed to. Her body, when it pressed against mine, seemed to fit so perfectly, like two puzzle pieces finally locked in place. The rhythm of her heartbeat matched the pulse of my own, and I felt it deep inside me.

I never realized how much I needed her until she was standing right in front of me, her energy lighting up everything around us. And in that moment, I realized I didn't care what the future held or what battles lay ahead.

All I knew was that I wanted to face them with her by my side.

My head fell back as my climax found me, and she followed me into the storm of ecstasy and passion.

When our bodies were spent, tangled in the soft aftermath of our joining, I felt her shift, slow and tender, until she nestled herself beside me. She moved with such quiet grace, curling against my side like she was meant to fit there. Her head found its place on my chest, her soft dark hair brushing against my skin as she settled in.

We didn't need words, just the steady rhythm of our breathing filling the space between us. It was slow, languid, a dance of hearts finding their natural cadence. Each exhale seemed to echo the calm of the other, a silent symphony of closeness that wrapped around us. I could feel the weight of her in the best way, the softness of her body against mine grounding me, making the world outside seem so far away.

"Sing with me for the trial," I whispered, my voice barely more than a breath. She lifted her gaze, her eyes meeting mine with uncertainty.

"Are you sure? I don't want to mess up your chances of keeping that guitar this time," she cautioned, a slight tremor in her voice.

I smiled softly, the tension in my chest easing. "I have a feeling, no matter what place I get in this trial, you won't let them take it from me again."

She smiled, her lips brushing mine in a gentle kiss. "Yeah. Maybe, if we're lucky, we'll stop them from taking anything from anyone ever again."

"Luck's got nothing to do with it, Hollis," I whispered, my heart pounding in the quiet space between us. "If we succeed. If we finally finish what my Ma started. It'll be because of you."

CHAPTER
SEVEN

BEX

THE STUDIO where we'd done our interview had been completely transformed for the Entertainment Trial. The stage was a towering display of lights and tech, like the rigs they hauled in every year for the vote, only bigger, bolder, more extravagant. It pulsed with energy, the air thick with anticipation and something sharp beneath it.

Nova swept in like a cloud of gold and glitter, her outfit catching the light with every movement. She rounded us all up and ferried us to wardrobe, my men being ushered down the hall, Briar and I sequestered into a separate dressing room where the expected happened. We were shoveled into black outfits, glinting with studs and sequins, tailored to perfection. Predictable, but still striking. Nova spent extra time at the makeup table, her hands surprisingly steady as she painted thick, dark lines across my eyelids, then turned to Briar.

And God, if Briar didn't already stop hearts, she did now. The heavy, smokey makeup made her look dangerous, otherworldly. I'd be lying if I said my skin didn't still hum from her 'singing lessons' earlier, and standing there now, watching her reflected in the mirror, the heat beneath my skin curled tighter, mixing with the steady hum of nerves about what came next.

Nova, for all her irritating qualities, had a gift with a brush.

"No one's ever done a duet in these trials," Nova commented, her voice light, but I couldn't tell if it was admiration or a veiled warning.

"Then we'll have the element of surprise, if nothing else," Briar shot back, squeezing my hand so tightly I was sure she could feel my pulse pounding in my palm. Nova's eyes caught the movement, lingered a second longer than expected, then flicked up to meet ours.

"Your little team," she began, and I braced for the blow, "has been very entertaining to watch." She gave the smallest of smiles. "I don't root for Challengers. Almost never. But if I did... I might root for you."

Nova was everything Praxis worshipped, wealth, excess, superiority masked as charm. So, if even a sliver of what we were doing had cracked something in her, maybe, just maybe, we weren't fighting a losing battle.

"Thanks, Nova," I murmured.

She gave a short nod, her expression slipping back into the familiar mask of calculated detachment. "Briar, I need you to come with me. Brexlyn has a visitor."

My stomach dropped.

"Who?" I asked, too quickly.

"You'll see soon enough." She held out a hand to Briar, who hesitated only long enough to cast me a worried look.

"I'm okay," I whispered, leaning in to brush a kiss against her lips. "I'll see you soon."

She gripped her guitar, her fingers white-knuckled around the neck, then followed Nova out, leaving me alone in the dressing room. The quiet felt heavier without her there. And all I could do was wait, my mind spinning with every possible name of who could be asking for me now.

After an agonizing stretch of silence, the door hissed open, and in stepped Archon Evanora Veritas. The woman was a vision of lethal opulence, draped in a shimmering gold pantsuit with a sharp, fanned peplum that flared like a blade around her hips. The fabric shimmered in the dim light, glinting like cracked glass, as though even brushing against her would leave you bleeding.

I instinctively stood, taking a few careful steps back, granting her a wide berth. The door slid shut behind her, and the suffocating weight of the room multiplied. It felt smaller now. Claustrophobic. Like the walls had shifted closer.

Her gaze moved over me with slow, measured precision, not like someone seeing a person, but like a predator weighing the weakness of its prey.

"Miss Hollis," she said at last, her voice velvet-smooth and laced with something sharp. Every syllable soft, every undertone venomous. "I've been... eager to meet you."

I swallowed, feeling the coil of sickness twist tight in my stomach. "I'm honored to have earned your attention," I managed, the words brittle and paper-thin.

Did she know? About the messages we'd been sending. About the song? About the veiled message Briar and I had woven into tonight's performance, a rally cry buried beneath metaphor and melody?

"I'm sure you are," Evanora murmured, stepping further into the room. I could feel the air shift as she moved, like the static charge before a lightning strike. "Do you know why I wanted to come see you?"

I shook my head, keeping my voice level. "I can't imagine it's to wish me luck."

She gave a low, humorless chuckle, dark as a grave. "No,

darling, I don't think you need luck." Her fingers trailed idly across the edge of a counter as she spoke, her nails clicking softly against the metal. "I've watched your performances, Miss Hollis. And I think you're clever enough to recognize the... influence you've accumulated during your time in the Reclamation Run."

Her gaze pinned me in place again, the room closing in. I fought the urge to shrink.

"I guess I've earned a few fans," I said carefully.

"Don't be modest," she hissed, like the words themselves were a warning. "And while you're at it, don't pretend you're pleased to see me. I intend to be very candid with you here tonight, Miss Hollis and I'd appreciate it if you do the same."

I swallowed hard. "Okay."

She smiled then, a thin, wicked curve of her lips. "You're popular in a way we haven't seen in years. The kind of popularity Praxis finds... dangerous."

The word hung in the air like smoke, and I tensed beneath her stare.

"Do you know why?" she asked, a brow arching.

"I have a sinking feeling you'll tell me," I said, truthfully.

Her smile sharpened. "Because you outnumber us."

The words landed like a blow. I felt my stomach drop, my pulse hammer in my ears.

"The Collectives," she went on, taking another step forward. "You're the kind of person who could remind them of that fact. Remind them that the power of the people could drown the people in power."

I didn't move. Couldn't. She was too close now. The room felt starved of air.

"You're wondering why I'm telling you this," she said, head tilting like a serpent before a strike.

I nodded stiffly.

"Because, Miss Hollis," she purred, "I didn't claw my way

to this throne by ignoring rebellion. I built Praxis by cutting the heads off snakes before they had the chance to slither through my gates."

I swallowed the knot in my throat. "Let me guess. I'm the snake?"

A real smile now, one that chilled the marrow of my bones. "You are, darling. But I'm feeling... charitable."

She circled me slowly, a predator savoring the moment before the kill.

"I have a deal for you," Evanora whispered. "Spend the next four trials showering Praxis with praise. Show them how grateful you are for all we've given you. Make the Collectives believe you're loyal. That you've been tamed."

"And if I do that?" I asked tightly.

"Then I'll save your brother's life."

The air rushed out of my lungs. My knees nearly buckled.

"What?" My voice was nothing but a rasp.

"I'll have a private physician assigned to him. All the medicine, all the treatments, everything he needs."

It felt too good to be true. It was. "Until the next Run, you mean."

She leaned in close, her perfume cloying, her voice a deadly promise. "I mean forever."

I stared at her, feeling the weight of the chains being fastened around my throat.

"And if I refuse?" I asked, my voice barely a whisper.

Her smile vanished, and something cold and ancient flashed in her eyes. "Then you'll bury your brother."

The room was silent, except for the ragged sound of my breathing.

"I look forward to you showing me what you decide during tonight's trial," she murmured, brushing a hand across my shoulder as she passed. It felt like ice.

The door hissed open behind her, and Evanora Veritas

stepped through it leaving nothing but her offer, and the suffocating presence behind.

I braced my hands on the cold metal counter, my breathing ragged as panic clawed its way up my throat, threatening to drown me. My whole body trembled under the crushing weight of what had just happened. The room felt smaller now, suffocating me with the memory of her voice, of those venom-laced words.

I didn't even hear the door open, but the moment a pair of hands gripped my shoulders, I flinched, a choked sound escaping me. And then I felt the warmth of familiar touch, grounding me. Slowly, I turned, my vision clearing enough to see my Wildguard. Each of them wore a different expression, but the same fear etched into their eyes.

"What's wrong, love?" Thorne asked, his voice low, but brittle as glass ready to shatter.

"Was that Archon Veritas we saw leaving your room?" Zaffir's words were tight, his jaw clenched so hard the muscles twitched.

Briar didn't say anything at first, she just took my hand, her grip firm, solid. A tether.

Ezra, though, looked like a man seconds from murder, his fists balled so tightly his knuckles were bloodless. His gaze flicked toward the door like he might chase her down and finish what Praxis started years ago.

I managed a shaky nod. "She knows..."

Thorne's face drained of color. "All of it?"

"Not... specifics," I said, my voice little more than a ghost of itself. "But she knows we have the power to start something. She knows that I know it, too."

Some of the tension eased from them, but not much. The threat still hung thick in the air, an executioner's blade suspended above us all.

"What did she want?" Ezra demanded, his voice sharp, brittle with barely restrained violence.

"She offered me a deal," I whispered.

"What kind of deal?" Briar finally spoke, his voice low, bracing for the worst.

"She said... if I calm the rebellion... if I convince everyone that I'm loyal to Praxis... she'll make sure Jax gets medicine. And doctors. For the rest of his life."

Thorne dragged a hand through his hair, his expression darkening.

"And if you don't?" Briar asked.

The words stuck in my throat. But I forced them out. "She'll kill him."

The moment they left my lips, a sob broke free. I collapsed against the counter, the grief and fear threatening to crush me. Zaffir was there in an instant, arms around me, pulling me close, holding me together when I was breaking apart.

"Shhh... shhh, it's alright. I've got you," he murmured against my hair, though his voice trembled too.

"What are we going to do now?" Briar asked, scanning the room, the question slicing through the silence like a blade.

"We call it off," Thorne said, his voice quiet but resolute.

We all turned to him, stunned.

"What?" I croaked.

"We knew it was a risk. We knew Praxis wouldn't sit idle if they caught wind of this. But she's made a direct threat now, love." His eyes found mine, so heartbreakingly kind and full of regret. "I won't ask you to choose between your brother and my mother's rebellion. That isn't a choice."

I hated the way he looked at me, like I'd already made the decision to surrender. Like the fight had drained from me. But hadn't it? Could I risk Jax's life for this? Could I live with myself if I didn't?

And yet... I could feel it. That rising heat. That storm

gathering inside my chest. The same storm Veritas had seen, and feared. She was afraid. It may have been hidden behind her threats and calm demeanor. But the truth of it was there, clear and vivid. She was afraid.

And I couldn't risk losing that momentum.

"I don't want to stop," I said. The words were true, but it felt like ash on my tongue. "I just... I wish I could tell Ava and Jax. Get them out. Warn them."

"Maybe you can," Thorne murmured.

I looked up sharply. "What do you mean?"

He gestured to the bag slung over Zaffir's back. "People from every Collective are in there. Eyes in every shadow. You send word, and they'll find your family. They'll hide them."

"You really think it'll work?"

"I do," he replied.

Zaffir was already unzipping the bag, pulling out the device. His fingers flew across the keys, breaking through encrypted firewalls, bypassing passwords. Opening the locked doors that the rebellion hid behind. He opened the message system and slid it toward me.

My hands shook as I typed.

'**Runaways. I need your help. I need someone to find Jax Hollis and Ava Torvich in Canyon. Praxis plans to use him against me. Hide them. Protect them. Get him and his guardian to safety. The guards are coming. Don't let them win. Not when we're so close.**'

Zaffir hit send.

We waited, the seconds stretching unbearably long. Then one by one, replies started to pour in. Dozens. Hundreds. A flood of strangers pledging to help us. To find him and protect him. Anonymous names I didn't know. Chances were they weren't Canyon... considering we didn't have this technology there. But maybe word could spread.

And then one message appeared that made my breath catch.

'He is safe with me. Where we're hiding, they'll never find us. I'll protect him until you can come home to us. Love, always. -A'

"Ava..." I whispered her name. A sob tore itself from my chest, raw and trembling, not from fear this time, but from a fierce, aching relief that I could barely contain. "She's a Runaway. How..." I stammered, wiping at my face uselessly. "I mean, we don't even have technology in Canyon. We don't have access to any of this."

"Maybe she's not in Canyon anymore," Briar offered gently, her voice threading through my panic. "She said she's in hiding now, didn't she?"

"According to the thread," Thorne said, picking up from her and turning the computer toward me, "the low-tech Collectives still participate. They have chapters. It's just... different. More analog. Symbols. Stories. Art."

He clicked through a few images until one stopped me cold. A street mural, painted right on the cracked pavement of Canyon's Market Row, a moth, shimmering with vibrant purples and blues, wings spread wide like it was ready to carry dreams on its back. I knew that moth. I'd seen it. Walked past it a hundred times without really seeing it.

And Ava...she loved moths.

The memories rushed in, unbidden and sharp, almost painful in their clarity. The tattoo on her wrist dedicated to the memory of her brother. Nights sitting on the roof of the shed behind her house, our fingers tracing patterns in the sky as she'd whisper about the stars, about stories that deserved more than endings forced on them by the Run. About her brother. Her voice, soft and secretive, *"The stars are still ours, Bex. No one can take that."*

All the tiny moments I'd overlooked, all the things she said that had seemed sweet or strange but harmless at the time, they crashed over me now with new meaning.

When I left for the Run, she'd hugged me so tightly I thought she'd never let go. *"May the stars shine on you, Bex,"* she'd said, voice shaking. I thought it was just a goodbye. I hadn't understood then.

But now, it was so obvious. She hadn't just been wishing me well. She'd been sending me off with a code, a Runaway blessing.

"She's a Runaway," I said again, the words steady and sure this time, no longer a question, no longer a wonder. They felt right in my mouth. Like they had always been true and I was just finally catching up.

"She's been keeping him safe," Thorne said, his voice low but certain as he stepped closer and placed a grounding hand on my shoulder. His thumb pressed lightly into my skin, a silent reminder that I wasn't alone in this. Ava had found a way to fight back, even from inside a place like Canyon. Even when the world said she couldn't. She'd fought with paint, with whispers, with stories, with stars.

I wiped my eyes, turning back to them. "If I don't play Veritas' game tonight...if she can't go after him. She'll go after us. Things are going to get worse. These trials will become deadly."

"They already are," Ezra said. "It's time for those stars to shine," he finished in a low, dangerous whisper.

We stood in a quiet circle, eyes moving from one face to the next. And in that stillness, I saw them...really saw them. These people have become my family. Chosen. Earned. Loved.

I wanted to protect them.

I wanted to save them.

I wanted to build a world where we could live without fear thrumming under our skin, without the constant dread of Praxis at our backs. A world where we could breathe freely and laugh loudly and touch without paying for it in blood and death.

This choice would put us in danger. It would make targets of all of us. But we'd made it through so much already. We could survive this too, as long as we had each other. And it was important.

I stepped forward and took my time, pressing soft, reverent kisses to each of their lips like I was sealing a vow.

Thorne tasted of the woods, pine and smoke and something grounding.

Briar was rain through trees, cool and soothing, a balm.

Ezra, sharp and burning like whiskey, left warmth lingering on my tongue.

And Zaffir was floral and light, once a scent reminiscent of the Praxis amenities, but now... now it was just him. Something reclaimed. Something real.

That was the kind of reclamation I believed in. Taking back the pieces Praxis had stolen, the scents, the symbols, the parts of ourselves they had tried to brand with their ownership and making them ours again.

I caught the subtle moment Zaffir reached for Ezra's hand, fingers curling around his, a gentle squeeze shared between them. Their eyes met, and though no words passed between them, the depth of feeling did. I could feel it too.

I wanted peace for them. I wanted Zaffir to be able to love both of us openly, without guilt or fear. I wanted Ezra's name to be cleared. I wanted to finish what Thorne and Briar's mother began.

We didn't speak as we left the room.

We didn't need to.

We walked together, step by step, toward the stage.

Toward the choice that would change everything.

Toward the spark that might finally light the fire.

CHAPTER
EIGHT

BEX

THE STAGE LIGHTS WERE BLINDING, hot and white and merciless. From the shadows of the wings, Briar and I stood pressed together, the harsh glow spilling just far enough to paint our faces in slivers of silver. Zaffir had made his way to the audience to set up his camera. Ezra and Thorne were lined up on the other side of the stage, but I could see their faces from our spot.

Annalese welcomed everyone to the trial with her usual cheery disposition. Then she introduced the first Challenger. Devrin entered the stage.

He sat at the grand piano with no introduction, no flourish, just stillness. Then his fingers found the keys, and the music poured out like a confession. It was a Saltspire folk song, familiar and aching despite never having heard it, the kind sung to children on long winter nights or whispered during stolen moments in the dark. He didn't sing, but he didn't need to. The piano told the story for him.

"He's good," Briar murmured beside me, her voice soft but full of something almost reverent.

The crowd was on their feet, hands raised high, chanting his name.

I narrowed my eyes at the sea of them. "I wonder if he earned those fans before or after he nearly killed me," I whispered, the words sour on my tongue. Were they cheering for the music, or the violence? Did they care about the art, or the blood?

Briar leaned her head gently against my shoulder. She didn't say anything, just comforted me with her touch. Praxis didn't earn its bloodthirsty reputation through rumor alone. These people had been trained to applaud destruction.

When the final note faded, Annalese swept onto the stage with her usual theatrical flourish, grabbing Devrin's wrist and raising his arm high into the air like he'd just won a boxing match.

The crowd roared. Devrin didn't flinch. No smile. No bow. Just a cold, defiant stare into the nearest camera.

"What's that song called, Devrin?" Annalese asked, pushing the mic too close to his mouth.

He paused for a heartbeat, then said clearly, "The Moth."

My breath caught. Briar's eyes snapped to mine.

"Did he just..." I started, glancing across the stage to see Ezra and Thorne having a similar silent shocked conversation.

"There's Runaways everywhere, I guess," she finished, her voice barely audible, like saying it too loud would collapse the moment.

As Devrin stepped off the stage, he didn't look at me. Not at first. But just before he vanished into the shadows, he flicked a single glance my way and gave the smallest nod. A signal. A promise.

He knew what I was planning.

And he was in.

Next up was Vivian Arlo of Ironclad. She wheeled out a massive canvas, easel already set, and began to paint with deft, confident strokes. We couldn't see the image from where we stood, but her hands moved with certainty, every flick of her wrist deliberate. The crowd stayed hushed, waiting.

When she finally stepped back, Annalese lifted the canvas for all to see, revealing a night sky, endless and full of stars. Briar and I exchanged a look.

Was it really happening? Were *all* of us making statements?

Thorne was next. Ever the lively one, he sauntered onto the stage with a cocky grin, unfolding a slightly crumpled piece of paper. I braced myself, half-laughing already, expecting the dirty limerick he'd teased me with earlier.

But what came out of his mouth wasn't crude. It wasn't even funny. It was soft. Reverent.

And it shattered me.

"She named the stars like lullabies, soft on her tongue, sweet in his skies. Each one a promise, burning true. A light to follow, a love he knew."

The room, previously loud with applause and laughter, fell still. You could hear the hush settle like snow. Even Annalese, standing at the edge of the stage with her mic poised, looked utterly invested.

"She taught him how to look above, to trace the constellations' love. To see in distance not despair, but all the ways that she'd be there."

Someone in the crowd sniffled. Another sobbed outright. A hush rippled through the audience, heavy with held breath and aching hearts. Briar's grip on my hand tightened.

"He'd sit and watch the night alone, like it still whispered through the stone. Her voice in starlight, low and clear. You're stronger, son, because I'm near."

I didn't even realize I was crying until Briar reached up

and wiped a tear from my cheek. She had tears streaking down her own face too. Wordlessly, I squeezed her hand.

"And though the sky is vast and wide, he carries her in every stride. In every breath, in every scar... he is her boy. And she is his star."

The final line landed like a quiet thunderclap. The crowd didn't erupt at first. They sat in silence for a second too long, like everyone needed a breath. Then the applause burst forward, raw and emotional, peppered with cheers and more than a few sobs.

Annalise stepped forward slowly, her eyes shining. "Thorne," she said gently, her voice filled with a kind of maternal awe. "That was stunning. You wrote that about your mother?"

He nodded, serious now, no trace of his usual swagger.

"Is she still with us?"

"No, ma'am," he said. "Gone nearly fifteen years now."

Annalese's gaze softened even further. "Do you think she'd be proud of you? For the work you've done tonight... and in this Run?"

Thorne didn't answer her right away. Instead, he turned his head to face the camera. To face everyone watching. His voice rang steady and clear.

"She'd be proud of what I've done," he said. "But I know she'll be even more proud of what I do next."

The crowd roared. It was thunderous. He turned and walked off the stage, but not before shooting me a flirty wink that made my already-tired heart twist in the best kind of way. Then he disappeared into the wings on the other side, leaving behind a stage full of silence and stars.

Cayal Orin of Ember followed. He stepped forward, book in hand, and began to read. His voice was rich and clear, pulling us into a tale of a young prince trapped in a kingdom haunted by a cruel dragon. The people cowered, afraid to speak, until finally, they rose together. Fought. Won.

"The prince decided," he read, "that his story didn't have to end like that."

The crowd laughed, clapped, cheered. But something cold and electric slid down my spine. Because I knew exactly who the dragon was meant to be.

One by one, they were standing up. Telling the truth. In code. In symbols. In song and story and paint. The Challengers were standing together instead of in opposition.

And then came Lark Harbor of Wildfold.

I'd spent the whole Run with a knot in my stomach every time I saw him, he was the other top contender for the medical trials. The one person who could take what my brother needed away from me. I'd told myself he was the enemy, because that's the narrative Praxis had manufactured.

Music started softly, and then he moved.

Not just moved, but danced. Every motion was poetry, every spin a declaration. He wore a long dark cloak that swirled like smoke around him, but halfway through the piece, he ripped it off, revealing wings painted across his chest and arms...moth wings.

The audience exploded. They didn't understand. Not really. Maybe some of them did. They thought it was beautiful, dramatic. They didn't see what the Runaways saw. The hidden message within the movements.

But we knew.

A moth. A starfield. A prince. A folk song.

A rebellion wrapped in performance.

Tears prickled behind my eyes. I blinked fast. I couldn't afford to cry right now.

We were in this together. All of us. Even Fenly. My throat tightened at the thought of his name. He should be here too.

And maybe, in some way, he still was. His absence only spurred me forward.

What was happening tonight was bigger than any one of us.

Ezra was next. He entered the stage with shackles on his wrists. I felt a jolt of shock and confusion as I watched him take his place center stage. The audience murmured with confusion as well. He made his way to a small pillar that was raised from the stage. Metal, sturdy, immoveable.

He began wrapping the chains connected to his wrists around the pillar. Slow deliberate movements. Circling the pillar like a vice grip. Then, with nothing but brute strength, ripped the chains apart, the shackles fell from his wrists clattering on the floor. The audience cheered as Annalese scurried in.

"My my, what a show of strength, Ezra," she began. "Why did you choose to share this talent today?"

Ezra leaned down to the mic and looked down the barrel of the camera before him. "Just a reminder that not every cage is inescapable." They cheered again, and Ezra slipped from the stage but not before shooting me a gentle look, and a soft smile meant just for me.

Then Annalese called our names.

Briar shot me a soft smile, one only I got to see, then stepped into the lights. I followed close behind, and the moment our bodies hit the stage, the crowd screamed. Ravenously. Their praise came like a wave, overwhelming and deafening. It echoed against the domed ceiling and crashed against the stage.

I scanned the audience, a sea of wealth and brilliance. The stage lights beamed hot on my skin, and the faces beyond were mostly smudges in the glare.

Until I saw him.

Zaffir.

My chest fluttered, just for a moment, and I allowed myself a small, fleeting smile. But I didn't linger, because as my gaze continued to wander, it landed on her.

Archon Veritas.

She wasn't in the crowd. Perched above in a box seat like a God in judgment. Her gaze was sharp, assessing, unblinking. She leaned slightly forward, elbows resting on the rail, the barest smirk playing on her lips...waiting. Daring me to make my choice.

And I held her stare. I didn't bow. Didn't look away. Not tonight. Not ever again.

Briar took her seat first, perched on the stool like she'd been born to do this, even if it had been years since her fingers last caressed a guitar string. She adjusted the mic, and her hands trembled just slightly as she set the guitar in her lap.

I stepped in front of the second mic. My own hands gripped the stand, clammy and shaking, though I prayed it didn't show.

I glanced at Briar. She nodded once. Then her fingers strummed the first chord.

The sound bloomed soft and aching. A dark tone, slow and haunting. And just like that, the room fell still again, just as it had for Thorne. Every sound seemed to hold its breath.

Then Briar began. Her voice came low, near the vocal fry, with a hint of gravel that made it sound worn and true. Not like a songbird, but like someone who had lived every word.

"When the run is over, and the lights grow dim,
When the songs are silent and the victors grin..."

I closed my eyes just briefly. Took a breath. And stepped into the next line. My voice was quieter than hers, but pointed. Steady. Like I was leaving behind a trail. A map.

"You'll find me by the old gold gate, where the wild roots grow,
With a pack on my shoulder and a heart you know."

Maybe they understood. Maybe they heard it. The truth under the lyrics. The message sewn into the melody. Then Briar and I sang together, our voices locking like pieces in a puzzle. Seamless. Like we were always meant to sing this one song, just this once.

"Raise your hands, raise your eyes, to the breakin' dawn,
There's a road past the border where the lost ones've gone."

The harmony built. An aching, longing sound.

"And when the run is over, when the reckonin's near,
We'll sing the old verses only runaways hear."

Someone in the audience gasped softly. Another clapped a hand over their mouth.

"Lay your tools by the riverside, leave your mark in stone,
Count the crows at midnight, you won't be alone."

My hands didn't shake anymore. They held steady to the mic, firm. Certain.

"Watch for the lantern in the hollow's bend,
It'll burn like a promise where the shadows send."

I looked back up. Straight at her. Archon Veritas sat like a phantom carved in gold, separated from the masses in her elevated box. All around her, the crowd roared with noise and light but she was stillness incarnate.

And I sang right to her.

"Raise your hands, raise your eyes, to the breakin' dawn,
There's a road past the border where the lost ones've gone.
And when the run is over, when the reckonin's near,
We'll sing the old verses only runaways hear."

The words...our hidden anthem...poured from my mouth. I didn't flinch. Didn't blink. Just held her gaze and let the truth burn its way through the melody. Briar's voice cracked just slightly at the start of the next verse, but it made it more beautiful. More real.

"Hold fast to the names they tried to erase,
There's a fire in the earth and it knows your face."

Veritas tilted her head, slow and deliberate, like a predator watching a challenge rise from the dirt.

Her eyes locked with mine, burning hotter than the stage lights overhead. A furnace of curiosity, calculation. No mask of neutrality now, just something sharp and feral gleaming behind the polish of power.

"Tie a thread 'round your wrist, red as dusk, tight as kin,
When the last winner's called, that's when we begin."

My voice rang out then, clear and strong as fire.

"Raise your hands, raise your hearts, to the breakin' sky,
We're the storm they forgot, we're the wolves runnin' high."

The crowd surged. I could feel the emotion crashing through them.

"And when the run is over, when the reckonin's near,
We'll rise from the ashes and they'll know we were here."

We held the last note just a little too long. Let it echo. Let them feel it. Then silence. The silence right before the flood.

Then came the roar.

Thunderous applause erupted like a tidal wave crashing through the arena. Some in the crowd clapped for the melody, oblivious to the coded defiance laced between each line. Others, those who understood, rose to their feet, the undercurrent of rebellion pulsing just beneath their praise. I had no way of knowing which was which, but I felt it. It was determination and celebration woven together, a perfect smokescreen.

Annalese spilled onto the stage, radiant and beaming, her heels clicking against the floor as she swept into the spotlight between us.

"You two sounded beautiful together, didn't they?" she gushed, turning to the audience with a grin that could sell sunshine. The crowd responded with a fresh wave of cheers, some whistling, some already chanting our names.

"What a charming little song," she continued, eyes twinkling with forced innocence. "Anyone special you're dedicating it to?"

She shoved the mic between Briar and me.

I met Archon Veritas's eyes across the space, her box seat looming like a throne above the masses. She hadn't moved. Not once. Still as a blade right before the strike. Her expression unreadable, but her presence burned.

"To Praxis," I said, my voice clear and steady. "And Archon Veritas."

The crowd roared again, some in earnest celebration, others catching the spark beneath the surface.

But Archon didn't move. Didn't clap. Didn't blink.

Her fury rolled toward me like smoke on the wind, cold and crackling. I couldn't tell if she had heard the message buried in our melody, if she'd unraveled the truth between the notes. But it didn't matter.

Because those who needed to hear it did.

The Runaways would be ready. When the final trial ended, we would strike.

We would fight back.

We would reclaim what was ours.

And she could try to stop us, but as she told me, *we* outnumbered her.

CHAPTER
NINE

ZAFFIR

I WAS a little more careful leaving the studio after the trial.
Can you blame me? The last time I walked out those doors, I
was kidnapped and tortured.

So, yeah. A little extra caution felt earned.

Ezra barely even waited for the final note of the show to
fade before he was stalking off the stage and coming to a stop
at my side, ignoring Nova's protests and cutting through the
chaos with a single-minded focus. He gripped my arm, not
rough, but firm, and pulled me away from the camera station
I'd barely had time to pack up. No hesitation. Just action.
Just me.

I shouldn't have liked it. The way he took control, the way
he didn't ask, just *did*. But God help me, I did. The protective-
ness sent wicked thoughts racing through my mind, sharp as
fire and twice as hot.

The crowd clawed for him, of course. He's Ezra. A star to
them. One of the Wildguard. But his focus didn't flicker. Not

once. He didn't see the fans, the lights, the cameras. He saw me.

And he wasn't letting me out of his sight.

I barely had time to gather my gear before he pulled me into a shadowy corner backstage, hidden from the mass of handlers and techs. I could hear the other Challengers being shuttled out toward their cars, the buzz of conversation and flashing lights still bleeding in from the stage. But here, tucked behind thick curtains and heavy velvet, it was just us.

"Subtle," I teased, trying to keep it light, trying not to let my pulse give me away.

He looked at me then. Really looked. Eyes burning with something dark and fierce.

"I told you," he said, voice low and trembling with restrained fury. "I'm never going to let her put her hands on you again."

Those words hit me somewhere deep, deeper than I wanted to admit. The kind of place that makes breathing difficult.

"Technically," I said, forcing a laugh I didn't quite feel, "she didn't touch me. She just ordered the guards to."

He didn't smile. Didn't ease.

Instead, he pressed me gently, *deliberately*, into the narrow alcove, the black curtain closing us in. The heat of him was overwhelming, our bodies just inches apart. I could feel him without him even touching me. My breath hitched, and I bit down on my lip.

His eyes followed the movement.

And for one sharp, suspended moment, I thought he was going to kiss me again. Finally. Put me out of my damn misery. My entire body was screaming for it. For him.

But instead, he blinked, leaned back just enough to break the spell.

"Okay," he said softly. "Coast is clear."

He reached for my bag, slinging it over one shoulder, and took my wrist with the other, leading me from the alcove toward the car waiting just outside.

My mind was a storm. My body was worse. Every step throbbed with unsaid things and unfinished moments. I wanted him to kiss me. I wanted him to do more than that. I wanted...

Ezra ushered me into the car, and I wasn't oblivious to the way he held his body like a shield with his head on a swivel until I was safely inside. Instantly, arms wrapped around me.

"Congratulations," I whispered as Brexlyn's arms wrapped tightly around me. She pulled me in close, her scent grounding me.

She'd won. Well, her and Briar. First place in the trial, announced just moments before the curtain fell. The audience had voted, and Brexlyn and Briar had earned it by a landslide. I didn't know what Briar's deal with the Entertainment Trial was, not really, I could just tell it was important to her. So, when they called her name, something in her shifted. Her whole body seemed to exhale, relief washing over her like a tide she'd barely kept at bay.

"I'm just glad you're safe," Brexlyn murmured, her lips brushing my neck in a way that made my breath catch all over again. I melted into her, my body reacting instinctively. I wanted her. Right here, right now, in front of everyone.

But I reined it in. Just barely.

"Don't worry about me," I said with a sly glance toward Ezra. "My bodyguard kept me safe."

Ezra, finally starting to relax, cracked the faintest of smirks as the car pulled away from the curb.

But Brexlyn wasn't smiling.

"I don't think any of us are going to be safe after tonight," she whispered, so soft I barely caught it.

And she was right.

Shockingly, every single Challenger had used tonight's trial to quietly pledge allegiance to the Runaway movement. We didn't coordinate it, not openly, but somehow, we all understood what was at stake. What was being asked of us. And we each found our own way to answer.

Maybe Archon Veritas didn't know what to look for. Maybe she didn't recognize our coded messages, the songs, the symbols, the stories slipped into the performances like knives hidden in bouquets. If she had known, truly known, she would've shut it down. She would've silenced us before we even reached the stage.

But she hadn't. Which meant she didn't know everything.

Not yet.

But she had to feel it now, the pressure drop, the static charge in the air. The quiet before the downpour. The storm was coming. And we were the eye of it.

None of us spoke on the topic anymore. Not with Nova up front. Brexlyn seemed to think Nova wasn't as 'Praxis praising' as she seemed. Still, it felt smarter not to risk it.

So instead, I shifted Brexlyn into my lap, tugging her back against my chest and wrapping my arms tight around her middle. Like I could shield her. Like I could hold the world together by holding her.

She giggled softly as I shifted beneath her, and I knew she felt it, the evidence of just how deeply she affected me as I pressed my hips and my hardening cock against her backside. Her almost lustful laugh made my stomach twist with hunger, and I leaned into it. Into her.

My fingers found her thigh, tracing slow, idle patterns across her skin. Each pass drifted higher, the touch featherlight but full of promise. Her breath caught, just a little, each time I passed the hem of her dress. She didn't stop me. She opened to me.

The air in the car changed. Thickened. Charged.

I didn't need to look to know we had an audience.

Thorne and Briar were watching Brexlyn like they'd forgotten how to breathe. Briar with barely restrained hunger, Thorne with a kind of reverent awe. Their gazes were locked on the triangle of exposed skin at the apex of her thighs, watching the way her legs drifted open, just enough to tease.

But Ezra watched both of us.

His eyes moved back and forth, slow and deliberate, heat blazing in every glance. There was no shame in it. No jealousy. Just want. Unfiltered and heavy.

I kept my eyes on his as I leaned forward, brushing Brexlyn's hair aside and pressing a kiss to the nape of her neck. Not soft. Not sweet. Claiming. And when she let out a low moan, needy and broken, the entire car seemed to pulse with it.

The temperature rose. The windows fogged at the edges. And still, no one said a word. We had risked everything tonight, our safety, our lives, to speak the truth, to make a plan hidden in melody and metaphor. And now, in this car, with Brexlyn moaning in my arms and Ezra watching like he wanted to burn, I realized that I wanted to make the most of every single second with this little family we've found. Because tomorrow wasn't guaranteed.

I pressed a palm against her inner high, urging her to widen her legs even more for me. Thorne had a wicked smirk on his face and he sat back, admiring the view. Brexlyn sighed softly as I brought my lips to her ear.

"Do you think you can stay quiet for us, Brexlyn?" I asked in that demanding tone that I saved for only her. My eyes flashed to Ezra. Well, only them.

She nodded, and I knew she was biting her lip. "That's my good girl," I praised and I felt her body tremble in my hold. "If you make a sound, I'll have to stop. Do you understand?"

She nodded again. Then I let my fingers dance along the seam of her panties. I felt her tense in my hold, like she was trying not to let the moan escape. When I slid the fabric to the side and exposed her center, Briar leaned forward. Her eyes feasting on our girl's glistening pussy.

I trailed a single finger through her slickness, using a featherlight touch. Her hips pressed forward, trying to encourage my fingers to slide inside of her. But I wasn't ready for that. I met Ezra's eyes, and began slowly circling Brexlyn's clit with soft gentle pressure. Her head lulled back against my shoulder, exposing her throat to me. I pressed another kiss to her heated skin as my finger danced along her sensitive and throbbing clit.

When I felt her body tightening, and could hear her soft muffled moans, I pressed my finger deep inside of her heat. She gasped, and I had to fight every urge to keep chasing that sound to pull my hand from her center. Completely withdrawing from her body. She whimpered.

"You promised you'd stay quiet, Brexlyn," I challenged.

"I will," she cried in a barely there whisper.

"I dunno baby. Not sure I can trust you," I teased, meeting her eyes over her shoulder. I lifted my fingers to my mouth and tasted her arousal on them. I, following my own rules, stifled the moan that threatened to pull from me. God, her taste was delicious. Tangy and sweet. I could savor her for hours. Brexlyn and Ezra's eyes were heated on my skin as they watched me taste her off of my fingers. Before I could change my mind, I was thrusting my fingers toward Ezra's lips.

He opened willingly, and eagerly, pulling the digits into his warm mouth. My cock, which was already hard as stone, felt painfully stiff as I watched this hulking man suck our girl's arousal off of my fingers. I had a quick thought of him sucking her juices off a different part of me and I had to take a stuttering breath to calm myself. Brexlyn was watching the scene unfold with dark sinful eyes. She liked what she was seeing just as much as I did.

I slid my fingers from Ezra's mouth and his gaze pinned

me to place. A dark promise. Then I returned my fingers to Brexlyn's center. Without a single moment of preamble or warning, I dove two fingers into her pussy. She bucked against my hand, but to her credit stayed silent save for her heavy breaths. My calm and collected mask of a dominant figure was slipping with each press of my fingers into her wet channel. As I fucked her with my hands, her hips met me thrust for thrust. The others were watching, and I could see Ezra's cock tenting in his pants. He wanted us. Both of us. And fuck it, tonight, I was going to give him exactly what he wanted.

"Say you'll spend the night in my room," I whispered to Brexlyn as her muscles coiled and tightened. Her orgasm climbing within her. "In our room," I amended, looking at Ezra who was eagerly awaiting her answer.

Her answer came in the form of a silent but powerful orgasm. Her release flooded my hand and I stilled within her, feeling her walls tighten around me. Everyone in the back of the vehicle groaned quietly. The scent of sex and lust was heavy and heady. I pulled my hand from her center and slowly slid her panties back into place. She slumped against my shoulder. Struggling to catch her breath.

"So, will you?" I asked her quietly, using my non-arousal coated hand to stroke her hair.

"Of course," she replied with a smile.

"No fair," Thorne whined. I shot him a teasing glare.

"You can monopolize her attention tomorrow," I vowed, surprised at just how easy it was to share her affection with them. All of them. I trusted them. I believed in them. And in a world where resources were withheld and people had to fight tooth and nail for even an ounce of anything. I firmly believed Brexlyn deserved every ounce of love she was offered. We all did.

When the car finally rolled to a stop in front of the cabin, I hated it, but I moved her off of my lap and slid out of the car first so prying eyes couldn't see just how much I wanted to touch her. The doors clicked open and I spilled out into the night, ignoring Nova entirely, not even sparing her a glance. Whatever tonight had awakened in us, it wasn't meant for her.

The second she crossed the threshold of the cabin, and the door was safely closed behind her, I didn't pause to think. I grabbed Brexlyn's hand in mine, warm and willing, and caught Ezra by the wrist with my other. I didn't look back. Just pulled them both behind me, moving with single-minded determination down the narrow hallway to the room I shared with Ezra.

"Have fun," Thorne called after us, voice dripping with amusement. Briar's soft laugh followed, musical and knowing. But I didn't stop, not until the door was shut and locked behind us.

Inside, everything stilled. The silence was thick. Charged.

The three of us stood there, breathing heavy, staring at each other like we'd already crossed the point of no return. Lust darkened every gaze, pupils blown wide. I could feel the tension thrumming in the air like the room itself was holding its breath.

There was something electric between us, some magnetic pull that drew our bodies closer without a word. Like invisible cords had been wrapped around our torsos and were being cinched tight, winding us toward each other, tighter, tighter.

Brexlyn's hand landed on my chest. Ezra's fingers curled around my waist. I hadn't even realized how close we'd gotten until I could feel their breaths on my skin. My heart thundered in my chest as I looked between the two of them, wild with want.

I leaned forward first, drawn to Brexlyn's parted lips like gravity had made the decision for me, and kissed her. She gasped against my mouth, then melted into it, greedy and aching and utterly consumed. Her lips were soft, eager, her hands clinging to my shirt like she needed something to hold onto or she'd fall apart.

Every sound she made, those breathy whimpers, those small broken moans, ignited something deep in me. She was finally free to make noise, and I was going to enjoy coaxing every sinful sound she had to offer.

When I finally pulled back, she looked dazed, drunk on sensation. Beautiful. Blissed out.

Before I could say a word, her hand moved, fingers curling around my chin, firm but tender. She turned my head slowly, deliberately, until I was facing Ezra.

She didn't have to speak.

Her message was clear. *You want this. So do we.*

And God, she was right.

I did. I needed it like breath.

And from the way Ezra's eyes had fixed on mine, blazing with hunger and something deeper, I knew he did, too.

We weren't just about to fall into each other.

We were about to set the room on fire.

Ezra's lips crashed into mine, unyielding, wild, full of all the want we'd been holding back for far too long. His hands rose to cradle my head, fingers threading into my hair, anchoring me to him like he was afraid I might slip away. There was no hesitation in him this time, no restraint. Just hunger.

When his tongue swept into my mouth, I welcomed it with a low moan, tasting him, *us*, with Brexlyn's arousal still lingering between us. The taste of the three of us, tangled and heady, was intoxicating. A perfect alchemy I wanted more of. Would never get enough of.

This kiss wasn't like the one in the kitchen, that one had been unexpected, an explosion of surprise and fleeting sexual tension. But this... this kiss was earned. Built from slow-burning glances across rooms, from hands that lingered too long, from every moment he'd stood between danger and Brexlyn. Between danger and me. This kiss had weight. This kiss had history.

When we finally parted, our breath came in short, ragged bursts. His lips were kiss-swollen, his eyes half-lidded and heavy with lust. He looked at me like I was something he'd always wanted and had finally been allowed to have.

And then, as if choreographed by instinct, we turned to face her.

Our girl.

Brexlyn stood across from us, silent but no less commanding. Her eyes were dark with desire, pupils wide, lashes low. Her bottom lip was caught between her teeth as she watched us with a heat that made my knees feel unsteady.

Ezra's hands were still on me, steadying me as we both stared at her like the rabid animals we were reduced to in her presence.

Slowly, without a word, Brexlyn lifted her hands to the back of her dress. Her fingers moved with purpose, and I watched, transfixed, as she slid the zipper down. The fabric slipped from her shoulders like a whisper and fell around her feet in a silky pool. She stepped free of it, unabashed, every inch of her lit by the low, warm light.

I ran my eyes along her body hungrily. She was wearing only the thin strap of panties. Her nipples were pointed and swollen. Practically begging to be tasted. So I did.

I sprang forward, pulling one of her hardened peaks into my mouth and she moaned, aching her back and pressing her breast into me. Ezra was quick to follow, claiming the other nipple for himself. I danced my tongue around the peak, and let my teeth graze across the skin there, letting her soft sounds spur me on.

I felt her hand drift down my torso until she reached the hem of my pants. I made quick work of them, without removing her nipple from my mouth, and slid them down around my knees so she could have the access she was desperate for.

Her soft hand wrapped around the base of my stiff cock and I groaned around her breast at the sensation. Her soft hands slid along my shaft, her thumb dancing over the slit and spreading the bead of precum for lubrication. When I heard Ezra moan beside me, I glanced down to see she was giving him the same treatment.

His cock was thick, round. Her hand barely fit all the way around it, and I suddenly found myself desperate to find out if I could fit my mouth around its girth. I pulled off of Brexlyn's breast with a soft *pop* then grabbed Ezra's shoulders and forced him back. I led him to the bed. My eyes were demanding and focused. He followed my lead, letting me direct his body to where I needed him. When the back of his knees hit the mattress, I pushed his shoulders. He fell back onto the bed. Catching himself and looking up at the two of us who were standing over him now. His body was a work of art. Taut and rigid. I smiled sinfully at him, leaning down over him to press a kiss to his mouth again, licking at his lips eagerly. I could feel his cock pressing against my stomach and if I moved just a few inches I knew that his would brush against mine. But as much as I wanted that, I had other plans first.

I leaned back, pressing a finger to his lips. "Have a seat, Brexlyn," I whispered, earning me a satisfied smirk from Ezra and a soft gasp of surprise from my girl. I turned to find her standing there, not moving. I quickly slid my fingers into the waistband of her panties and pulled them down, revealing her glistening pussy to us.

"Now, don't make me ask again, Brexlyn," I warned darkly. "Climb up there and sit on his fucking face."

Ezra's eyes tracked Brexlyn's movements like a predator

watching his prey, he was eager to have her cunt on his tongue. I knew it, because so was I.

As if my command gave her a boost of confidence, she made her way to the bed and climbed up his body, peppering promising kisses along his bare skin on the way until her knees came to a rest on either side of his head, but she sat up, hovering over his willing mouth.

I came to the side of the bed and pressed a palm against her pert ass. Then, with a quick flick of my wrist, I smacked the flesh there. She gasped, jolting in Ezra's hold, her hands braced against the wall in front of her.

"I said sit down," I commanded. "Or should I spank you again?"

She met my eyes, and I saw it then, the hint of challenge. The little brat in her that wanted to be punished.

"Oh," I whispered. Gently caressing the spot on her ass where I had hit her. "Did my girl enjoy that?"

She nodded.

"Do you want me to do it again?"

Again she nodded. And before she even finished the motion, I brought my palm down against her skin again. The sharp sound echoed in the room. She cried out, leaning forward. "Now, be a good girl for me, and sit down," I cooed into her ear. Pressing a kiss to her cheek.

I took a step back and watched then as she lowered her core to Ezra's waiting mouth. He didn't waste a single second before devouring her. The sounds were downright sinful. Ezra's hands clamped onto her legs and held her down on his face. She began to buck her hips riding him, chasing her release on his tongue. The erotic display was nearly as good as if I was a part of it.

Speaking of. Ezra's cock was thick, rigid, and severely unappreciated. I climbed onto the bed between Ezra's thighs and laid my hands on his thighs. I felt them tense beneath my touch. His cock twitched as if searching for my mouth.

I gave him what he wanted.

I started slow, licking from base to tip, which drew a fucking glorious groan from Ezra which vibrated Brexlyn who then cried out. When my tongue reached the tip, I let it swirl around the head, savoring the taste of his precum. Then I took him into my mouth. Swallowing him inch by inch and relishing in the way his body reacted to mine and the way my throat adjusted so I could fit him.

I drove my hips into the side of the mattress, desperate for some sort of friction as I bobbed up and down on Ezra's massive dick. He seemed to be spurred on by my attention and was devouring Brexlyn within an inch of her life. She bucked on him, pressing hard down onto his tongue. When she came I listened to the sounds of Ezra lapping it up and moaned around his cock before slowly lifting off of it.

I grabbed Brexlyn, maneuvered her until she was now straddling Ezra. I grabbed his cock in my hand and positioned it at her entrance. Then I gripped onto her hips and slammed her down onto him. They both cried out, in desperate throaty cries. I wanted nothing more than to hear those sounds for the rest of my life. I kept my tough grip on her waist and helped her ride Ezra's cock until they were both panting. Then I pulled him out of her and replaced him with my own cock. Then I was slamming into her. Her pussy clamped down onto me, as if welcoming me home. I pressed into her, driving my hips with fervor as I made fast, reckless, passionate love to the woman of my dreams.

I pulled out and returned Ezra's cock inside of her. They continued their passionate fucking while I dipped a finger into her cunt alongside his dick. They both groaned. When my finger was nice and slick, I slid it out and then pressed it against the tight ring of her ass. Her body stilled.

"Tell me to stop," I challenged even though I knew she wouldn't. She wanted this. Instead, she pressed her hips back, begging my fingers for more. As she bounced on Ezra's dick, I spread her arousal around the opening until she was ready for me to press a finger inside. Her body stilled, like a statue as she adjusted to my finger. Her head fell back and I grabbed her hair in my fist. I slid another finger in and she cursed under her breath.

"Fuck," I whispered. "You're so fucking tight, baby."

"Please, Zaffir," she begged.

"Please what?" I teased.

"More."

I started pressing my fingers into her harder and faster, scissoring them just enough to stretch her. Ezra was still beneath her, just content to feel her body pulse around his as I readied her to take both of us.

I pulled my fingers from her and stepped up alongside the edge of the bed until my cock was level with Ezra's face. He watched me like a predator.

"Get me wet enough to fuck our girl, Ezra," I commanded. And for a brief moment, he paused, and I wondered if my dominance didn't work for him the way it worked for Brexlyn. But then he surged forward, his hot mouth clamping down on my shaft. I hissed as he worked his tongue along me. Brexlyn was watching us, her eyes burning with bright white heat as he slammed his cock into her and devoured me with his mouth. I would have been content to stay here for hours, but I had very specific plans, so using every ounce of my willpower, I withdrew from Ezra's perfect mouth, and pressed a kiss to them, before moving back to my place behind Brexlyn.

My slick cock, now wet with his saliva, was ready for her. I pressed the head of my length to her now stretched entrance. "Relax for me baby," I said before slowly pressing my hips forward. She winced, but didn't say anything as the tip slid past the ring of muscles. "Ezra," I strained through clenched teeth. "Her clit."

He listened and began giving her clit the attention it deserved. And the moment her body relaxed under that touch, she opened for me and soon enough I was bottomed out in her tight ass.

The three of us sat perfectly still for an instant just soaking up the feeling of it. The intimacy. The charged emotions.

"I can feel you inside of her," Ezra groaned, meeting my eyes. I gave him a small smile, then a quick nod. And we began moving within her. She gripped onto the headboard with every ounce of strength she had left in her sexy little body as the two of us picked up the pace and began fucking her the way we were desperate to. My balls slapped against his, which only heightened the experience. All my thoughts disappeared, all reservations, all fears. There was only Brexlyn, and only Ezra. They were my saving grace. They were my wake up call. They were mine.

Brexlyn's body tensed as another release built and when she came, her body convulsing with waves of pleasure, she took both Ezra and I with her. We emptied ourselves into her like we were claiming her. Owning her.

But really it was she who owned us. And I wouldn't want it any differently. When I was finally spent, I slid out from her and she lifted off of Ezra. And I couldn't help but stare at her spent pussy. The way it gaped and dripped with the remnants of us. Of what we did to her.

I couldn't resist. I bent down and let my tongue run from top to bottom, tasting us on her. She bucked out of the way with a gasp then turned to gape at me, shock on her face.

I shrugged. "Couldn't help myself."

After cleaning up, showering, and pressing our two beds together, we fell asleep, a tangle of limbs, hands, and hearts.

I wished this little bubble of perfection could last forever. But even if it couldn't, at least we had tonight.

BEX

Only one trial stood between me and the medical trials, and after that, if our secret message had been heard and understood, the Runaways would gather at the gates of Praxis.

The rebellion we had been working toward, the uprising that had simmered for years, would finally ignite.

All that Praxis stole from the Collectives would finally be reclaimed.

It was almost time to find out if the Runaways were brave enough to honor their word... and if we were strong enough to finish what Briar and Thorne's mother started.

Last night, the five of us sat right here in this living room, the air heavy with nerves. We talked about what it would mean if the Runaways didn't show up, how everything we were fighting for could collapse before it even began.

The song we sang was catching fire in the forums, spreading faster than we could have hoped. But all the noise in the world wouldn't matter if it didn't turn into action. Plans didn't change the world. People did.

We wrestled with it for hours, how to convince them to move past their fear, to take the risk.

And in the end, the answer was simple, even if it wasn't easy.

We had to do it first.

We had to show them that we were just as scared, and that we were standing up anyway.

"As I was saying," Nova's voice broke through my thoughts, high-pitched, strained, entirely too screechy for this early hour. "You're all required to arrive at today's trial separately. And there's nothing I can do about it," she added, exasperated, pinching the bridge of her nose.

"What's the trial?" Ezra asked, his voice a low, gruff rumble thick with irritation.

"Lumber," Nova answered simply.

"We know that," Ezra snapped back. "I mean, what are they gonna make us do?"

"You know I can't tell you that yet, Ezra," she said, meeting his glare evenly. She wore a cotton dress today, simple but with a shimmering silver sheen, still undeniably Praxis, but somehow... softer. Less imposing.

"Why separate us?" Thorne cut in, frowning.

"Because this is an individual challenge," Nova replied flatly.

"And it's physical," Briar added, more a grim statement than a guess.

Thorne leaned back, arms crossed. "For the lumber trial a few years back they had to build a structure. Then they blasted the roofs with water. Whoever stayed the driest won."

"Last year," Briar chimed in, "they dumped the challengers on an island and made them build rafts to sail back to the mainland."

I nodded. I remembered both. But Praxis wasn't likely to make the rest of this Run simple ...especially not for me.

Not after everything.

"Something tells me," I said carefully, catching each of their eyes in turn, "we're not going to have it quite that easy."

They all understood. I could see it in the tightness of Thorne's jaw, the hard set of Briar's mouth, the way Ezra's hands curled into fists at his sides. Even Nova, usually so practiced, so distant, let something flicker across her face. A brief, raw glimmer of regret before the mask slammed back into place.

Veritas knew I wasn't her pawn anymore.

She knew exactly how dangerous we were becoming.

And she wasn't going to let us reach the finish line without trying to break us.

"Ezra, your car is out front. Please don't make this difficult and just get into it," Nova urged, her voice edged with impatience.

Ezra didn't even look her way. Instead, he crossed the room with purposeful steps, his gaze locked on me. As he reached my side, his hands slid around my waist, pulling me close. Without hesitation, he tipped my chin up and pressed his lips to mine. The kiss was soft at first, a fleeting brush, but it deepened quickly as I rose up on my toes, molding against him as he guided the kiss. The weight of the moment settled between us, the unspoken words, the promises that couldn't be said aloud.

When he finally pulled back, he gave a small nod to the others. His eyes flicked briefly to Zaffir, a silent, almost regretful glance that lingered just a moment too long. I could see the longing in him, the desire to show the world, to show him that he deserved a goodbye kiss too. But Nova was here and the camera was running, so brief longing glances was all he could offer. Ezra's lips pressed into a tight line before he turned and slipped out the front door.

Next was Thorne, and his approach was a contrast of

energy. He practically swept me off my feet, his arms pulling me into him with a laugh, his lips brushing against my cheeks and neck in a flurry of playful, almost frantic kisses. His touch was light but insistent, full of warmth, the kind that made it hard not to smile. By the time he was done, I was giggling, and Nova was already moving to pull him away, her hands on his shoulders, as if trying to wrangle him back to reality. He winked at me over his shoulder before heading out the door, his presence already fading like a shadow. "Don't miss me too much, love."

Briar was more subtle in her approach, stepping up quietly to my side. She took my hand in hers, her thumb brushing the back of it as she gazed at me with a soft intensity. Her eyes were a mix of love and fear. She cupped my cheek gently before kissing my lips, the kiss tender, a promise wrapped in fragility.

"I'll see you soon," she whispered against my lips, her voice thick with emotion before she slipped out the door, leaving me with the space between us now feeling heavier than ever.

Finally, it was just me, Nova, and Zaffir. The air between us seemed to crackle, charged with tension. Zaffir stood in front of me, his camera trained on me like a silent observer. I swallowed the tightness in my throat and forced myself to stand tall, fighting the nervous tremor in my hands. I didn't want to appear weak, not for the Runaways, not for anyone. They needed to see me as strong, resolute. They needed to know that I was ready to lead this fight, even if I didn't always feel like it.

"How are you feeling, Brexlyn?" Zaffir asked, his voice quiet but insistent, the camera steady between us like a tether. He was handing me the floor. Giving me a chance to say what needed to be said.

I smiled, but it didn't touch my eyes. I shifted my weight, letting my fingers brush against my thigh to hide how tightly I was clenching my fists. When I turned to the camera, I knew exactly who I was speaking to.

"I think the right answer is that I'm eager to go out there and compete for my Collective again," I said, the words easy, almost rehearsed.

Zaffir tilted his head slightly, lifting an eyebrow. "And the real answer?"

I let the silence stretch just long enough to feel heavy, then drew a slow breath and let the mask slip. "I'm scared," I admitted, the words low but firm.

Out of the corner of my eye, I caught Nova watching us, sharp and calculating, like she could feel the shift in the air but couldn't quite predict where it would lead.

"Why?" Zaffir pressed, a subtle nudge. He wanted me to share this with those watching. He needed me to be vulnerable. They all did.

I locked eyes with the lens, not flinching. "I didn't want this," I said, my voice barely above a whisper. "I didn't want to be a Challenger. I didn't want my brother's life resting on my performance in the Run. I didn't want to survive by watching others fall. I didn't ask for this pressure."

The honesty burned on my tongue, raw and real. But I didn't let it stop me.

"But now?" Zaffir prompted, his voice barely a breath.

"Now, I understand." I straightened my shoulders, letting the fire inside me show. "I can be scared. I can doubt. I can want to run. But I won't. Because fear doesn't get to decide who we are...we do."

I leaned forward slightly, speaking directly to the Runaways now, to the ones hidden behind screens and shadows.

"Because some people think pressure makes things break. But it doesn't. It makes them easier to shape," I said, my voice calm. "If you push hard enough, long enough, you can become something else. Something stronger. Something reinforced."

The promise was there, in every steady beat of my voice.

"So you're not afraid anymore?" he asked.

"Of course I am. Maybe I always will be. But standing still because of it? Not fighting? That's not who I am. Not who I want to be, at least."

For just a second, Nova's mask cracked, the faintest flicker of something like regret or understanding flashing across her face, before she snapped it back into place.

But I wasn't looking at her. I was staring down the barrel of the camera, sending a message to everyone who needed it.

"Fear will always be a part of me," I said, my voice steady now, anchored by something deeper than anger. "But my courage doesn't come in spite of my fear. It exists because of it."

For a beat, the room was utterly still. Then Zaffir lowered the camera, clicking it off with a soft, final sound. He studied me through the dark fringe of his lashes, a rare smile tugging at the corner of his mouth, quiet, proud. He gave a single, deliberate nod.

"Brexlyn," Nova's voice cut through the moment, cool and sharp as glass. I turned toward her, catching the way she gripped the edge of the table, knuckles whitening. "You're playing a very dangerous game," she said, her words low but laced with something that almost sounded like fear. Not for herself, but for me.

I met her gaze without flinching. For the first time, I saw past the polished surface she always wore. Beneath it, her worry was real. Tangled. Raw. She cared about what happened to me.

"The game was already dangerous, Nova," I said, my voice quiet but unshakable. "I'm just not letting them be the only ones writing the rules anymore."

Her lips pressed into a thin line. She nodded once, a reluctant surrender. Not agreement, not approval. Just acknowledgement that I had crossed a line I could never uncross. And she knew it.

"I can't..." she whispered. "I don't want you," she swallowed hard then cleared her throat. "I mean," she began again. "It's been an honor watching you thrive in these trials, dear."

I nodded. Genuinely thankful for her words. But it wasn't what she said that meant the most to me. It's what she couldn't say. The words of support that were sitting there on her tongue were unable to spill off because of who she was conditioned to be.

"Your car is here," she said after a beat, pulling open the front door, the night spilling in around her like a living thing.

I shifted my gaze back to Zaffir for just a heartbeat, a silent message passing between us. If things were different, it would have been a kiss. A goodbye wrapped in something warmer, something braver. But all we had was this look, this understanding stitched in the space between us.

I tucked it into my heart like armor, straightened my shoulders, and stepped out into the cold night, toward the waiting car.

CHAPTER
ELEVEN

BEX

I was on a plane again. This time, no parachute strapped to my back, no blindfold over my eyes. It was a smaller plane than I'd been in before, and I was alone, well, alone except for the pilot. He sat in silence, staring ahead, his grip firm on the controls as we flew northwest, away from Praxis. We'd been flying for over an hour now, and the landscape below had become increasingly unfamiliar, confirming what I already suspected, we were heading deeper into unknown territory, farther than we'd gone for the transportation trial.

The plane hummed steadily in the air, but there was an undercurrent of tension that I couldn't shake. Eventually, the pilot started to slow the plane, descending smoothly over a wide expanse of water. As we lowered, the view below began to come into focus. A scattered group of small islands dotted the water's surface, like a chain of forgotten rocks poking up from the depths. A sharp breeze swept through the open cockpit, and I could see eight other small planes like mine, scattered across the sky. They were flying lower as well, heading toward the islands, and my thoughts immediately turned to my Wildguard. Where were they? Which plane carried them?

Before I could process that thought, the speaker in the plane crackled to life, and Annalese's voice cut through the static, smooth and cheery.

"Good morning, Challengers, and welcome to the lumber trial!" she began, her tone unnervingly upbeat. "Today, your task is simple. You'll be dropped off on your own small island. Each island has a watchtower, but they're broken, unsafe, beyond repair... mostly. Your task is to use the resources on your island to fix your watchtower and call for a rescue by lighting the rescue lamp at the top. If your light is lit at dawn tomorrow, you will be rescued, and you will pass the trial!"

I felt my chest tighten, the words sinking in. It sounded too simple. And I knew better than to trust anything that sounded simple in the Reclamation Run. There was always a catch.

"Fix your tower, survive the night, light the lamp, and signal the rescue team," Annalese repeated, her voice almost sweet in its simplicity.

Survive the night.

There it was. Survival. She wasn't just talking about building the tower or lighting the lamp. There was something else. Something on those islands that would make survival far from easy.

I glanced out the window, the first signs of the island coming closer. Each one was small, isolated, and rugged. There were no signs of habitation, no markers to indicate anything beyond nature's cruel beauty. But I could sense it, the looming danger, the unknown that lay in wait for us. This wasn't just a test of strength, skill, or even willpower. It was going to be about outlasting whatever threats the island would throw at us.

The plane banked hard to the left, the pilot starting the descent. I could already see the craggy shores of the island that would soon be mine to survive below, the jagged rocks and thick forest that stretched up toward the sky. Somewhere on that island was my watchtower, or what was left of it. I could feel my pulse quicken as the plane swooped lower. What else would be waiting for me there?

I swallowed hard, trying to keep my thoughts focused. The sky was bright and filled with the midday sun. The plane began its final descent, and I braced myself for whatever was to come.

The pilot pressed a button on his dashboard, and with a soft mechanical whir, the side door of the plane slid open. A rope ladder unfurled from the doorway, dangling thirty feet above the sandy shore below. The engine hummed steadily, the only sound accompanying the rush of wind as I swallowed hard, trying to steady my nerves. This was it.

They hadn't provided us with a pack this time—not even a stick of jerky. At least Thorne had insisted on feeding us a hearty breakfast before we left. I was grateful for it now. A solid meal in my stomach would have to sustain me through the night. I could make it until tomorrow without food if I had to.

I turned my attention to the rope ladder, my fingers wrapping around the rough fibers. Carefully, I tested each step with my foot, feeling the sway of the plane still hovering above. I wasn't sure how I felt about jumping off into the unknown, but there was no turning back now. My hands and legs moved with deliberate care as I made my way down. The cold air stung my skin, and my heart raced in my chest, but I focused on my breathing. One step at a time.

Finally, I felt the sand beneath my boots. My feet sank just a little into the soft texture, and I paused, steadying myself as I glanced back at the plane. And once I was free from the rope ladder, they pulled away, leaving me standing alone on the island.

I turned back toward the shore, the shoreline stretching

thinly across the island, the water lapping gently against the sand. I bent down, letting the cool water wash over my hands and took a deep breath, the scent of lake water filling my lungs. It was thick and murky, tinged with the acrid scent of fish. The smell was sharp, but not inherently not unpleasant.

When I lifted my gaze, my eyes fixed on the island's dense terrain. Towering, thick trees crowded the space, their trunks reaching up toward the sky, and the steep cliffs rose sharply at the edge of the land. Roots snaked outward, crawling up the rocks as though trying to claim the whole place. It would be hard to scale these cliffs.

As I looked around, something caught my attention, a camera perched against one of the trees, its small lens turning in my direction. I could hear the faint whirring as it adjusted to focus on me. I wasn't surprised. These islands were much smaller and much more contained than the Wilds were. It would be easy for every inch of this island to be under the watchful eye of Praxis.

The air had a strange scent now, too, something warm, almost smokey. For a moment, it reminded me of a meal Thorne had cooked for us a few nights ago. The thought hit me harder than I expected. I missed them. I hoped they were alright and that their towers weren't beyond repair.

I pushed those thoughts aside, focusing on the task ahead. My heart tightened, but I steeled myself, lifting my chin as I approached the island's rocky base. There was no time to dwell on homesickness. I had a tower to fix.

I started up the exposed roots, grabbing at the rough bark to pull myself higher. Each movement was slow, deliberate, as I navigated the tough climb. When I reached the top of the island, sweat began to bead on my forehead despite the warmth of the sun. I wiped it away with the long sleeve shirt they had insisted I wear, sweat clinging to the fabric despite the heat.

Pushing through the thick trees was no easier. The dense foliage made every step a challenge, and I had to duck and weave around low-hanging branches. After several minutes, I finally emerged into a small, almost circular clearing. In the middle of the clearing stood a wooden tower.

Or at least, that's what it used to be.

"Shit," I whispered under my breath as I took in the sight. The structure was barely recognizable. Eroded beams hung loosely, swaying slightly in the breeze. There were no solid stairs to climb, just a hollow step leading to a gaping hole where once there had been a platform. It looked like one of the old water towers from back home in Canyon, dilapidated and dangerous. Four large posts jutted out of the earth, their support beams cracked and splintered. It was a death trap waiting to happen.

I circled the structure, taking in the damage. No amount of patching up could make this tower safe again. My heart sank, but I knew I had to make do.

To the right of the tower sat a workbench, a pile of tools scattered haphazardly across it. I walked over, heart sinking further. There were hammers, saws, and hatchets, but not much else. A bucket of used nails, some rusty scrap metal, and a pile of lumber that looked barely enough to repair a fraction of the tower.

I let out a frustrated breath. This wasn't going to be easy. I was going to need more than just tools and scrap wood to make this tower even remotely functional. I glanced back toward the thick forest, my mind racing. The trees were my only hope. I'd have to cut branches down and use what I could find.

The smokey scent hung thick in the air now, clinging to my senses. I looked around again, trying to spot the source, but saw nothing. Perhaps it was just the island's natural scent.

I rolled my shoulders back, pushing through the exhaustion that had already begun to settle in. There was no time to waste. I had to get to work.

Grabbing the hatchet, I started chopping at the nearest tree, my arms aching with each swing. The sun hung heavy overhead, and the sweat on my brow stung my eyes. But I couldn't afford to stop. The clock was ticking.

A few hours later, the sweat poured down my face, stinging my eyes, as I stood surrounded by a growing pile of thick, sturdy branches. It would have to be enough. The sun was sinking lower in the sky, the golden hue fading to a soft orange that spread across the water. The day was slipping away, and I had to move faster. I couldn't risk being left in the dark when the island's challenges could be lurking just beyond the fading light.

I took a moment to study the broken tower again, eyeing the decaying beams and rotting wood that barely clung to the four posts in place. The structure was in terrible condition. Tentatively, I placed my weight on different sections of the tower, testing the stability. The creaking wood sent jolts of panic through my chest, but I forced myself to breathe. I had no time to be afraid.

The tower was falling apart at the seams, and I only had a small pile of branches and a handful of tools to fix it. I ran the plan through my head again. If I reinforced the bottom structure first, I could build a kind of ladder instead of traditional stairs to reach the top. It wouldn't be ideal, but it might be enough to get me up there safely.

I glanced up at the sky. The last of the sunlight was flickering against the water's surface, casting long shadows over the island. Hours had passed in a blur of sweat, blood, and exhaustion. My hands were rough, palms split open by splinters that dug deep into my skin. Each hammer strike sent pain shooting up my arms, but I couldn't stop.

The sun was almost gone now. The orange glow was

barely visible through the trees as dusk crept in, and I could feel the weight of time pressing down on me. Whatever dangers lurked on this island would soon be here, and I had to finish this tower, fast. The nervous energy in my stomach twisted tighter with each passing moment, and I pushed harder.

Gripping the hammer with raw, aching hands, I worked furiously, nails biting into the wood as I secured a cross beam along the base. The four posts groaned under the strain, but this time when I leaned against it, the tower didn't sway. It was solid. Good. I had made some progress.

With my heart pounding, I climbed up onto the newly reinforced beams, making sure to keep my weight balanced as I repeated the process around the tower. Every movement was deliberate and calculated, but the exhaustion was catching up with me. My muscles burned from the constant strain, my arms trembling as I worked faster. The tower was slowly taking shape, but night was fast approaching.

When I reached the top level, my body was screaming in pain. My hands were cut and swollen, the skin raw from the constant friction against the wood. My vision was starting to blur, cloudy from exhaustion, and my eyes watered from the pain. I didn't care. I reached the platform, only to find that it was a fragile, skeletal wreck. The structure wasn't even close to being sturdy enough to stand on.

But maybe I didn't need to stand on it.

I glanced over at the lamp positioned in the center of the platform, the amplified light that would signal my rescue. It was fragile and required a fire to ignite the back, which would then reflect off mirrors and light the signal. If I could light the lamp from here, I wouldn't need to step onto the platform at all.

I felt a momentary surge of hope, but it quickly faded as the weight of the tower's instability hit me again. The wind shifted, sending a soft creak through the beams. My pulse quickened.

I could do this.

Carefully, I climbed back down, the tower groaning beneath me with every move. The creaks and cracks in the wood made my heart race, but I focused on making each movement as slow and deliberate as possible. Every time a beam shifted under my weight, my stomach dropped, and I had to force myself to ignore the panic.

Once my feet finally hit solid ground again, I collapsed against the earth, my breath coming in shallow, strained gasps. I closed my eyes, trying to steady myself. The coolness of the ground beneath me felt comforting for a moment, but I couldn't let myself rest for long.

I had been working non-stop for hours. My body was bruised, battered, and starving. My throat was dry, and I longed for something to drink. There was nothing I could do about the hunger or the pain right now.

I just had to survive the night.

The sky was dotted with stars, their pinpricks of light scattered across the vast expanse above me. I lay on my back, taking slow, steady breaths as the exhaustion from the day's work began to wash over me. My body felt heavy, sinking into the earth beneath me, but it was a comforting weight. The ground was warm, warmer than I would've expected, though I guessed it was from the sun beating down on it all day. Either way, it was a welcome sensation.

I turned my gaze back up to the stars, studying their patterns and shapes, watching the way they painted the sky. Out here, the night sky was so clear. It reminded me of Canyon, where the darkness swallowed everything, the stars bold and bright against the backdrop of nothingness. I hadn't realized how much I missed it, how much I missed the true night sky. In Praxis, the lights from the city drowned out any hope of seeing stars. The neon glow and the constant hum of artificial light had kept the heavens hidden from view. But out here, like in the Wilds with Thorne, or on the rooftop with Ava, the stars were visible in all their glory, clear as day, as though they had been waiting for me all along.

For a moment, I felt like those stars, small and distant, yet still shining in spite of everything. In spite of Praxis, in spite of all the obstacles in my way. It was as if no matter how dark the world became, there was always a glimmer of light that could refuse to be dimmed.

I stared up at the sky for a while longer, letting the peacefulness of the moment wash over me. But eventually, my eyelids grew heavy, and the exhaustion from the day claimed me. My eyes slid shut, and sleep took over.

IT WAS the heat that first woke me.

I felt a sharp, burning pain spreading across my back, the warmth seeping through my long-sleeve shirt and licking at my skin with a fierceness that felt vicious. The comfort I'd felt before had been replaced by an unbearable sting. My back was on fire.

I jerked upright, my body stiff with pain as I tried to stretch out the tight muscles, but nothing could ease the burn. My shirt felt as though it had been pressed against a scorching surface. I winced and stood quickly, the heat still radiating from my skin.

That's when I noticed the smoke.

The air was thick with it, swirling in a hazy cloud around me. The smell, that same almost-smoky scent from before, was even stronger now. It clung to everything, coating my throat, my clothes, and my skin. I glanced around, squinting through the smoke, trying to figure out where it was coming from. The smoke didn't seem to have any particular direction, it was just there, heavy in the air, creeping from the ground itself.

My chest tightened as I inhaled the smoke, and I couldn't suppress the cough that rattled through my body. It felt as if my lungs were on fire, and my eyes watered from the sting. I reached for the hatchet I'd left by my side, instinctively wrapping my fingers around the handle, feeling better just having something solid in my grip.

The heat and smoke seemed to be coming from the ground. I walked carefully, trying to avoid breathing too deeply, but the smoke was inescapable. Every step I took felt like it led me deeper into a furnace.

I stumbled down the path, following the curve of the island toward the shoreline, the roots of the cliffside smoking as I drew closer. As I reached the edge of the water, I hesitated.

I pulled my shirt off over my head, the fabric damp with sweat, and dunked it into the lapping waves. The coolness of the water felt like a relief against the oppressive heat. I wrung it out, then tied it around my mouth and nose, hoping it would help filter out some of the smoke.

With the hatchet in hand, I moved closer to the roots of the cliff, where the smoke seemed to be pouring most fiercely. My grip tightened on the weapon as I swung it at the thick, twisted roots. The first swing struck with a dull thud, and I felt the resistance in the wood. I took another swing, harder this time. The earth beneath me seemed to cave in, and with a sudden jolt, a blast of heat erupted from the hole I'd made.

The force of the explosion sent me sprawling back onto the sand. A wave of intense, searing heat washed over me, and I cried out as my arm instinctively came up to shield my face. The exposed skin burned against the air, and I realized that without my shirt to protect me, I stood no chance against the fire's heat. But the pain didn't matter. The fire was roaring, spilling out of the hole I'd made, hot and furious.

Flames licked at the sky, dancing wildly as they erupted from beneath the cliff. The roots, those thick, twisted things, were consumed by the fire. It spread quickly, the earth beneath the cliffside igniting in a blaze that seemed to have been building all day, just beneath the surface.

I groaned, pushing myself up off the sand, my body screaming in protest. Every inch of me was sore. The sting in my arm was unbearable, and my lungs felt like they were being scraped raw with every breath. The fire beneath the cliff was still blazing, crawling ever higher, threatening to swallow everything in its path.

I glanced toward the water. The sky was dark, but I could see the faintest hint of orange on the horizon, a sign that dawn was on its way. All I had to do was survive until then, and I would be rescued. I could already taste freedom, if I could just make it through this.

But as I stared out at the water, a sinking feeling clawed at my chest. The fire was not contained to my island. I could see a handful of other orange glows in the distance, flickering along the shores of nearby islands. The flames were claiming them too. I felt my heart tighten at the thought of Briar, Thorne, and Ezra. I could only pray they were safe and that they had the smarts to stay alive long enough to make it out.

I had nothing with me, aside from the hatchet still gripped tightly in my hand, and my soaked t-shirt, now pressed against my face to mask the smoke that was thickening around me. The water was close, but it did me no good if I couldn't reach the fire and put it out. I didn't have time to waste.

Ignoring the fire's growing intensity, I forced my legs to move. The air was stifling, thick with smoke, but I couldn't let it stop me. My lungs burned with each breath, but I pressed forward up the cliff's edge.

I needed to get to higher ground, needed to protect my tower. The flame had to be kept away. I scrambled through the trees, the smoke pressing in on all sides. It made the air feel oppressive, heavy with heat and ash. I was disoriented, my mind fogged with pain and exhaustion, but I pushed on, driven by the need to protect what little hope I had left.

Eventually, I reached my tower again. I barely noticed the way my palms were scorched from touching the burning roots on the climb back up. The heat was unbearable, but there was no time to stop. I couldn't stop. The fire hadn't reached this spot yet, and I was determined to keep it that way.

I moved fast, snatching up the last of the branches and broken lumber from my earlier pile. My fingers fumbled clumsily with the wood as I staggered around the base of the tower, laying it out in a wide, rough circle. Every breath was a struggle, my lungs clawing against the thick smoke curling in the air.

Inside the ring, I dropped to my knees and, using the hatchet, carved a shallow trench into the dry dirt. It wasn't deep, my arms shook too badly for that, but it was something. A pitiful line of defense. A thin scar against the oncoming fire. It wouldn't hold the flames for long. Maybe not even for an hour. But maybe, just maybe, it would buy me enough time to see the sun rise. Enough time to survive.

The fire was growing louder now. I could hear it snapping and tearing through the trees, a living, breathing thing. Flames leapt hungrily at the leaves overhead, and the tall grass around the edges of the clearing swayed as it was devoured.

I finished the circle best as I could, and then, heart pounding in my ears, ran toward the inferno. I needed a torch.

Near the edge of the blaze, I found discarded brush, already dry and brittle. The heat was unbearable this close, suffocating and thick, but I didn't hesitate. With trembling hands, I fashioned a crude torch, thrusting it into the searing edge of the fire. Flames clung to it instantly, racing up the dry twigs.

Torch in hand, I turned and sprinted back toward the tower. Every step was agony, the smoke was a living thing inside my chest. When I reached the base, I didn't stop to catch my breath. I jammed the hatchet into my belt, gripped the ladder tightly with my free hand, and began to climb.

The smoke climbed with me.

It was thicker up here, curling in heavy plumes around the structure. My muscles screamed with the effort of hauling myself upward one-handed, the other hand desperately clutching the burning torch.

I reached the top platform, panting, my vision swimming. The lantern was mounted too far from the edge, I couldn't reach it from the ladder, not with the condition of my arm. I had to step onto the rickety platform itself.

The rotted wood would surely give out, but then again, I'd die if I didn't try.

I slid under the railing, gritting my teeth as I eased onto the brittle, splintering wood. Every step had to be deliberate, precise. I didn't reinforce a damn thing up here, a fact I was now regretting. I kept the torch held high above my head, terrified of brushing it against the dry, crackling boards underfoot.

I spared a glance outward and immediately regretted it. The fire had reached the perimeter of my makeshift barrier. It roared and spat in defiance, wicked and bright. To my left and right, across the water, matching infernos danced on matching islands, consuming everything in sight. It looked like the whole world was burning.

I forced myself to look back at the lantern. Focus. Get it done.

I edged forward, one careful step at a time. A board beneath my foot snapped with a loud crack.

I gasped as my leg plunged through the floor. Sharp wood tore into my shin, slicing deep. Pain exploded up my leg. I screamed, the sound ripping free of my raw throat, but some-how, somehow, I kept the torch aloft.

Tears blurred my vision as I hauled myself up, my blood dripping steadily down my ruined leg. Every part of me shook, my nerves fraying, but I staggered the last few feet and shoved the torch into the lantern.

The flame roared to life.

Light burst outward, caught and magnified by the polished mirrors around it. It was bright enough to cut through the heavy smoke, bright enough to be seen even from miles away.

I stumbled back against the railing, nearly collapsing. Through the haze, I spotted the small black eye of a camera mounted in the corner of the tower, its cold lens watching me. Watching and recording every miserable second.

Good. Let them watch.

With what little strength I had left, I hurled the torch out beyond the defensive ring, praying it wouldn't land inside it. It landed with a thud and sputtered out into darkness beyond my barrier.

And then there was nothing to do but stand there.

Blood poured hot and fast down my leg. My burned arm throbbed with every heartbeat. My lungs, scraped raw and broken, strained with each shallow breath.

I stood there, broken and burning, the tower creaking beneath me, and stared toward the horizon, waiting for the first fragile light of dawn to break.

Waiting to be saved.

My makeshift barrier had held for longer than I'd dared to hope, the fire slowing at the edge, dancing hungrily along the rim of scorched branches and half-burnt wood. But already, it was beginning to breach, licking over the trench I'd dug like it barely existed.

The horizon began to glow. Pale light bled over the glistening water, the deep purple of night giving way to bruised orange and gold. Dawn was here.

But where was the rescue?

I clung to the railing, scanning the line where sea met sky, heart hammering against my ribs so violently it hurt. I searched desperately for any sign, any shimmer of wings, any flash of silver, but there was nothing. Only the rising sun and the thick columns of smoke billowing from the islands.

Six lanterns burned against the creeping fire, small stars of hope in a sea of smoke and devastation. I sent a silent prayer for the others. Please let my Wildguard be among those six. Please let them have lit their lanterns. Please let them be waiting like I was, perched at the tops of their towers, injured maybe, terrified definitely, but alive.

The minutes dragged on. The sun rose higher, gilding the world in indifferent light. Still, no rescue.

Fury bubbled up inside me, raw and bitter.

"We've passed your trial!" I screamed, my voice ripping through the smoke and up toward the camera still mounted in the corner. "We did what you asked!"

My blood, sticky and dark, was pooling around my boots as I gripped the railing, each word soaked in desperation.

Below me, the fire surged forward. The barrier finally gave way completely, and the flames spilled into the clearing. I watched helplessly as they danced toward the tower from every side, embers spinning like vengeful spirits.

"No," I whispered, my voice cracking as the fire crept closer.

Was this it? Was this the punishment Veritas had planned all along? Was this the cost of rebellion? Would they make me burn, live on camera, to warn the others what disobedience meant?

Would I ever see Jax again? Ava? My Wildguard?

I staggered upright, coughing violently as I pulled the strip of cloth from around my face. The smoke filled my mouth and nose immediately, harsh and searing, but I forced myself to meet the camera's unblinking gaze.

If they were going to let me die, then they would damn well look me in the face as I did.

"For the will of the people," I said, forcing the words out, steady and strong even as my body trembled.

The heat coiled up around the tower like a living thing, the wooden structure groaning under its assault.

"For the will of the people," I repeated, louder this time, louder than the crackling flames, louder than the part of me that screamed to run even when there was nowhere left to go.

I thought of Zaffir. Somewhere, he would be watching. Somewhere, he would see this footage. He would have to watch me die. But maybe he'd leave this final rebellious act in the edit. Let it slip through the cracks so everyone could see. Even if it put him in danger. Especially if it did.

I set my jaw, locking eyes with the camera, and screamed it again, "For the will of the people!"

The tower shuddered under me. I could feel it begin to give, the wood at the base devoured and crumbling.

Then, faint but growing louder, I heard it. The distant, beautiful buzz of engines.

I jerked my head up, squinting through the smoke. Small planes. Several of them, dotting the sky like black-winged angels.

My heart leapt in my chest.

The tower creaked alarmingly as it swayed, and I clung tighter to the railing. The planes came closer, slicing through the thick, smoky sky. I could have waved them down. I could have screamed for them.

But I didn't. I refused to give Praxis the satisfaction of seeing me grateful for a rescue they had orchestrated the need for in the first place.

Instead, I stood tall. Bloodied, burned, and broken, but still standing.

The first plane hovered directly over me. A rope ladder uncoiled, swinging wildly in the smoke and turbulence.

I reached for it, but my arm, battered and raw, screamed in protest. The ladder swung just out of reach.

And then the tower groaned one last time and began to fall.

I had no choice...I jumped.

I caught the rope, pain exploding through my body as my injured arm wrapped instinctively around the rungs. The tower collapsed beneath me, the world a roaring chaos of fire and ash, as the plane began to lift me away.

I climbed, slowly, gritting my teeth against the agony, blood pouring freely from my leg, my muscles spasming and locking with every movement. The plane's ladder swayed violently in the hot updrafts from the inferno below.

Hand over hand, I pulled myself higher.

When I finally reached the open door of the plane, I spilled onto the metal floor, my body too broken to do anything but collapse. My chest heaved in shuddering, painful gasps.

I'd made it, alive. Bleeding and injured, sure, but alive nonetheless. And I could only hope that my Wildguard managed the same.

CHAPTER
TWELVE

EZRA

THE ENTIRE LEFT side of my body was on fire.

Literally.

As I scrambled up the ladder toward the plane hovering above, I cursed, swatting at the flames clinging to my clothing. They were eating through the fabric, slicing into my skin, but I couldn't swing too hard, not without risking a fall. The ladder swayed as the plane began to lift, dragging me away from the burning island I'd just been plucked off.

The pain was worse than anything I'd ever felt. I bit my lip, hard, forcing myself not to scream. There was a camera above me, and I wasn't going to give Praxis the satisfaction of recording my agony.

"Lower me into the water!" I shouted as I reached the top of the ladder. The pilot didn't respond. Maybe he couldn't hear me. Maybe he didn't care.

"Lower the plane!" I yelled again, louder this time. His head tilted slightly in my direction, but he still didn't move.

This asshole was just going to let me burn—same as all of Praxis.

"Maybe I should go hang out by the fuel tank! I'm on fucking fire, and unless you want this whole damn plane to go up with me, dunk me in the goddamn lake!"

The aircraft dipped. Thank God. I climbed down a few rungs, gripping tight as the cold water rushed up. The moment it hit me, I let myself sink beneath the surface.

Relief came fast then left just as quickly. Now the burns screamed under the water's pressure, the sting like a thousand needles driving into every raw patch of skin.

When the ladder lifted and the plane rose again, I climbed into the belly and collapsed in the open seating area, breath coming in ragged gasps. My heart pounded. My skin felt like it had been peeled back.

I stripped my shirt off next, or at least what was left of it. The fabric clung to the scorched skin, and I had to tear it free from the charred holes. I bit down on my tongue to keep from crying out. My entire left arm, shoulder, and half my torso were angry and raw, the skin bubbled and blackened. I didn't even want to look at my leg yet.

I leaned back, head against the wall, eyes squeezed shut, trying to keep my mind from spiraling.

Out the open belly of the plane, I saw other aircrafts rising, Challengers dangling from their own rope ladders. I squinted, trying to make out who was still alive, but the figures were too small, just blurry shapes against the smoke and sky.

I needed Bex to be okay. Thorne and Briar too. Maybe they had an easier time with this trial, wooded terrain was more their style. But I doubted they faced off with fire frequently in their childhood.

My head swam, adrenaline wearing off. My skin above my heart felt tight, like the flames had tried to burn straight through to the muscle underneath.

My breathing was shallow. I forced it slower.

The ride was bumpy, brutal, really, and far too long. Every jolt of the plane rattled through me like shrapnel. I knew we were heading back toward the mainland, but I wasn't sure I'd survive the two-hour flight to Praxis without collapsing entirely. Part of me hoped someone onboard recognized how bad I was, how much blood I'd lost, how unsteady my breaths had become. But I also knew—without question—I wouldn't say a damn thing if they didn't. I wouldn't give them the satisfaction.

Each jostle felt like a red-hot iron stabbing into my skin. I curled inward, trying to make myself small, to focus on the single, agonizing rhythm of breathing. In. Out. In. Out.

After what felt like an eternity, the plane began its slow descent. I tilted my head just enough to peer out the open cargo door, the cold wind slapping my face. Below us, a lake gleamed like fractured glass, and given the direction and distance we'd traveled from Praxis, I had a pretty solid idea of where we were. And more importantly, where we were landing.

Tall steel buildings pushed up from the horizon like jagged teeth. An urban sprawl emerged, a city base, no doubt. The Steelheart Collective. I recognized it from the broadcast screens. I'd seen its skyline during past Runs, but never in person. The buildings looked weathered, more worn than anything in Praxis, but still... functional. Strong.

Kade had always been obsessed with other Collectives. Always talking about seeing them for himself one day, getting out of Canyon. I don't think this is what he meant when he said that. I don't think he imagined our freedom from Canyon coming in the form of the Run.

"It's as beautiful as I always thought it would be," said a voice, low and soft, beside me.

I flinched. An involuntary, sharp movement that sent a

spear of pain through my neck. I turned, teeth gritted. My eyes widened as they landed on the figure before me where once there was nothing.

"Kade?" I breathed.

There he was. Just... there. Unchanged. His dark skin gleamed like the sky at midnight. His eyes, that light, sand-colored brown, full of fire and mischief. He looked like he always had.

My heart lurched, skipping painfully in my chest.

"How are—?"

"I told you I was right to want out of Canyon," he interrupted, flashing me that familiar, cocky grin that I had missed something fierce.

I shook my head, even though it hurt like hell. "You're dead," I said, more to myself than to him. Maybe if I said it out loud, I'd believe it. But it didn't change what I saw. He looked real.

He felt real.

He tilted his head, gaze drifting out the door to the Collective below. "That's unfortunate," he said. "I think I really would've liked to see this."

A lump swelled in my throat. I couldn't take my eyes off him. I wanted to reach out, to touch him, but I didn't. I was afraid of what I'd find, or what I wouldn't.

"Am I...?" I began, my voice weak and hoarse.

"Dead?" he asked, meeting my gaze. I nodded. "No. Not yet, anyway."

The hum of the plane's engines roared around us, and somewhere in the corner of the cabin, a camera blinked its steady red light. I couldn't imagine what they were seeing, me whispering into the empty air. I just prayed the noise drowned out my voice.

Tears welled in my eyes. "I'm so sorry, Kade," I whispered. My voice cracked like glass underfoot.

His brows lifted. "For what?"

"For... for you. For what happened." I swallowed hard. "It's my fault."

"Don't be a dumbass," he said, lips twitching in amusement. "You really think this is on you?"

"I've been convicted," I choked out. "I'm guilty."

He rolled his eyes. "Yeah, and I'm *not* lying six feet under right now." He laughed under his breath. "Bunch of horseshit. You're as much a killer as I am alive. Which is to say not at all."

He said it like a joke, but I didn't really find the humor in it.

I stared at him, at the easy way he spoke, the way his smirk softened into something kinder.

"How are you here, Kade?"

He shrugged. "I'm not. Not really."

"I don't want to die," I said. The words spilled out before I knew I'd spoken them. Raw and bare and honest. And I was surprised to realize just how true they were. There were nights, locked in that cell after he was gone, when I wondered if dying would be easier. But somehow, somewhere along the way, I found a reason to fight.

Her name was Brexlyn Hollis.

"I know," he said gently, the ghost of a smile on his face. "You found a new family."

"You're still my family," I said, the words aching in my chest. "You always will be."

"I know that too." He looked proud. Sad. Peaceful. "I'm glad you found them."

"I'm in love with her," I admitted, gasping through the words, dragging her image into focus, long dark hair, porcelain skin, eyes like blue fire. The scent of her skin. The sound of her laugh.

Then, unbidden, another face flickered into view, mischievous red hair, a lopsided grin, all bravado and warmth.

"And him too," Kade added with a teasing wink. "You sly dog."

I barked a short, strangled laugh that turned into a grunt of pain. My vision blurred. My limbs felt like sandbags. I was slipping.

The wheels hit the tarmac and the impact ripped a fresh scream of pain through me, but just as quickly, the agony receded. Something else was pulling at me. A void, soft and dark and strangely comforting.

I couldn't move. Couldn't sit up. Couldn't even lift my head. I was weightless and trapped all at once.

I heard shouting. Distant, desperate.

"Your Wildguard is coming," Kade said. He stood, looking out across the runway, eyes narrowed toward the noise.

I wanted to turn. I wanted to see them, Brexlyn, him, all of them. Just one more time. But my body refused.

"I don't blame you, you know," Kade whispered. "And they won't either. If you have to go."

My eyelids fluttered. I fought to hold them open, to see, but I was losing. Losing everything.

"Goodbye," I whispered. I didn't know who I was saying it to. Kade, Brexlyn, the world maybe, but the word felt final.

Then the darkness took me.

And this time, I wasn't sure I'd come back.

CHAPTER
THIRTEEN

THORNE

The moment the plane jolted to a stop, I was out of it, my boots hitting the tarmac before the engine fully powered down. My legs were heavy, stiff from yesterday's grueling task of rebuilding the watch tower and this morning's battle against the flames. Every muscle ached. My lungs still held the smoke. My arms trembled, more from adrenaline and desperation than fatigue.

The trial had been brutal. Not just physically, but emotionally. And I was filled with unrelenting fear and worry, not for myself, but for the people I loved. I needed to see them. *Now.*

I whipped my head toward the runway, scanning frantically as the other planes touched down in staggered intervals. I counted them. One. Two. Three. Four...

Where were they?

Then I spotted her.

Briar.

Relief cracked through the tension in my chest like sunlight through storm clouds. My shoulders sagged, my breath catching, and then I was running, full tilt, legs burning, dust kicking up behind me.

"Briar!" I shouted.

She turned just in time for me to crash into her, wrapping her in a desperate, aching hug. She melted into me with that same breathless relief, her arms tightening around my back. We stood like that, holding each other upright with nothing but the knowledge that we'd both made it.

"You're okay," I whispered into her hair, still disbelieving.

"I'm okay," she murmured, her voice rasped and hoarse. "Just a few burns. Nothing I can't handle."

My hand slid down her arm, checking for injuries. Bruises. Burned fabric. It was all there. She was wounded, but standing. Alive.

"Have you found Bex? Or Ezra?" she asked.

I shook my head, already scanning the horizon again. My fingers caught hers, and we took off in sync, two shadows streaking across the landing strip.

The air still smelled like scorched wood and metal. I spotted Lark and Devrin stumbling off their planes, both of them coated in soot. Their clothes were torn, melted in places, skin blistered and blackened. But they were walking. Conscious. They'd survived.

I sprinted past them, and that's when my eyes landed on Bex.

She was climbing down from her plane slowly, each movement deliberate. She cradled her right arm against her chest, her steps uneven. No shirt, just the soot-smeared skin of her torso beneath her black bra and a thick burn running the entire length of her arm. Blood streamed down her leg in dried rivulets. Her lips were pale. She looked like a ghost.

But she was here.

My lungs caught. My heart roared in my ears. I was

running again, reaching her just as she reached the bottom step.

Without thinking, I tore off my shirt and wrapped it around her shoulders, shielding her from the staring eyes of whoever was watching us now. Her skin was hot beneath my hands. Too hot.

I didn't hug her. I wanted to. I needed to. But I didn't dare risk causing her more pain. Instead, I hovered my hands just above her, my fingers trembling in the space between us. Our eyes locked.

And for a moment, the world dropped away.

I had no idea how it had happened, how this woman had become my everything. But she had. Like my heart had stepped out of my chest and started walking around on two battered legs.

"I'm okay," she said. But it didn't sound like the truth. "I've got a pretty bad burn on my arm," she added, her voice quiet, "and I lost a lot of blood from my leg, but the bleeding's stopped now. At least, I think it has."

Her skin was too pale. Her lips had no color. She needed help. Soon.

Briar leaned in and pressed a soft, grateful kiss to her cheek. A silent thank-you for surviving.

"Ezra?" she asked.

I turned, eyes scanning wildly. Eight Challengers had made their way to the islands.

Only six planes had landed.

Six.

My stomach turned to ice.

Lark. Devrin. That was two.

My plane. Three.

Briar's. Four.

Bex. Five.

One more.

One left.

And no one had disembarked.

A cold sweat broke out across my back. I saw the same fear flicker across Bex's face. The blood drained from her cheeks as she looked toward the final plane.

Then she was moving, running, limping, pushing her body past its limit.

"Ezra!" I called. My voice cracked in the cold air. "Ezra, come on, answer me!"

The world narrowed to that last plane. No movement. No sound.

Bex cried out his name again, her voice raw.

Please let it be him. Let him be okay.

Let him be on that plane.

Let him be alive.

We stormed the plane the second we could, and for one brief moment, I felt a wave of relief crash over me at the sight of Ezra lying there on the floor. But it shattered just as quickly.

He wasn't moving.

His entire left side was blackened, raw, the skin blistered and peeling. Smoke and blood clung to him. His face was ghost-pale, and his chest wasn't rising.

I froze.

"Ezra!" Bex screamed, dropping to her knees beside him in the plane. Her hands trembled midair, hovering above him unwilling to cause more pain. "Ezra, please! Wake up. It's me. We're here," she sobbed, her voice already fraying.

I dragged my eyes away, blinking furiously, and found Briar. The terror in her expression mirrored my own.

Where the hell were the medics? The Architects? The film crew? The fucking audience that watched every second of our suffering. Why were we alone now, when it mattered most?

Then I spotted it. A bus, waiting on the far end of the tarmac. Lark and Devrin were already walking toward it.

"We need to get on that bus," I muttered, barely able to speak past the lump in my throat.

Bex turned to me, eyes red. "He's unconscious."

"We'll carry him."

I stepped forward. My hands hovered uselessly. Where could I touch him that wouldn't hurt? But the truth was, pain was inevitable. He needed help more than comfort. I slid my arms beneath his torso, the searing scent of burnt flesh making my stomach turn. Briar gently took his legs, and Bex supported his head with both hands, her jaw clenched to keep herself from breaking.

We moved together, quick but careful, toward the bus. I didn't know what waited for us there, hope, maybe. Help, I prayed.

Inside, the driver sat behind a thick cage of plastic. When I asked where the medics were, he didn't respond. Not a word. Not a glance.

We laid Ezra across one of the bus seats, his body so still it made me feel like screaming. I reached for his neck, fingers searching desperately.

"I can't feel a pulse," I whispered. My throat burned from the words.

The engine growled to life, and the bus lurched forward.

Only six of us remained.

Maybe.

I looked down at Ezra, my teammate, my friend. Then at Bex, pale and trembling, blood soaking her pant leg. She could barely stand on her own. How much longer could she hold on?

She leaned over Ezra, her fingers clutching his, her tears falling freely. "Please," she whispered. "Breathe."

She bent and kissed him, soft and desperate.

"You have to give him CPR," Devrin said suddenly.

We all turned to him. The bus was eerily silent. He met

Bex's gaze, calm and steady. I hated it. Hated him for what he did to her in the canals. I nearly lost it when Bex let him win the trial he wanted, felt the rage boiling in my chest like acid.

But then I remembered the talent show. The way his music had echoed through the room as he played *The Moth*. Like it or not, he had stepped up when it counted. He was a part of the Runaways, tangled in it just like the rest of us. And in this moment, when Ezra was slipping away, we needed every ally we had.

Even Devrin.

"What's that?" Bex asked, panicked.

"It's a way to keep his heart beating," Devrin said. I'd heard of it before, in passing, but our Collective never placed high enough in medical trials for me to ever have learned it.

"Can you do it, Thorne?" she asked, eyes pleading with mine.

I froze. "I—I don't know how. I'm sorry."

Bex's shoulders shook. She looked to Devrin. "Tell me. Please. Tell me how."

He met her gaze and nodded slowly. Despite everything he'd done, everything I still held against him, in that moment, he was the only one who could help us.

"You have to pump his chest, and give him rescue breaths," Devrin said, still seated, his voice eerily calm. We all stared at him, wide-eyed. It didn't make a lick of sense to me, and judging by Bex and Briar's silence, it didn't to them either. "And you need to do it fast. If he's out too long, he'll lose oxygen to his brain."

That sent Bex into a full-blown panic. I grabbed her shoulders, trying to steady her, then turned to Devrin.

"Help us," I begged. "Please."

His eyes locked on mine, and for a long, breathless moment, he didn't move. Silence swallowed the bus. Fear wrapped its fingers around my throat. Was he going to help or just sit there and let Ezra die?

My heart pounded. Every second felt like a scream.

"Please," I said again, my voice cracking.

Still nothing.

Then finally, he moved. A small nod, almost imperceptible, and Devrin slid down onto his knees beside me. Relief slammed into my chest, but there was no time to feel it.

I had to drag Bex back, her hands clutching Ezra like she could anchor him to this world. She resisted, but I guided her just enough, giving Devrin the space he needed. She hovered close, trembling, watching every move like her own life depended on it.

Devrin knelt beside Ezra. I watched, helpless, as he began, his hands pressing into Ezra's chest, each motion cracking through the silence. Blood welled beneath his palms, the burns splitting further with every pump. It was horrifying. But necessary. We'd focus on the burns when he was breathing. One horrible problem at a time.

He paused, then leaned in to breathe into Ezra's mouth. His chest rose, just a little. Then again.

Then again.

And then—

"There," Devrin said, his fingers pressed to Ezra's throat. "He's got a pulse."

Bex let out a sound between a sob and a laugh, collapsing against the nearest seat. My body sagged with relief, knees shaking.

"He needs more than I can give him," Devrin added, glancing up. "But he's alive."

"Thank you," Bex said, her voice barely audible through her tears.

The bus rolled to a stop beneath a broad, crumbling

awning. A massive building loomed ahead, once grand, now shadowed in dust and decay.

"What now?" Briar asked, scanning the space.

"I think... we get off," Lark said. He was already standing.

Devrin followed. The rest of us lifted Ezra carefully, moving down the aisle, out into the open air.

The building before us was huge, long, grey, skeletal in its abandonment. But the layout, the shape of the entrance...

"This is a hospital," I breathed.

Bex pushed forward, hope reigniting in her eyes. "Help! Somebody help us!" Her voice echoed down the hollow corridors as we stepped inside.

The abandoned hospital was dark, cold, and humming faintly with a low pulse of electricity that vibrated through the floor beneath our feet. A few overhead lights flickered, casting long, twitching shadows down the hallway. Discarded machines sat in corners like dead animals, their screens black, wires trailing like veins. The beds were coated in thick dust, untouched for years.

In the far corner, however, several trays of medical instruments gleamed, clean, orderly, and suspiciously dust-free. Vials of medicine. Bandages. Scalpels. Burn cream. Syringes. Everything looked untouched... or perhaps, recently touched.

"This is the trial," I breathed, eyes scanning the corners of the ceiling. Cameras blinked red in every corner. Watching.

"What?" Briar asked, trying to follow my gaze.

I adjusted Ezra's weight in my arms, his body unnaturally limp. "This is the medical trial. We're already in it."

The words sank like stones into the room.

Bex's face paled as realization struck. "Nobody's coming to help us save him, are they?" Her voice wavered, but it wasn't a question. Not really.

I shook my head slowly. "No."

"Oh my God," she whispered, choking back a sob.

"Bry, strip that bed," I ordered. "We need something clean to lay him on. Infection's the last thing he needs right now."

Briar nodded and got to work, yanking the linens off with furious precision.

"Are we... all supposed to help?" Lark asked, inching closer, uncertain.

"They probably didn't know who would be injured, or how," Briar muttered, teeth clenched. "I'm sure Praxis intended for us to save ourselves if it came to that." She yanked the last sheet free, then turned to one of the cameras, her glare cold. "But we're not that selfish."

Bex was already at the trays, hands flying through instruments and supplies. "I don't know what any of this is for," she admitted, voice tight with panic as she picked up a tube with a needle attached then set it down just as fast.

I laid Ezra gently on the stripped mattress, fingers pressing against his throat. There, faint, but present. A pulse. I let out a shaky breath.

"Thorne, look." Briar rolled over a machine on wheels, her eyes searching mine. "Is this something?"

I stared at it. Dials, cords, blinking lights. "Maybe," I said bitterly. "But I don't know how the fuck to use it." My hands clenched into fists. I felt useless. This must've been how Ezra and Bex felt in the tech trial, completely out of their element.

But Ezra survived that one. I'd be damned if he didn't survive this.

"It's a heart monitor," Devrin said, appearing at Briar's side, hands steady. "I don't know how to set it up either, but if we can, it'll at least track his vitals."

"How do you know all this?" Lark asked.

"Saltspire's always done well in these trials. And education too. My mom works as a healer in our Collective."

I didn't like him. I never had. But right now, I needed his brain more than I needed to hate him.

"Lark!" I barked. "Look for some kind of manual, check those desks."

"On it!" he shouted back, already digging through drawers like a tornado.

Briar joined Bex at the supplies, creating order out of chaos. "I'm sorting what I recognize here, stuff I think I can use, and putting what I don't over there." She pointed to a growing pile of instruments and vials. The pile of things she didn't know was much larger.

"Lark, anything?" I called.

"A lot of books," he replied, popping up from behind the desk with a stack in his arms. "No manual, but these are medical textbooks, maybe there's something useful?"

I looked at Bex. She was already moving.

"Get to reading, love," I said.

She grabbed the top book and flipped through the pages at lightning speed. "This one's on machines, yes!" She scanned the diagram, then bolted to the heart monitor with a kind of desperate grace.

Wires were connected. Thin white disks pressed to Ezra's blistered skin. A button flipped.

The monitor whirred to life. And then—*beep... beep... beep...*

His pulse echoed through the room. Everyone exhaled. But it was *slow*. Too slow.

"Okay," I said, voice trembling as I met her eyes. "Time to read about how to treat burns."

I glanced at the supplies. Praxis had left us with the tools, some of them, at least. That was always their way. They didn't make these trials impossible. Just cruel. Twisted. Designed to break us before they tested us.

But we weren't broken yet.

And Ezra wasn't dead. Not yet.

We still had time.

The heart monitor's steady rhythm was a fragile thread we all clung to. *Beep... beep... beep...* The sound filled the silence like a lifeline, until it didn't.

It stopped.

A single, flat tone screamed into the room.

"No, no, no, no," I whispered, whirling toward the machine. The monitor displayed a flat line. Ezra's pulse was gone.

"Bex!" I shouted.

She was already moving, flipping furiously through the pages of the textbook. Her hands shook, but her eyes scanned with laser focus. "There, page 142," she muttered, voice tight with panic. "I think...I think I can do this."

"Just tell us what you need," Briar said, stepping to her side.

"AED pads. Syringe...adrenaline." She read off the list. "There's a chart, wait, I've got it." Bex yanked the supplies she'd previously sorted into the 'what the fuck is this' pile. Her fingers trembled, but her grip was sure. "Turn on that machine." She said pointing at a bulky device. I quickly turned it on, it whirred to life.

I stayed by Ezra's side, watching helplessly as she worked. Her face was pale under the flickering light, her hair matted to her face with sweat and soot. She pressed the pads to Ezra's chest, following the instructions in the manual like her life depended on it. Because his did.

"Nobody touch him," she barked, all of us pulled our hands away and watched her.

She hit the button.

Ezra's body jerked once, violently.

"Fuck," she cried.

Still nothing.

Another shock.

"No no no no no no. I'm so sorry, Ezra," she cried out,

tears streaming down her face. My vision blurred as my own tears began to pour. We couldn't lose him. Not like this. Not now.

Then, *beep... beep...*

A ragged sob escaped Briar. And someone gasped. I realized it was me. Ezra's pulse was back. Shallow. Weak. But back.

"We need to," she closed her eyes recalling the words on the page she'd just read. "Give him fluids," Bex said, her voice a hoarse whisper. She was swaying now, tilting slightly as she crouched beside him.

"Bex," I said quietly, moving toward her. "You okay?"

"I'm fine." Her answer was automatic. Too fast. She pressed gauze to Ezra's burns and fumbled with a vial of fluid. Her fingers slipped. The vial clattered to the floor. She didn't go after it.

I stepped forward, catching her elbow as she tried to rise. "You're not fine. You're..."

"Not now," she snapped, her voice sharper than a blade. "Not until he's okay." She grabbed another vial with shaking hands and attached it to an IV, threading the line with frantic determination.

But her body gave out before her will did.

She slumped forward, catching herself on the edge of the bed with a weak grunt before her knees buckled. I caught her just before she hit the floor.

"Bex!" Briar cried, rushing to her.

"She's out cold," I said, easing her to the ground. The puddle of blood pouring from her leg was gushing now. "Shit. She's burning up. And she's bleeding out."

"She needs meds too," Briar whispered, brushing hair from Bex's face.

"I'll take care of Ezra, You go focus on her" Devrin said suddenly, reaching for the creams and gauze on the supply tray. His voice was calm, steady.

I stepped between him and the bed, my body locking like a wall of iron. "Like hell. I'm not leaving him with you."

Devrin didn't flinch. He met my glare dead-on, focused. "His story doesn't end like this."

That made me falter. Just a fraction of a second. My mother's voice echoed in my head, those same words wrapped in a lullaby of defiance.

Something shifted in me.

"Take care of him. Okay?" I said, with a quick nod, and turned to Briar. "Get her on another bed. Now."

Briar was already moving, ripping the dust covered sheet off the nearest cot. We got Bex between us, barely able to lift her deadweight. Her skin was pale and tacky with sweat, and her breathing had grown too shallow.

"Lark!" Briar barked. "Book. Blood loss. Find it."

Lark scrambled, fumbling through the mess of medical textbooks like they might explode. His hands shook so hard I thought the pages might tear. He landed on a thick volume, nodding at me with wide eyes. "Got it."

"Talk to us," I said, kneeling beside Bex. I swept her matted hair from her face. "What do we do?"

"Is she still bleeding?" He asked, reading off something.

I looked down at her leg, coated with dark red blood. I took some gauze and cleaned around the wound, watching it to see if blood pumped out of it anymore. "No."

"That's good," Lark said, nodding and turning the page.

"So, what's next?" Briar asked, voice tight.

Lark's eyes darted across the page. "We need to give her blood. Fast. If she's gonna survive this..."

Briar was already sprinting toward the supply room. "That door, there was something locked behind it."

She gripped the large handle, and pulled the door open. A moment later, a hiss of cold air swept into the room, and Briar's voice rang out. "Blood. There's blood in here."

"Does anyone know her blood type?" Lark asked, voice pitching.

I looked at him like he'd grown another head. "What the fuck does that mean? It's blood, right?"

Lark stayed calm, luckily not reacting to my aggressive tone. "Okay. We need O Negative then, universal donor."

Briar's voice echoed from the cooler, "Give me a second. I'm looking."

"Hurry!" I yelled, feeling the panic rise again.

Behind me, I heard Ezra groan in pain.

"Devrin. Talk to me, what's going on?" I turned and saw Devrin cleaning the burns.

"Stable," Devrin said, not looking up. "He's breathing, and in a lot of pain. I'm cleaning him up now."

I watched, stunned, as he cleaned Ezra's burns with practiced hands, spreading salve and wrapping gauze like someone who'd done it a hundred times before.

Ezra would probably punch him later. Or hug him. Maybe both.

"Thorne," Briar called. "I've got it. O Negative."

I turned back to Bex. Her lips were starting to blue.

"What now, Lark?" I asked, trying not to scream. "Tell me what the hell to do."

"You need to start a transfusion. Get a needle in her. There's a diagram but...I'm not sure how to..."

"Come here," I said, already rolling up my sleeve. "Just show me the picture."

Lark moved beside me, pointing with trembling fingers. I scanned the diagram, matched tools from the tray, my hands shaking harder than his. Sweat burned into my eyes. I couldn't afford to be clumsy.

Briar arrived beside us with the blood bag. "It's cold."

"She's colder," I said, taking the IV line from Lark. I held the needle over Bex's arm and froze.

My hands wouldn't move.

"She needs it, Thorne," Briar whispered. Her hand settled on my shoulder, grounding me.

"I don't want to hurt her."

"If you don't, she's already gone," Lark said softly.

That did it.

I inhaled sharp and hard, then guided the needle beneath her skin. A tiny bloom of red in the tubing let me know it was working.

"I got it," I whispered, heart hammering.

"Open the valve," Lark said, adjusting the line. The blood began its slow crawl down the tube and into her.

Time lost all shape. Each second stretched, twisted. I could only watch and wait.

Then, Bex stirred. Her eyelids fluttered. Her fingers twitched. And relief flooded through me. My muscles relaxed and I didn't even realize how tight I had been holding my body.

"Ezra?" she rasped, her voice more breath than sound.

"He's okay," Briar said quickly, tears springing into her eyes as she cradled Bex's hand. "Thanks to you."

"You passed out, love," I murmured, brushing a clean cloth across her sweaty forehead, then pressing a kiss to her warming lips. "Don't do that again."

A weak, tired smile curved her lips. "I'll try to schedule my collapses better."

Behind me, Devrin looked up from where he was finishing Ezra's last wrap. "His burns are treated. He won't be dancing anytime soon, but he's alive."

Briar squeezed Bex's hand. "Both of them are."

"Let me take care of that leg," I said, reaching for the ointments and salves lined up on the tray beside us. Because Praxis hoards their supplies, and gatekeeps their doctors and their medicine, they've been able to develop some truly miraculous stuff. Stuff that could change lives. Maybe even save them, if they cared to share. I uncapped one of the jars, the smell sharp and sterile, and carefully dabbed a bit of the shimmering cream along Bex's torn skin.

It was like watching frost melt off glass, slow but unmistakable. The angry red of the wound softened almost immediately. By the time I wrapped the bandage around her leg, she was out of danger. At least for now.

Only then did I let myself stumble back, collapsing onto the nearest cot like a puppet with cut strings. My hands shook. My vision blurred at the edges. Exhaustion burrowed into my bones, thick and aching. I sat forward, elbows on my knees, burying my face in my hands. The quiet was overwhelming, just the soft beep of machinery and the low, steady breaths of the living. Which, no thanks to Praxis, was all of us.

"Thank you," Bex said, her voice faint but steady. She looked at me first, then over to Briar. "All of you." Her eyes continued to Lark, and then—after a beat—to Devrin.

Devrin met her gaze. There was something in his face then, something fast and fractured. Guilt, maybe. Good. He should feel it. He'd nearly killed her.

"It's the least I could do," he murmured, voice clipped. He looked away.

Bex sank back into the cot, exhaling a long, tired breath.

"So... is that it?" Lark asked. His voice barely reached above a whisper, directed more at the still air than anyone in particular.

I scanned the room. Six of us, all that was left from the original twenty Challengers. Two more gone just this morning. The medical trials were always separate, and typically more mental than physical. Although today, I guess, was a healthy mix of the two. Supplies. Then personnel. But this... this one felt like a full stop. Like we'd done both in one vicious fell swoop.

"I don't know," I admitted. It was the only answer that felt honest.

Lark drifted toward the supply table. His fingers lingered over the items there until they closed around a mask, filter-lined, made for prolonged wear. He turned it over in his hands like it was something sacred.

"Your people... they've been suffering, haven't they?" Bex asked. Her voice had gentled, softened like cloth soaked in light. She was looking directly at Lark now.

He blinked, surprised by the question. Then nodded.

"Our air's been poisoned for years," he said, lifting the mask slightly as if to explain it. "We wear these to breathe. Long exposure without one... it breaks you down. Lungs. Brain. Even the skin, sometimes." His voice cracked at the edges. "We've lost a lot of people."

"I'm so sorry," Bex said, and she meant it. You could see it in her eyes, the way they shimmered, not from pain, but from empathy.

"It's not fair," Lark muttered, almost too low to hear.

We all stilled.

"It's not fair," he repeated, louder this time. His voice splintered, and then the dam broke. The tears came hard, sudden and silent at first. Then sobs wracked his frame as he dropped the mask and buried his face in his hands.

Bex slid off the cot, slow and careful. Briar and I instinctively reached out to steady her, but she waved us off. She was still pale, but color had started to return to her cheeks. She wasn't trembling anymore.

She crossed the room and wrapped her arms around Lark without hesitation. He cried into her shoulder, the sound echoing through the sterile space. Raw and human in a place designed to strip that away.

We let the moment stand.

Then, overhead, a sudden crackle. The speaker system

flickered to life, its mechanical hum slicing through the silence.

Our heads lifted in unison, breath caught in our throats.

"Congratulations, Challengers." I expected Annalese's voice. But it wasn't. It was thicker. Darker. Carried something sharp beneath it. This was Archon Veritas.

"You are the lucky survivors of this year's Reclamation Run."

Relief hit me like a wave, then crashed just as fast.

If the Run was over, that meant...The real Reclamation was about to begin. Briar and Bex had left the breadcrumbs in the lyrics of their song. Tomorrow, the Runaways were supposed to meet us at the gates. That was the plan. *Take Praxis down from the inside.*

Suddenly the doors to the hospital swung open and about a dozen Praxis guards filed in. More than it would take to escort us out. My heart stuttered. Then sped. Why did they send so many?

"You've sacrificed and risked your lives for the Collectives. You've proven that Praxis rewards those deserving of it," Veritas continued. And I felt my blood heat. Deserving? That word tasted like poison.

"Now, your time as Challengers has come to an end. So your Collectives thank you. Praxis thanks you. I thank you." But there was nothing thankful in her voice. It was hollow. Mechanical. Like a script read before an execution. The guards moved in from the corners of the room. Slow. Deliberate. Closing in like a net.

My blood ran cold. My skin prickled. Something wasn't right.

"Your sacrifice for the greater good of Nexum will always be remembered."

The speaker cut out. A sharp, unnatural silence followed. I glanced up at the corners of the room. The cameras. The red lights that always blinked, always watched... they were off. No one was watching anymore. Whatever came next wasn't meant to be seen.

I heard a crackle coming from the radio on one of the guards belts. "Captain. You may proceed."

"Time to go," a guard said.

Lark stood slowly, cautiously, following the direction of the nearest guard. I watched their movements. Too stiff. Too ready. Not like escorts. Like hunters.

"Wait," Bex said, stepping forward. "How are we supposed to transport Ezra? He needs to rest."

She pointed to where he still lay slumped in the corner.

"We can come back for him," the guard replied without hesitation.

"Um, no," I cut in. Too fast. Too loud. "We're not leaving him."

"You're going back to your respective Collectives now," another guard said, stepping behind me, pressing a heavy hand onto my shoulder to steer me toward the door.

I twisted out of his grip.

"No," I said, louder this time. "We're not splitting up. Not until he's awake. Not until he's safe."

"That's not your concern," the guard said flatly. And that was it. The moment I knew.

We weren't going anywhere.

Not alive.

This wasn't a transport mission. It was an execution. Archon was going to cut off the head of the rebellion before it began.

The guard near Lark moved faster than I could scream. Steel flashed. A line of red appeared across Lark's throat. His eyes went wide. His mouth opened. But no sound came. Just blood. Thick and fast, pouring down his chest as he dropped to his knees, then the floor. Still

"No!" I surged forward, grabbing the nearest sharp object from a tray and launching myself at the closest guard. We were outnumbered. But we were done running. Done being pawns. We were pissed off, and that made us more dangerous than they knew.

The room erupted into a flurry of movement.

I knocked one guard to the ground, landing on top of him, slamming his wrist against the floor until his weapon skittered across the tile. Another rushed behind me. I spun, dragging the fallen guard into the path of the next attack. The knife meant for me sank into his back instead. He sputtered, then went still.

I shoved him off and swept my leg toward the guard still standing. He crashed down. I drove my heel into his face with a satisfying crunch. "We need to get out of here!" I shouted.

Devrin had already dropped two.

Bex was grappling with a third, slamming him into a glass cabinet. Shards stuck into his arm, his neck, he shrieked.

Briar, behind the desk, was hurling anything she could find. A lamp. The medical books. A steel tray.

I rushed over, grabbed the attacker from behind, and slammed his head into the desk.

Hard.

He slumped down, nose crushed, out cold.

Bex flipped her guard just in time to parry another with a pain filled grunt.

Briar and I jumped in. The three of us moved together, fast and furious, until the guard was on the floor groaning in pain.

Devrin was pinned now on the floor, a knife to his throat. I pivoted. Ran. Kicked the guard square in the gut. Devrin twisted, got just enough room to slam the blade into his attacker's chest. The man went limp.

Devrin shoved him aside, met my eyes, nodded once, and then we both turned, because we weren't done yet.

The last two guards braced themselves, eyes flicking across the blood-slick floor, scanning the aftermath we'd left behind. The room reeked of iron, sweat, and death.

Bex, Briar, Devrin, and I stood in the center of it all, blood on our hands, our clothes, our faces. Chests heaving. Eyes locked. But still we didn't flinch.

Let Praxis see what happens when they push too far. Let them learn that we weren't afraid of bleeding anymore. Not if it meant survival. Not if it meant justice.

The guards made their move. Fast. Sharp. Trained. But we weren't the same people who'd been marched into the Run weeks ago. We were hardened, sharpened by trauma and fear. We were weapons all in our own right.

I ducked low and drove my shoulder into the nearest one's stomach, hard enough to hear the air knock out of him. His blade still caught me, ripping a line of fire across my shoulder, but I gritted through the pain. He doubled over, and Briar was there. Her fist cracked against his jaw like thunder, sending him crashing to the ground.

The second guard didn't stand a chance. Devrin moved in first, faking to the left, drawing the man's attention. Bex followed from behind and swung. The medical textbook, thick and heavy, slammed into the side of his skull with a sickening thud. He dropped instantly.

I almost laughed. A book that saved her life... now nearly ended someone else's. Fate had a wicked sense of humor. "I don't think they're all dead," I said, already sprinting toward Ezra. "We've got minutes, maybe seconds, before one of them wakes up or reinforcements show."

Bex was beside me in an instant, unhooking wires and tubes with clinical precision.

"Briar, we need a vehicle. Now." I barked. Without a

word, she turned and bolted, vanishing into the hall. I looked at Devrin. Hesitated. "Watch her back?" I tried to keep my voice even, but I was already failing. She was my family. Devrin didn't hesitate. He just nodded once and took off after her.

Behind me, something crackled. A burst of static. I spun, heart thundering, and saw a guard's personal radio sputtering to life. I snatched it from his vest and raised it slowly, dread pooling in my stomach.

"Captain?" It wasn't Veritas' voice this time. But someone else. Another guard maybe? "Is it done?"

Bex froze, eyes snapping to mine. Fury lit her face.

I pressed the button, forced my voice low and gruff. "Affirmative."

There was a pause. Then, "Return to base immediately. I'll send a crew for cleanup and disposal."

Cleanup. Disposal. Like we were trash. Debris to be swept away. I didn't reply. I clipped the radio to my belt and quickly moved about the room. Pulling each guard's radio and smashing it beyond repair against the ground. Didn't need them calling for help before we could get out of here. Then I turned back to Bex. "Let's get him up. Fast. We've bought ourselves a head start."

She nodded and we lifted Ezra carefully. He was stable, for now. Breathing steady. Still unconscious, but alive. The miracle medicine Praxis had been hoarding from the Collectives already working its magic on his raw skin.

As we passed Lark's body, I felt Bex falter. Her eyes slid toward him despite herself. The blood. The stillness. The sight of yet another victim. Her sob came sudden and sharp, like a breath she'd been holding broke inside her.

I whispered, barely audible over the chaos still ringing in my ears, "It won't be in vain."

She nodded once, hard, and we kept moving. We pressed

forward, and when I glanced back at the cameras, there was a small red light on. Maybe someone was watching after all.

When we reached the exit, Briar and Devrin were already on the bus. Briar held the keys, her knuckles white around them. "It's all ours," she said.

We loaded Ezra gently into the back. He looked... better. His wounds were cleaned and dressed. The meds had taken hold. Still a long way to go, but he'd most likely wake up soon.

I reached for the keys and headed to the driver's seat, the cage now open and empty.

"Wait," Bex said, stopping me.

She turned to Devrin, her voice clear and strong, stronger than I'd ever heard it.

"We're going back to Praxis. No more running. No more hiding. Are you coming with us?"

Her words didn't tremble. She was giving him the option to back away. To choose relative safety instead of certain risk.

Devrin studied her for a long moment. Then glanced at me. At Briar.

Finally, he stepped forward and held out his hand. "For the will of the people," he said.

Bex took his arm. Gripped it. "We survive," she answered.

With the team in place, I slid into the driver's seat. I'd never driven a bus like this before. Didn't matter, I'd figure it out. I threw it into gear and hit the gas. The doors shut behind us with a hiss. We pulled away from the clinic. Away from the blood. Away from Lark. And through the industrial streets of Steelheart, the city of metal.

We drove straight toward Praxis.

Straight into the storm.

Toward the fight.

Toward the real reclamation.

PART TWO

THE RECLAMATION

CHAPTER
FOURTEEN

BEX

The bus groaned beneath us, a low, guttural sound that rattled through the floor and into my bones as Thorne drove us away from Steelheart and back toward Praxis. The engine sounded angry as we made our departure, like it knew what we were on our way to bring down Praxis' pristine golden walls.

The sun was setting outside the cracked windows, casting long orange shadows across the aisle, painting everything in gold and rust. Ezra's hand lay in mine, limp but warm, and I gripped it like a tether. He was still breathing. Still here. And yet the fear of losing him hadn't left my chest. Not really. It just sat deeper now, quieter, but no less sharp.

Down the aisle, Briar and Devrin were deep in conversation. War plans. Strategy. Phrases like "flank positioning" and "staggered team sweep formations" drifted through the noise of the bus, and I let them. I didn't understand half of what they were saying, but I was grateful they did. It freed me up to do what I needed to, keep Ezra alive. And hold myself together.

I smoothed the hair off Ezra's forehead, fingers lingering there longer than necessary. He was sleeping, peaceful, at last. I'd nearly lost him. So close. One breath, one heartbeat away from never hearing his quiet laugh again. From never seeing those forest-green eyes light up in the morning sun. From never telling him how much I loved him.

The engine was loud, but not loud enough to drown out the echo of my thoughts. No engine could do that.

We'd set this whole rebellion in motion, called the Runaways together, reignited the spark that Thorne and Briar's mother lit years ago. We had pulled on the string, and now the whole tapestry was unraveling.

But what if no one came?

What if we marched on Praxis alone?

The image haunted me, our ragged team stumbling into the capital, outnumbered and outgunned, only to find a country too afraid, too broken to rise up. What if all we had done was not enough?

I squeezed Ezra's hand again as my thoughts drifted to my brother. Jax.

It all started with him. This fight, this mission, this Reclamation. It began with a promise I made in the quiet of our broken home, that I'd find a way to give him a better life. That I'd fix a world that told him his body wasn't worth healing. That I'd come back with doctors and answers and hope.

But what if I didn't come back at all?

What if I never saw my little brother again? Never got to hold him close or tell him I loved him one more time? I could only hope Ava would tell him everything, that she'd explain why I had to go, why I had to risk it all. Why the fight was worth it.

God, please let him understand.

"Bex?"

My name, barely a whisper, but unmistakable. My eyes shot down to Ezra.

He stirred, lashes fluttering against his cheek, and I leaned in, barely breathing.

"Ezra," I gasped. "Oh my God, Ezra. You're awake." Tears spilled before I could stop them, warm and unrelenting. I pressed kisses to his mouth, desperate and grateful all at once. "You're awake."

His fingers tangled gently into my hair as he kissed me back, the touch soft and sure.

"Good morning to you, too," he murmured, the hint of a chuckle in his voice. He tried to sit up, and I moved instantly, wrapping an arm around his back, steadying him. He was stronger but still groaned in pain as he shifted upright.

"Nice to see you awake," Briar called softly, glancing over her shoulder with a tired smile.

"Thanks for staying in the land of the living, man" Thorne added over the roar of the engine, eyes catching us in the rearview mirror.

"Thanks for keeping me here," Ezra said, stretching. He winced as the motion tugged at healing skin, but he managed a smirk through the discomfort.

"How are you feeling?" I asked, running a hand down his unburned arm, grounding myself in his presence.

"Like someone tried to roast me over a spit," he said dryly. "But honestly? Better than I should be."

"Bex restarted your heart," Briar said, nodding toward me. Ezra's eyes locked on mine, wide with something I couldn't name. He gripped my hand, his thumb tracing slow, deliberate circles into my skin.

"Yes, she did," he said, voice low. The double meaning true and clear.

"And Devrin dressed your wounds," I added. His gaze snapped to the man sitting beside Briar. For a moment, confusion crossed his face, then realization, then something softer...acceptance.

"Thank you," Ezra said, sincerity laced through the words like steel. Devrin gave a small nod, already turning back to Briar.

Ezra looked back at me. "How long was I out?"

"Long enough for the Run to end," I said quietly.

His eyes widened. "The medical trials?"

"You kind of... were the medical trials," I replied. "We both were," I added, lifting my bandaged leg for him to see.

He let out a dry breath. "So, I'm guessing that means I didn't place very high."

A smile pulled at my lips, but it didn't last.

"When the Run ended, Veritas sent guards to execute us."

Ezra's jaw tightened, but he didn't look surprised. Of course he wasn't. None of us should've been. We should've known.

I should've known.

We could've saved Lark.

The guilt punched through me like it had every night since it happened, hollowing out a fresh pit in my chest. My vision blurred.

Ezra's hand found my jaw and gently tilted my face back to his.

"What's wrong, baby?" he asked softly.

"They got Lark," I whispered. "We couldn't save him."

He didn't speak right away. Just pulled me into his arms, the warmth of him anchoring me again. And for a long moment, I just let myself be held. We'd had to be so fucking strong through everything, but as the bus rattled forward, I allowed myself this one, precious moment of vulnerability.

Just a brief surrender to what we were carrying and what we had survived.

"We're headed back to Praxis now," I said, my voice trembling just slightly as I wiped the tears from my cheeks, steadying myself. "With any luck, the Runaways will be there waiting."

"They will," Ezra replied, his voice solid and unwavering, like a promise. His conviction grounded me in a way I didn't realize I needed.

"I hope you're right," I muttered under my breath, uncertainty still curling in the pit of my stomach.

The radio attached to Thorne's hip sounded, but I couldn't make it out. He listened.

Thorne's voice broke into the moment, his tone rough but carrying that steady certainty of his. "They found the guards. They know we escaped." I nodded, feeling the tension build in my chest. "We'll be there early morning. Might be a good idea for you all to get some rest," he called from the front.

"You too," Briar added, her voice laced with a rare kindness. "Wake me up at some point, and I'll drive us the rest of the way."

"Deal," Thorne responded, a slight shift in his voice that hinted at the exhaustion we all shared.

Briar and Devrin split off, claiming empty rows near the back of the bus to lay down, their bodies eager for any bit of rest they could find. But before she settled, Briar stopped by our row. She leaned over and pressed a soft, fleeting kiss to my lips. I kissed her back, absorbing that simple gesture of intimacy, a momentary sanctuary amid the chaos.

The sun had dipped below the horizon, and the last streaks of light bled into the night sky. The weariness settled deeper into my bones, but I wasn't ready to sleep. Not yet. Not when Ezra was here, breathing beside me.

I turned to study his face. His eyes were closed, but the

furrow between his brows told me that his mind was still miles away, trapped in thoughts I couldn't reach.

"What's on your mind?" I asked gently, reaching out to trace the wrinkle that creased his forehead. "There's worry painted all over you."

He met my eyes, his expression distant but soft. "I saw Kade," he said, his voice low, like a secret shared in the dark.

My heart skipped a beat. The words hit me like a jolt of lightning, but before I could fully grasp their meaning, he continued.

"Well... I know it wasn't really him," he said slowly, almost apologetically, "But it sure felt like it."

I ran my hand down his cheek, a soft, comforting gesture, and he leaned into it, the exhaustion on his face giving way to a deeper ache.

"No matter the reason," I said quietly, "I can imagine it must have been nice to see him."

He nodded, his jaw tightening as a fresh wave of emotion washed over him. "Yeah." His voice cracked just a little. "I never thought I'd ever see his face again, or hear his voice. But there he was. And God, it felt so real." His eyes softened, unfocused as he drifted back into the memory. "I think I was always afraid I'd forget him. That time would erase pieces of him. But he's still right there. Ya know?"

I leaned in, pressing a soft kiss to his cheek, feeling his warmth bleed into me. "Yeah. I know." My voice caught. "I don't think the people we love ever disappear. Not from here." I placed my palm gently over his heart, letting it linger.

He covered my hand with his, holding me there. His touch was firm, like he was trying to ground us both.

"You're here now too, Brexlyn," he whispered, his breath warm against my face. "Etched on this heart like you've always belonged there."

I smiled, feeling the weight of his words. "And I'll always

be there," I promised him, my voice steady, though the world around us was anything but. No matter what happened next, I knew that much to be true. Our hearts were linked, eternally, no matter what. Even if one of them stopped beating.

"I know you will." He kissed my forehead softly, and for a moment, everything felt right.

I've always loved the quiet, tender side of Ezra, the part of him he only let a few people see. Me mostly. And maybe Zaffir too. It felt like a privilege, to see his vulnerability.

But the thought of Zaffir broke the moment. A cold, tight knot twisted in my chest at the thought of him. Was he okay? Did he know that Archon sent guards to kill us? Did he see us escape? Or did he think we were dead?

"Now you're the one with worry all over your face," Ezra said, his thumb brushing over the crease between my brows.

"I'm just thinking about Zaffir," I answered quietly, my voice dropping, carrying the weight of unspoken fear. "If they sent guards to execute us..." I couldn't finish the sentence. But Ezra knew.

"He's smart," Ezra said, his tone steady, unwavering. "He's been watching this all from both sides. We had to focus on staying alive, but Zaffir... he's been able to watch things from the other side of the camera. If he saw what was coming for us, then he knew what would come for him too." He took a deep breath, his eyes locked on mine. "He's safe. I feel it. I know it."

I nodded slowly, the tension still tight in my chest, but the certainty in his voice made it easier to believe. Zaffir was safe. I had to believe that. Just like I had to choose to believe that the Runaways would be waiting for us when we arrived at Praxis.

"I was really worried about you," I said quietly, my voice barely above a whisper as I studied his face, his color nearly completely returned thanks to the medicine working its way through his system. "I thought we lost you."

"For a minute there, you did," Ezra replied, his voice rasped and low, tinged with something haunted, but there was warmth there too. The kind of warmth you can only feel after crawling your way back from the edge.

I leaned forward and pressed my forehead to his, our breaths mingling in the small space between us, syncing like they always did, like they were made to. A steady rhythm. A promise. Then he kissed me.

Soft. Gentle. Reverent. Like this was our first kiss again, not our thousandth. Like he'd clawed his way out of death's grasp just to feel my lips on his. I melted into him, my hands curling around the back of his neck, careful not to brush the bandages, mindful of his wounds, but needing him close all the same.

My own injury ached with the movement, but I didn't care. The salve had dulled most of the pain, and what was left was nothing compared to this moment. Compared to him.

His tongue ghosted across my lips, asking, not demanding, and I opened for him, letting him taste me, slow and languid. My fingers threaded into his hair as I leaned into him, needing to feel the life in him, to prove to myself that this wasn't a dream.

His teeth caught my bottom lip and tugged lightly, coaxing a soft, involuntary moan from me.

"Love," Thorne's voice came from the front of the bus, barely audible over the purr of the engine. "You'd best keep quiet... or you'll wake our guest."

I froze, breath caught in my throat. Then slowly turned, locking eyes with Thorne in the rearview mirror. His gaze was molten, simmering with mischief and warning both. My whole body ignited under it, flushed and buzzing and very, very aware of how close Ezra still was, how his breath was hot against my cheek.

Ezra chuckled darkly beside me. "Yeah, love," he echoed, mocking Thorne's pet name for me, though the way it rolled off his tongue made my stomach flip. "Keep quiet."

His lips trailed to my neck, his teeth grazing my skin as he nipped at the soft spot beneath my jaw. I bit down hard on my lip, struggling to stifle the noise building in my throat.

The memory of the limo flared hot in my mind, their hands, their eyes, the way I came undone beneath Zaffir's touch while Thorne, Briar and Ezra watched. My body pulsed at the thought, need curling low and urgent in my belly.

"You're barely recovered," I managed, swatting at Ezra's wandering fingers. My voice trembled, not from fear, but from how badly I wanted to surrender to this. To him. To them. But also how much I needed him to recover from his brush with death.

"I'm fine," he murmured, voice low and playful, fingers ghosting along my thigh again. Teasing.

"Don't you think Ezra deserves a reward," Thorne said, his voice syrup-slick and dangerous, "for clawing his way back to you from the grave, love?"

His words sparked like a match to dry kindling. I felt the heat rise in my chest, pooling between my hips. Thorne's eyes were still locked on mine in the mirror, as they flicked back and forth from me to the empty road ahead, challenging, coaxing. He was worried, I could tell. Just like I was. Ezra shouldn't push himself. But maybe there was another way.

I leaned in close, brushing my lips against Ezra's ear, my voice just a whisper.

"You survived death for me, Ezra. Let me remind you what living feels like."

His breath hitched, and I felt his hands tighten ever so slightly where they rested on my hips, as I peeled out of his hold and knelt to the ground between his legs. My leg protested a little, but I found a comfortable spot and looked up at him. Behind the wheel, Thorne didn't say a word. But he didn't look away either.

Devrin had stripped him to his boxers already when he was taking care of the burns on his legs, so all I had to do was slide the band far enough down to release his massive and hardened cock. Ezra's eyes were burning into me, and I could feel the heat of Thorne's gaze on the back of my head. I wrapped my hand around his length, and gently let my fingers stroke him. He groaned and I shot him a warning glance. "Now it's your turn to be quiet," I warned, just as I darted out my tongue to circle the tip of his cock. He grunted, low and quiet, his hands coming to tangle in my hair.

The bead of precum on my tongue was tangy, and sweet all at once, and I needed more. I opened my mouth and took him into it as far as I could. He slid into my warm and waiting mouth easily, his tip pressing against the back of my throat. The pressure was familiar and welcoming, I loved feeling filled by them. Being full of them. I ran my tongue along the underside of him and then slowly, gently, began bobbing up and down on him. He had a hold on my hair, but he didn't drive my movements, content to let me steer the ship.

But he still led, whether he knew it or not. I watched his body's reaction carefully. Taking his cues and driving him crazy with need.

"Fuck baby," Ezra whispered through gritted teeth as I sucked on the tip of him.

"She looks so good on her knees," Thorne replied, quietly. I could hear the strain in his voice. I knew he was as turned on as the two of us were. I wished I could reach his cock to stroke it with my fingers. Or better yet, slide him into my wet and desperate pussy.

At the thought of it, I dipped my fingers lower, beneath the band of my pants and into my heat. I found myself wet and throbbing as I circled my fingers against my clit. I moaned around Ezra's cock, which muffled the sound, but sent a wave of vibrations through him and he grunted, before pressing his hands in my hair and jutted his hips up until he was well and truly fucking my mouth. I let him take over now, content to let him use my mouth while my fingers chased my orgasm.

His cock twitched, his cum painting my tongue. I swallowed his every drop as I found my own release.

There was a glorious few seconds of stifled euphoria, then when his body and my body stilled, he helped me up and pressed an eager kiss to my lips.

"Bring me those fingers, love. I'm starving," Thorne demanded. I shot a glance at Ezra who gave me a sated and satisfied smile.

He nodded, smacking me on the ass playfully as I took careful steps toward the front of the bus. I came to a stop near the open driver's cage where Thorne was sitting, and without tearing his eyes from the road he opened his mouth for me.

It was sinful, dirty, and so incredibly hot as I slipped my fingers into his open mouth and he closed his lips around them. His tongue drank my release from them, and I had to bite my lips to keep from releasing another loud groan of pleasure. When he was sure to steal every drop from me, he let me pull my fingers back. He licked his lips with a devilish grin.

"Like a five-course meal, love," he teased. I smacked his shoulder playfully.

"Now both of you, get some sleep," Thorne said, his voice low but firm, the kind of command laced with care. His eyes found mine, steady and soft around the edges, before shifting to Ezra's in the rearview mirror. "I mean it."

I bent and brushed a kiss against his lips, quick and careful. A silent thank you, a wordless I love you, before pulling away before I could tempt him into more or distract him from the road ahead.

Then I turned to Ezra, whose eyes hadn't left me. He

looked exhausted but fulfilled. I leaned down, letting our foreheads touch for a breath before I kissed him too, short, sweet,
but lingering just enough.

"Sleep," I whispered against his lips.

He nodded, fingers brushing mine as I moved away.

I claimed the empty row behind him, curling up against
the window as best I could. The seats were stiff and narrow,
but I was exhausted enough to feel comfortable anyway. My
body was worn and aching, but my heart felt light. Whole.

I closed my eyes and let the rhythm of the road lull me, the
low hum of the engine and the occasional creak of the frame
wrapping around me like a lullaby until finally, rest came.

I AWOKE to golden light spilling softly through the bus
window, warming my cheeks. It was the kind of light that
didn't demand your attention but coaxed you gently back to
the world.

Blinking against the sun, I sat up slowly, my muscles stiff
but not screaming, just a quiet ache that reminded me I was
still alive, still healing. And that felt like a gift.

There was a low hum of voices around the bus. Briar was
behind the wheel now, alert and focused. Devrin and Ezra sat a
few rows up, speaking in hushed tones, voices low and familiar. Across from me, Thorne lay curled into the bench seat,
still fast asleep, his chest rising and falling in a steady rhythm. I
smiled down at him, quietly grateful that he hadn't been too
stubborn to hand over the reins to Briar for a few hours of real
rest.

I stretched, letting out a quiet groan as my spine cracked
into place. It hurt, but in a clean, satisfying way.

"How are you feeling?" Ezra asked, his voice drawing my
gaze. He was watching me now.

"I'm alright," I said, studying his face. "You?"

He looked good. Some color had returned to his cheeks, and while the burns still peeked from beneath the bandages wrapped around his neck and arms, the skin looked better. Healing, if scarred. He'd carry those marks forever, but they didn't seem to drag him down.

My stomach growled violently.

Ezra chuckled and tossed something toward me. I caught it midair, an apple, slightly bruised, but still firm and vibrant red.

"When did you get this?" I asked, examining it like it might be a mirage.

"When Briar and Thorne switched shifts," Devrin answered from up front. "We passed through a grove on the outskirts of Steelheart, near the Wilds. Picked up some fresh stuff. Not a feast, but it'll hold us."

I nodded gratefully and bit into the apple. The juice exploded across my tongue, sweet, crisp, cold. It was possibly the most delicious thing I'd ever tasted. I closed my eyes for a second to savor it.

Then I glanced at Ezra again and felt a slow blush creep into my cheeks.

Okay. Maybe not the *most* delicious thing.

"How close are we?" I asked, wiping my mouth with the back of my hand.

"Any minute now," Briar called from the driver's seat. She met my eyes in the mirror and grinned. "Good morning, beautiful."

The compliment sent a flutter spiraling through my chest. I smiled back, warmth blooming across my cheeks. "Good morning," I replied softly.

"It's the moment of truth," Devrin said, adjusting his seatbelt. "Time to find out if the Wildguard was enough to rally the troops."

He didn't mean it like a challenge, but it landed in my chest like one. My heart tightened. I could only hope we'd done enough, that the Runaways believed in us as much as we believed in them. That they knew, like we did, the time for waiting was long past.

Ezra nudged Thorne's foot with the toe of his boot. Thorne startled awake, sitting up sharply with sleep-mussed hair flopping into his eyes. He blinked at me, confused for half a second, then smiled, slow and crooked. So damn adorable.

"We're almost there," I explained softly.

My pulse quickened as we crested a small hill, the tires rumbling over uneven ground. I pressed my forehead to the cool glass, trying to steady my breath.

In the distance, the gleam of Praxis's outer gates shimmered gold in the rising sun. But it wasn't the city that stole the breath from my lungs.

At the base of the hill, thousands of people stood waiting.

Tents. Weapons. Painted banners bearing the moth symbol fluttered in the wind. Supplies. An army. My throat went tight. My heart pounded against my ribs like a war drum.

We drove slowly into the crowd. As we passed, heads turned. Eyes widened as they saw us through the windows. Then came the cheers, wild, uncontainable sound breaking through the morning stillness like thunder.

They knew who we were. They had been waiting for us.

"They came," I whispered.

"Holy shit," Devrin breathed.

"I wish Ma could've seen this," Thorne murmured. His voice cracked slightly as he looked up into the mirror, meeting Briar's eyes. She glanced at him with something like pride and sorrow tangled in her gaze.

I reached out and took Thorne's hand. Gave it a squeeze. Then looked at Briar and offered her a soft smile full of gratitude.

She slowed the bus to a careful stop.

We were dirty, scraped, bloodied, and barely clothed in anything that resembled dignity. But I had never felt more powerful.

The Runaways were here.

CHAPTER
FIFTEEN

ZAFFIR

THE SHOW CENTER was chaotic and buzzing with the frantic energy that always came from the final moments of the Run. Screens flickered with live feeds, editors shouted time-stamps back and forth, and the air buzzed with an electric kind of tension, something between excitement and dread. The final trial had begun.

They'd called all the editors on-site for the last two trials. Nearly every moment was going out live now, or as close to real time as possible. Where usually we did our work hidden behind the curtain, we were suddenly given a front-row seat. I had been working faster than I ever had in my life, stitching together footage from the islands.

Thorne and Briar had made it out mostly intact. Scraped, bruised, but moving with the unshaken calm of people who knew how to survive the wild. I'd expected as much from them.

But Brexlyn and Ezra...

Their screams had embedded themselves into my skull.

Ezra's trembling hands, and fire covered body. Bex's voice, ragged with panic. I could still see the way the camera caught the moment Ezra spoke to the air then collapsed, eyes wide with something that looked too much like acceptance of death, and then nothing at all. Blank.

I had sent off the latest cut to the producers, but I couldn't move from the main screen now. I couldn't pretend to be useful. Not when Ezra was lying still, too still. His chest wasn't rising. His heart wasn't beating. The feed didn't lie.

He was dead.

And I felt it like someone had taken a sledgehammer to my ribs.

There were too many eyes around. Executives, security, media reps, high-ranking officials from Praxis excited and eager for the carnage of the end of the Run. I couldn't fall apart. Not here. Not now.

I forced my body to remain still, to breathe evenly. But my jaw ached from how hard I was biting my cheek. I could taste the metallic tang of blood. My palms were sweating so badly they left streaks on the desk. I clung to the edge of the table as I watched Brexlyn pull the machine up beside Ezra. Her hands shook, her voice cracked, but she worked. She wouldn't let him go.

"Come on," I whispered. "Come on, Ezra. Please."

"Stark."

I jerked my head up. A producer stood near another terminal, her dark eyes scanning me too closely. I snapped back into the practiced cool I wore like armor. Hoping she couldn't see the cracks.

"Yeah?" My voice was hoarse but steady. Trying to focus on her face and not the endless flatline coming from the screen behind me.

"You got the victory feed ready? For your team?"

The Victory Montage. A propaganda-laced highlight reel

that aired whenever a Challenger survived the Reclamation Run. A heroic story, a manufactured anthem of triumph over terror. Each year, they played one for each survivor, crafted from their best and bloodiest moments.

I'd spent weeks pulling footage. I'd poured myself into it. Every frame, every cut, every beat of music. But not for Praxis. It was for them. My team. My family. My Wildguard. Their battle deserved to be remembered as the spark that changed everything.

Brexlyn and Briar's song played under the edit, layered with moths flitting across burning trees and stars falling like embers from the sky. The whole montage screamed rebellion. Screamed Runaway. The minute it played they would know that Rebellion was coming.

"Yeah," I said, voice thick. "I got it."

"Well, plug in. If they survive, we'll need it on standby. The stream's going to be basically uninterrupted from here on out."

If.

That word sank into me like a blade. She said it casually, but it echoed like a death knell.

"And get Ezra Wynstone's death montage ready too, just in case he doesn't wake up."

The words made me nauseous. My eyes burned, but I kept my expression steady, nodding slowly, pretending I had everything under control. I'd been putting off that montage for weeks. It should have been nearly finished. Ready. If I were a good editor, it would be.

But how do you cut together the last moments of someone you love? Create a highlight reel of their best moments only to lead to their bloody and horrific end? How do you score the end of their story? I never started it, because some stubborn part of me still believed none of them would need one.

"Please, Ezra," I whispered.

I turned back to the screen, just in time to see Bex press harder into Ezra's chest. The flatline beep stretched on, endless and merciless.

Then...

A sound.

A blip.

A heartbeat.

I gasped quietly, my whole body shaking with the exhale. I hadn't realized I was holding my breath. Around me, no one even seemed to notice the miracle.

He was alive.

Barely, maybe. But alive.

I walked to my terminal and loaded up the montages. One for each of them. Ready to go, should the universe show mercy. I lined up the files, fingers trembling.

On the screen beside me, live metrics scrolled in dizzying waves. Millions were watching. More than ever before. The numbers just kept climbing. People all across the Collectives and hell maybe even beyond were seeing what Praxis was doing.

Were they moved by it? Were they sickened? Were they finally ready?

Were they going to meet us at the gates tomorrow?

I didn't know. But I knew this, if my team survived this trial, if they made it through the hell Praxis threw at them, then I was going to make damn sure the world saw them for what they really were.

Not just Challengers.

Not just Survivors.

Symbols.

When Brexlyn collapsed, something inside me ruptured. My breath hitched, a searing pain stabbed through my chest, and I clutched the edge of the console to stay upright. Not her. Please. God, not her. I'd watched the pallor creep into her skin, the way her hands trembled from blood loss. She was stronger than all of us, had been from the start, but how much could a body take before it gave out?

Movement flickered at the edge of my vision. Across the hall, the studio door cracked open. Archon Veritas slipped inside. The mask she wore for the cameras, composed, regal, untouchable, was cracked at the edges. Her fingers twitched at her side, and there was a tightness in her jaw I hadn't seen before. She was nervous.

I snapped my gaze down to the editing terminal, pretending to fiddle with the feeds. I couldn't let her see me watching. Not yet. When the door clicked shut behind her, I turned my attention back to the main screen. Thorne was cradling Brexlyn, blood staining his shirt. Briar and Lark were screaming about blood bags, trying to find the right supply. I had to trust them now.

It was my turn to do my part.

I slipped out of the pit, avoiding the floorboards that creaked. Every step was calculated. I kept my head low, my breathing shallow. The studio Archon had entered was mostly used for high-production post-Run segments, clean lighting, acoustically sound, pristine for propaganda. She was recording the "victory" message. The one they aired every year. I needed to know what she planned to say... and what she planned to hide.

Circling the perimeter of the corridor, I kept to the shadows. The building had once been a broadcast center before Praxis repurposed it into a weapon of misinformation. I remembered taking a tour once, there was a back stairwell that led to the grid above the studio. If I could reach it, I could monitor everything from above. No one ever looked up.

The door to the stairwell stuck. My heart pounded as I forced it open with slow, steady pressure, wincing as it gave a low groan. Once inside, I closed it behind me and bolted up the stairs two at a time, ignoring the ache in my chest and the burn in my legs. There was no time for pain.

At the top, I stepped onto the grid, a suspended metal walkway of crisscrossed bars and cables that overlooked the studio floor. It swayed beneath me. My palms were slick as I grabbed the nearest rail and pulled myself into a crouch. Down below, Archon Veritas was already in position. She sat in the studio's throne-like chair, haloed by key lighting. A gold serpent on a marble pedestal.

"Alright, Archon," the cameraman said. "End of Reclamation. Take one."

She didn't blink. "Good evening, Nexum. And thank you for joining me on this day, the final trial of the Reclamation Run." Her voice was smooth, oiled with power. "Below me, you will see the final standings for each Challenger, and the resources they've secured for your Collectives during their trials."

A chill crawled down my spine.

"I know many of you have grown attached to these Challengers, rooted for them. Some of you even loved them." She nearly spat the word. Her distaste for my Wildguard was clear and evident in her wicked tone. "And while we traditionally celebrate their victories with interviews and tours..." Her lips curled into something cold and amused. "...I'm afraid this year, we will be taking a different approach."

No.

She continued. "Your Challengers have elected to forgo the fame and festivities, choosing instead to return home to their Collectives quietly, where they can live out their lives with the resources they've earned."

She was lying. I knew the ritual. The post-Run circuit was always mandatory. Smiling faces. Public interviews. Glory for the winners. If they weren't going to parade the survivors, it was because there were no plans to have any survivors.

I felt my breath catch. I couldn't move.

"By the will of Praxis, you are always welcome."

"And cut," the cameraman said. "That's perfect, Archon."

"Good," she replied.

The camera man slid from the room while her assistant slinked forward like a rat. "Guards are stationed, ma'am," he said.

She didn't look at him. "Give me the radio."

My heart hammered.

"Captain, do you copy?"

"Copy, Archon," came the response.

"When the trial ends, wait for my signal. I'll call the moment the feed is cut. Then... execute the protocol."

Protocol. I didn't need to ask what that meant.

She was going to kill them.

I was moving before my mind caught up. Back across the grid. Down the stairs like death itself chased me. At the bottom, I ducked behind a wall, scanned for guards. Clear, for now. I bolted toward the editor pit, rejoining the others as silently as I'd left.

I collapsed into my chair, forcing my hands to stop shaking. Brexlyn was alive. Barely. And I was going to keep her that way.

Moments later, the unmistakable click of high heels echoed behind me.

"Congratulations on another successful year," Archon said, and the room clapped politely. I did too, though my palms barely touched. My eyes stayed locked on the screen.

"Patch me in," Archon said, reaching for a microphone. "Congratulations, Challengers," she said, and I watched as the figures on the feed looked up at the source of the sound.

"You are the lucky survivors of this year's Reclamation Run."

They all looked so relieved. God. If only they knew what was about to happen.

Suddenly the doors to the clinic swung open and Praxis guards filed in. I felt my heart in my throat. "You've sacrificed and risked your lives for the Collectives. You've proven that Praxis rewards those deserving of it," she continued.

"Now, your time as Challengers has come to an end. So your Collectives thank you. Praxis thanks you. I thank you." But there was only malice in her tone.

"Your sacrifice for the greater good of Nexum will always be remembered." She set the microphone down.

"Joree," she called. "Cut the feed. Begin the montage loop."

She obeyed. The screen went black. My family disappeared.

She raised the radio again. "Captain. You may proceed."

No.

I set to work immediately. My fingers danced across the keys, bypassing the surface interface. I dropped into the raw feed from the clinic, just behind a firewall. I found the live camera in the clinic, the one they'd just cut. I rerouted it. Hid it behind the visual mask of the montage loop, burying it so deep inside a web of code and locks that no surface-level technician would know where to look.

The image popped up. Guards were surrounding them.

It's now or never, Zaffir.

I activated the stream. Sent it out live

And suddenly, millions were watching.

I stood. Walked briskly but evenly toward the back exit. I passed the corridor where, not long ago, she had me beaten bloody. My ribs still ached when I breathed too deep. But I was on my feet now.

This time, I would walk out on my own terms.

I kept my head down, moving quickly toward the exit, heart pounding like war drums in my chest. I had nearly reached the threshold when a figure blocked my path. I jerked to a stop, eyes rising, and found Nova.

Her stance was rigid, her arms crossed tight across her chest like armor. Her calculating eyes scanned my face like she was searching for a code to break.

"Where are you going?" she asked, voice calm but edged in suspicion.

"I'll tell you later, Nova," I muttered, attempting to side-step her.

She shifted cleanly, blocking me again. "You're acting strange," she said flatly. "What happened?" Her eyes shifted to the screens behind me. "Did something happen to the Wild-guard?" She almost sounded concerned.

"I can't—" I tried again to slip past her, but she was quicker.

Shouting erupted from the control station behind us.

"The feed from the clinic is still up!" someone barked.

"You were supposed to cut it!" Archon Veritas's voice sliced through the air like a blade.

My breath froze. The blood drained from my face.

"I did, ma'am, I swear! I don't know how—"

"Shut it down! NOW!"

Nova's eyes flicked to the chaos unfolding behind me, then snapped back to mine. Her brow creased. "Zaffir..." she whispered. "What did you do?"

I didn't need to lie to her. She already knew.

"Please, Nova," I whispered. "Let me go."

Joree's panicked voice rang out. "I can't! The feed's hard-coded, I'm locked out!"

My body was already shifting to bolt, but Nova wouldn't move. I could see the war she was fighting in her mind.

"You didn't," she said, voice tight.

"I had to," I whispered.

She blinked, her jaw trembling for half a second.

"They'll kill you for this," she said.

"I know."

"Did those guards just kill a Challenger?!" Someone screamed from behind us.

The room plunged into a stunned, electric silence.

"Cut the feed before they see anything else!"

I stopped cold. Every muscle in my body turned to stone. My lungs refused to work. I twisted, desperate to see the feed, to catch a name, a face, *anything*.

But instead, I saw her. Archon Veritas. Her face was twisted into fury, icy, righteous, seething with betrayal.

"It was him," she hissed. "Stop him!"

I turned back to Nova. Our eyes locked.

She didn't say anything.

There was a moment, a small, sacred beat of silence between us. Then she nodded once. Slow. Reluctant. But resolute.

"Get out of here," she whispered.

Then, without warning, she lunged forward. But her move was choreographed, telegraphed a second too long. Her hand barely grazed my shoulder before I twisted, easily ducked under her arm, and sprinted down the left corridor.

Behind me, I heard her shout, "He headed right!" But there was no heat behind it. Just the sound of someone trying to give me a head start.

She let me go.

And I knew—no matter what happened next—Nova had just chosen a side.

Mine.

Ours.

The Runaways.

And if she could choose us. Maybe we stood a fighting chance.

The hall blurred. My boots slammed against concrete. I didn't care about silence anymore, I just needed distance. I threw myself through the back door and didn't stop. No guards yet. Good.

I shoved the thought down, buried it beneath the roar of blood in my ears and the thunder of my feet pounding against the ground. I couldn't let myself imagine who the guards had reached. Who might be crumpled, lifeless, on the sterile tiles of that clinic. Not Thorne. Not Briar. Not Ezra. Not Brexlyn. God, please, not Brexlyn. But I didn't have the luxury of fear, not now. Grief was an emotion I couldn't afford to feel until I was safely beyond the golden gate, until I knew Praxis and its lies were behind me. Only then would I allow myself to collapse. But until that moment, I ran like my family's lives depended on it. Because they did.

If I could reach the perimeter of the city, if I could make it to the Runaways, maybe they'd have seen what I broadcasted. Maybe the world had, too.

Maybe Praxis had finally overplayed its hand.

And just maybe... When I reached that gate, I wouldn't be alone.

CHAPTER
SIXTEEN

BEX

WE MOVED toward the exit of the bus, stepping one by one into the waiting crowd. The air crackled around us with something electric, hope, tension, anticipation. Their cheers didn't just lift me. They wrapped around me like armor.

Then a flash of movement in the crowd caught my eye. Flame-red curls parted the sea of bodies like a beacon.

Zaffir.

He stepped forward, expression lit with disbelief and joy. Relief crashed through me so hard it nearly buckled my knees.

He was safe.

The Runaways were here.

And Praxis was going down.

I ran and I didn't stop. Not when my lungs burned. Not when the noise of the crowd blurred behind me. Not until I crashed into Zaffir's arms.

He caught me like he'd been waiting every second of his life just to hold me again. The impact stole my breath, but I didn't care. His arms locked around me, grounding and desperate, his face buried in the crook of my neck. His whole body shook, a quiet tremble rippling through him like he was exhaling a grief he hadn't dared feel until now.

"Hello, beautiful," he murmured into my skin, his voice raw, reverent. Then he pressed a kiss to my throat, gentle and trembling, a promise written in touch.

"You're safe," I whispered, my fingers clutching the fabric of his shirt. Dark grey and soft beneath my hands. It was such a small thing, the color of his clothes, but it knocked the wind out of me. No more gold. No more silver. No more polished Praxis sheen trying to claim him.

He wasn't theirs anymore.

He looked like himself, like the version I always knew was under the surface. He's been one of us for a long time, but this was the first time it showed on the outside. No disguise. No uniform. Just him. Real, and here, and finally free to be who he was without having to hide it.

"So are you," he breathed, his hands roaming down my back like he needed to map every inch of me to believe I was really there. Really whole. Really alive.

He leaned back, just enough to find my lips. The kiss was grateful, urgent, aching. I melted into it, tasting love, and relief so much that it made my knees weak. I never wanted to let go of him again.

When we finally parted, his gaze flicked past me.

To Ezra.

He stood near the bus, arms loosely crossed, his expression unreadable, like he wasn't sure he was invited into this moment, like maybe he didn't want to intrude. But Zaffir didn't hesitate. He reached out with one hand.

Ezra stepped forward slowly, and then Zaffir pulled him into him. Their embrace was different, careful, but just as fierce, and when they kissed, it was like something in the air was still. Like the universe exhaled with them.

I felt something bloom in my chest. I couldn't help the smile that broke across my face.

"Thought you were a goner there for a second," Zaffir said, voice cracking just a little.

Ezra smirked. "And leave you unsupervised? Not a chance."

We laughed. It felt good. God, it felt so *good* to laugh and not have it hurt.

Then—

"Briar! Thorne!" Zaffir called out as the twins approached, blood and ash still clinging to their uniforms. We could all go for a nice shower right about now. "Glad to see you two are still alive."

He reached out a hand to shake theirs, but Briar bypassed it completely, throwing her arms around him in a fierce hug. Thorne followed, his arms looping around them both.

I blinked hard, my throat tightening.

Because I *knew* how much this meant.

Zaffir was Praxis-born, raised behind their walls, shaped by their rules. I always knew that, even if unspoken, there was a thread of tension that tugged between him and the rest of the Wildguard, maybe even Ezra at times. A flicker of doubt, a sliver of blame. It showed in the way their eyes followed him when he first walked through our doors wearing that polished gold and silver. In the way silence hung heavier when the memory of their mother surfaced. Praxis had taken everything from them, and he had worn its colors.

But now?

Now, those colors were gone. So was the distance.

Thorne and Briar pulled him into an embrace like he'd always belonged. And maybe, finally, he did. There was no Praxis on his skin anymore. For the first time, they held him not as a symbol of what had gone wrong...but as one of us.

As *Wildguard*.

That word has always encompassed Zaffir in my mind but seeing it expand to him in theirs, too, made my heart stutter.

"I assume the little camera stunt back at the hospital was your doing?" Thorne asked, pulling back just enough to eye Zaffir with a raised brow.

"Camera stunt?" I asked, wiping a tear from the corner of my eye.

"Of course it was," Zaffir said, half-grinning. "Wasn't about to let her get away with that."

I turned from one to the other, confused.

"They cut the feed," Zaffir explained. "Right before they sent the guards in. Ended the Run, said they were sending you all home without a victory parade and told us to run the victory montages."

I nodded slowly. I remembered those montages. I used to watch them with awe, never knowing one day I'd be the star of one.

"But your boyfriend here," Thorne said with a pointed, charming look, "got the feed back on."

"So, everyone saw what she did?" I asked, stunned. "To.. Lark?"

Zaffir nodded. "Every last viewer."

My heart skipped. *That*...that changed everything. They couldn't edit that out. Couldn't change that history. Just the truth, broadcast wide and unfiltered.

"Nice work, Zaf," Ezra said, a soft smile blooming on his face.

Zaffir shrugged, trying to play it cool. But I saw it, the way his eyes softened under the praise, the way his hand found mine and squeezed like he needed the anchor. He was happy he could do something substantial for this cause.

And there we stood, a messy tangle of scars and love and loyalty. Battered. Bloodied. But together.

Then I turned for the first time toward the small audience we'd garnered, and my breath caught all over again.

"They came," I whispered, eyes sweeping over the small crowd that had gathered at the edges of our reunion. I didn't know how long they'd been there. But they watched us like we were the sunrise after a long, brutal night.

"They did," Zaffir said, smiling as he followed my gaze. "Look."

He nodded toward a group stepping closer, slowly, deliberately. There was something about them that made my stomach twist. Recognition flickered at the edge of my mind. Familiar faces. Familiar posture. Scars. Stance. *Eyes.*

And then it hit me.

"Oh my god," I breathed. "They're... they're Challengers."

They were older now. Weathered. But unmistakable. The ones who had walked the path we now tread, years ago. Survivors of the Reclamation Run.

One figure stepped forward from the group. Tall. Solid. Gray hair cropped close to his skull. His frame was broad, but not bulky and coiled with the kind of strength that didn't come from lifting weights but from a lifetime of hard work. He walked like he'd faced death and made it blink first.

His eyes found mine and even before he opened his mouth, I knew.

"Edgar Soonwater," I whispered, the name catching in my throat. The most decorated Reclamation Run winner in the history of Nexum.

He gave a short nod, the faintest smile breaking the hard line of his jaw. "Brexlyn Hollis."

"You're here?" I said, stunned. "You're a Runaway?"

"I am," he replied. "We all are." He turned, gesturing behind him. The figures I'd only just started to register fully, people hardened by time, by memory, by loss. Veterans of the Reclamation Run. The ones who survived.

"It's about damn time someone lit the fuse," Edgar said.

Emotion surged in my chest, sudden and sharp, catching me off guard. My gaze drifted past Edgar to the camp unfolding behind him—rows of tents set in perfect lines, gear stacked neatly, paths cleared and purposeful. People moved with intention, like they knew exactly what they were doing and where they were needed. It didn't look thrown together at all. No chaos, no scrambling. Nothing like I would expect in response to the less than organized call for action that Briar and I sent out. "What is all this?" I asked.

"We've got four primary camps, spread out by skill focus," Edgar explained, voice even but passionate. "Fighters in the east quadrant, they're combat ready and mobile. Engineers and builders to the west, weapons, fortifications, mobility units. To the north, we've got the techies, signal scramblers, drone runners, sabotage teams. And in the south, the healers. Med tents, supply coordination, emergency evac prep."

I stared at him, my brain tripping over itself to process.

"We've also got ration stores, backup comms, transport hubs. Teams rotating on recon watching the guard towers."

I blinked. "How... how did you do this so fast?"

He chuckled, low and dry, like I'd just asked if rain was wet.

"We didn't do it fast," he said. "We've been doing it quietly. For years."

My breath caught.

"When I came back from the Run, I thought I'd bought change for my people. That my wins would mean something. That Praxis would finally shine on us. But nothing changed. I was nothing but a fucking propaganda tool. A distraction. And when I saw that, I snapped. That's when I met your mother." His eyes flicked to Thorne and Briar.

Their eyes widened.

"She told me about the Runaways. Together we spread the

word, started expanding our underground network..." His eyes turned sad. "I was incredibly sorry to hear of her passing. She was one of the best people I ever knew."

Briar and Thorne nodded, soft saddened smiles on their faces.

Edgar glanced behind him again at the other Challengers. At his people.

"But she started a legacy. And we've been building ever since. Piece by piece. Underground. Off the grid. Waiting."

"Waiting for what?" I asked softly.

"For someone brave enough to strike the first blow," he said. "Someone who wouldn't just talk about justice but risk everything for it. We were waiting for you, Brexlyn."

I felt the Wildguard behind me, Zaffir, Ezra, Thorne, Briar, felt the way they steadied, drew closer.

"You all gave us the opening we'd been waiting for," Edgar said. "And now we're all in. We're done hiding. You lead, we follow."

I didn't know what to say. My chest burned with hope so bright it scared me.

Edgar took a step closer holding a hand out for me. "Let's finish what the Runaways started. Let's reclaim Nexum."

I gripped his hand and felt like we'd just made history.

BRIAR

I'D ALWAYS BEEN DRAWN to strategy. Not just the rules, but the rhythm. The way problems unfolded like puzzles. Goals mapped out, options weighed, assets positioned just right. I understood how people thought, how they moved, how they could be steered or inspired or shattered. Strategy was all about reading the field. Reading people.

It had served me well in the past.

But I never imagined it would come to this...standing over a battered map of Praxis, planning the overthrow of the very system that raised me.

Planning a rebellion. A rebellion that my own flesh and blood started.

Devrin stood beside me, arms crossed, jaw set. As much as a part of me still burned with resentment over what he pulled in the canals, I couldn't ignore what he'd done since then. He helped save Ezra. And no matter how murky his past, he was just as much a victim of Praxis's cruelty as we were.

That counted for something. Maybe not forgiveness. But something close to trust.

Edgar was sitting on an overturned crate, his eyes narrowing at the map in front of him, deep in thought..

"A direct assault would be a bloodbath," I said, gesturing at the city's outer sectors. "They've got guard towers at every approach. We'd be walking into a grinder."

"I agree," Devrin said, nodding. "We can't win head-on. The only way to slip past is to disarm them, make them chase shadows."

Bex sat on a crate a few feet away, unusually quiet. Her eyes flicked between us as we spoke, unfocused. Distant. Thorne was still out with Ezra and Zaffir, finishing the final tally of who had shown up for us.

And it was a lot. More than I expected.

Brexlyn had done that, rallied people from the fringes of Praxis, from the slums, the wastes, and the broken Collectives. She pulled them into the light. Gave them something to believe in. Gave us all a reason to hope.

And now, sitting here, she looked like it was all weighing on her at once.

She kept picking at her fingertips, rubbing the raw skin around her nails. The silence around her was louder than the rest of the camp.

I moved to kneel in front of her, gently taking her hands in mine. She had washed up and donned some new clothes courtesy of Edgar's supplies, but she still faintly smelled of campfire. I found that the scent wasn't as offending on her. She startled slightly, but met my eyes.

"Hey you," I said softly.

"Sorry. I'm listening," she murmured.

"I know. I just..." I hesitated, dropping my voice. "Are you okay?"

She gave a small nod. But I saw the way her shoulders hunched inward. The way she bit her lip.

"You don't have to lie to me, Hollis," I said gently, brushing a knuckle across her cheek.

She swallowed hard. "I guess I'm just scared," she admitted. "I brought all these people here...thousands. And what if this plan fails? What if we led them out of hiding just to get them killed?"

I let the silence settle for a moment. I knew that fear. I carried it in my bones too.

"My Ma started this fight with nothing but a whisper and a fire in her chest," I said. "And I don't know if I have her courage either. But I do know what she'd tell both of us right now if she were here. We fight because the alternative is living in chains."

I wish I'd let myself get to know that version of my mother.

Not just the caretaker. Not just the loving woman who rocked us to sleep. But the fire underneath...the rebel. The leader. The one who chose to resist when silence would've been safer.

The truth is, I did see it. Even if I didn't care to admit it. The small acts of defiance. The way her eyes would harden when a patrol passed. The quiet protests no one else noticed, the things she fixed, the people she sheltered, the questions she dared to ask.

But I turned away.

Because if I looked too closely, I couldn't pretend I didn't know. And if I acknowledged it, it became real. And real meant risk. Real meant danger.

And I was terrified for her.

So I looked past it, played blind. Convinced myself that protecting her meant not speaking it aloud, not calling attention to it. But all I was really doing was keeping myself safe from the fear. From the truth.

Thorne knew her in a way I didn't. He saw that part of her fully, fought beside it, believed in it. He understood what she was building long before I did.

I regret that now.

I regret not sitting beside her in the dark, asking why she was willing to risk everything. I regret not hearing the full story of the rebellion she was trying to start, or how she held onto hope like it was armor. I regret not letting her see that I could've been brave, too.

It's too late to know her like that, now.

But it's not too late to finish what she started. To carry the torch she lit, even if I was too scared to touch it back then.

"I just don't want these people to fight and die for nothing," Bex replied, tears stinging her eyes.

From across the tent, Devrin spoke up. "They know the risks," he said, voice low but firm.

Bex and I turned toward him.

"You don't want to feel responsible for them. I get it," he continued, standing straighter. "No one wants to be the reason someone doesn't make it home. But these people showed up anyway. They chose this."

Her fingers tightened around mine.

"They know there's a chance they won't walk out of here. That we might fail. That Praxis might erase this rebellion and spin it into some bedtime cautionary tale about what happens when you defy the Archon," he said, his eyes locking on mine then hers. "But they also know there's a chance we win. That we finally get to breathe air that isn't rationed by a government who doesn't protect us."

He stepped closer.

"They're not looking for guarantees. They're looking for leaders. People willing to stand up and say, 'We'll give everything for the chance to live free.'" Edgar spoke up. He looked between Bex and me.

Devrin finished by meeting Bex's gaze. "So don't mourn them before the fight. Honor them by leading like they deserve."

Bex stared at him for a moment, then let out a slow breath. She stood, walked toward him, and offered her hand. Devrin took it.

"Thank you," she said quietly.

"I'm sorry about almost killing you in the Trials," he replied, that familiar glint of cockiness softening at the edges. But it sounded real this time.

Bex gave a small laugh. "I'm sorry you felt like you had to."

Just then, the tent flaps opened and the rest of the Wild-guard stepped inside, freshly cleaned and dressed thanks to Edgar's foresight, faces set with resolve. Ezra was walking under his own power, still pale, but upright. Zaffir and Thorne flanked him, silent sentinels.

Thorne strode up to Bex without warning and scooped her up around the waist. She let out a surprised yelp that quickly turned into a breathless laugh, her arms flailing before she gave in to the moment.

"I'm cool with sharing you with these idiots," he said, nodding toward the rest of us, "but I draw the line at *that* one." He pointed dramatically at Devrin.

Devrin sighed and rubbed a hand down his face, a tired smirk tugging at the corner of his mouth. "Ridiculous," he muttered.

"Put me down, Thorne," Bex giggled. "I'm not looking to add to my little harem."

"Good," he murmured against her skin, pressing a quick kiss to her lips before spinning her in his arms and settling her against his chest, arms wrapped protectively around her waist. He rested his chin on her shoulder, content.

I turned from their affection to face Ezra and Zaffir. The two of them stood shoulder to shoulder, united in that quiet way trauma often binds people. I'd be lying if I said I hadn't struggled to trust Zaffir at first. Maybe because he was born in Praxis. Maybe because he got to sit out the trials while the rest of us bled for our survival.

But when we stepped off that bus and I saw Zaffir in a new llight, arms wrapped tightly around Bex and Ezra as if he could somehow hold all their broken pieces together with sheer will alone...I *saw* it.

The pain.

The devastation.

The truth that he had been carrying it all in silence, tucked behind that sharp Praxis-born composure.

He wept like someone who had spent every hour of every day watching the people he loved be torn apart and could do nothing to stop it. And that's exactly what he'd done. He hadn't been on the front lines with us in the trials, hadn't bled in the dirt, hadn't taken the hits or felt the fear rise in his throat every time the speakers crackled to life with a new decree, but that didn't mean he hadn't suffered.

He suffered *differently*.

He suffered *alone*.

He watched Bex fight to stay human. Watched Ezra get burnt half to death. Watched me nearly fall to my death. Watch Thorne struggle to keep his humor amongst the pain. And through it all, he could only watch.

So when he broke, when his sobs cracked the air around us and his hands clutched his people like lifelines, I realized something...he really was one of us.

Cut off from the fight but not from the pain. Not from the guilt. And now, finally, he was here. With us. Ready to do something. To take Praxis apart from the inside.

I was glad Bex had him.

I was glad Ezra did too.

And even though I hadn't trusted him at first, I did now.

Beyond a shadow of a doubt.

"So, we ready to make a plan?" Ezra asked, a spark in his eyes.

"Edgar, how many people do we have out there?" I asked.

He glanced up at me, a soft smirk on his weathered face. "Just over seven thousand."

Devrin gave a low whistle. "Damn." He chuckled. "Didn't think I'd live to see the day."

"Wow," Bex whispered. She leaned into Thorne, and he pressed a kiss to her temple.

"It's a hell of a showing," I said.

"But we're still outnumbered," Zaffir added cautiously. "I'm not trying to kill the mood, but if we charge in blind, we lose."

He was right. We had momentum, but not numbers.

"The Praxis defactor is right," Edgar added and I didn't miss how Zaffir flinched at the moniker. "They've got numbers and training."

"Then we don't charge blind," I said, stepping forward. "We go in waves."

Devrin nodded beside me. We'd discussed this on the bus ride. It was as good a plan as we could conceive. The numbers we had would help.

I pointed to the map we'd laid across a makeshift table of bark and old crates, Praxis stretched across the parchment, its towers, relays, and walls marked in crimson ink.

"If we go slow, methodical, we can pull their legs out from under them," I said. "They know we're coming, so we have to be smart about this."

"The first wave will go at night." Devrin said.

"We need those high-tech Collectives," I added, looking to Edgar "People with hacking and sabotage experience, any of it. They'll disable the outer surveillance, jam the perimeter frequencies, and create blind zones across the city grid."

"We've got a team," Edgar replied.

"Silent entries only," I confirmed. "No conflict unless absolutely necessary. That buys us stealth and time."

"Once the perimeter is compromised," I continued, "Wave two moves. We need the Collectives with engineering experience."

"Or explosives," Devrin added with a shrug.

"These teams will target the power relays, weapons caches, and the guard towers' core systems," I continued.

"Then comes wave three," Devrin said. "Strike squads assigned to each tower. With comms down and defenses failing, they'll move in to neutralize the remaining guards and take control. Lock down the towers."

"Healers and Medics can push in but hang back to care for the injured," Edgar added, pointing to a few spots on the map.

Bex leaned in, tracing a finger along the route. "That clears a path..."

"For us," I said. "Wave four. The tip of the spear."

Thorne's eyes lit up at that, and Ezra gave a short nod of approval.

"Our team. We'll move straight down the center once the guard is neutralized. If things go according to plan. We can slip right through."

"We take the Show Center," Zaffir said, his voice steady. He pointed to a cluster of buildings at the city's heart.

"If we can take control of the network," he said, "I can plug in, I can show them the real Praxis. Everything they've hidden. I can put it on every screen, every frequency. I can wake them up."

"It could spark support from the inside," Ezra added. "And at the very least, it ensures they can't rewrite this later. We'll have already told the truth."

I nodded, drawing a clear circle over the Show Center. "Then that's our first stop."

Zaffir met my eyes. "I'll show them. No more propaganda. No more filtered feeds. I'll show them what Praxis really is."

"And after that," I said, closing my hand into a fist over the location of the Archon's command quarters, "we finish this."

Bex's voice was soft but firm. "We try to negotiate surrender first."

Everyone nodded. No one here wanted to kill unless there was no other choice.

"But if she refuses to step down," Edgar said, "we end it. One way or another."

Silence fell across the tent. The map lay covered in scribbled notes and routes and names, our plan written in ink and desperation.

Outside, the distant murmur of thousands of voices hummed against the wind.

Tomorrow, we'd make history.

"I'll organize the strike teams," Edgar said, already rolling up the sleeves of his battered shirt like he was ready to dive into the trenches right then and there.

I gave him a firm nod. "Good."

"Do you have leaders for each group?" Devrin asked Edgar.

He nodded. "Yeah."

"Think you can gather them for a debrief?" Devrin asked.

Edgar stood from his crate. "Absolutely."

"Think it'll work?" I asked Edgar. He was the one who'd been planning this rebellion, I didn't want to steamroll him with our idea if he had a better thought.

"It's better than the one I came up with," he said with a smile.

"What was your plan?" I asked.

"It included a lot of explosives," he shrugged before stepping out of the tent.

"Think you two can go help him brief the teams?" I asked

Thorne and Ezra.

They nodded, each leaning down to press a quick kiss to Bex's cheek before slipping from the tent with a quiet resolve. Watching them both walk out, shoulder to shoulder, felt like watching the heart of this rebellion leave to start beating.

Devrin lingered a moment longer. He turned to me, extended his hand, and we clasped forearms like soldiers do.

"It's a hell of a plan," he said, voice lower , serious.

"It'll work," I replied, my voice firmer than I felt, but I had to believe it.

He smiled faintly, a curve of something both weary and hopeful. "I hope you're right." Then, without another word, he disappeared through the flaps.

Only Bex and Zaffir remained now.

Zaffir had drifted silently to Bex's side. He pulled her into a soft, protective embrace, wrapping his arms around her like she might still vanish if he blinked too long.

I watched him touch her gently, brush a strand of hair from her face like she was something fragile, sacred.

"I'm so glad you're okay," he murmured, pressing a kiss to her cheek, almost reverent.

"You too," she whispered back, and I could hear the truth trembling in her voice.

"I never felt as scared as I did when I heard Veritas give the order" he said. "I've been gathering footage for years. The things Praxis cut, manipulated, erased entirely. I've got drives full of their darkest secrets. Edited trials. Fabricated charges. Executions dressed as disappearances. Didn't know what I'd do with it, if anything. But I think deep down I knew one day I'd need it."

His voice tightened, fury brimming beneath it.

"I'm gonna take everything they buried," he said, "and make sure the whole damn world sees it."

Bex leaned forward and kissed him. There was nothing

rushed about it, just something deeply grateful, and quiet, and alive. His hands found her waist, held her like she was gravity itself.

And strangely... I didn't feel jealous.

Maybe it was the way he loved her, fierce and loud and without apology. Or maybe it was because, after everything we'd been through, watching the girl I loved be loved so openly felt... right. Maybe love, in its truest form, was meant to be shared, not owned.

When they finally parted, Zaffir turned to me. There was something different in his eyes now. Purpose. Fire.

"I've got some editing to do," he said with a small smile.

I gave him a nod.

He slipped through the tent flaps without another word, the momentum of revolution humming in his wake.

And just like that, Bex and I were alone.

CHAPTER
EIGHTEEN

BEX

BRIAR STEPPED toward me in the hush of the tent.

The plan was made. The waves were set.

Tomorrow, the first wave was going to infiltrate Praxis. Hopefully.

"You look nervous," she said softly, stopping in front of me. Her fingers lifted to gently cradle my chin, and I leaned into her touch without hesitation.

"Aren't you?" I asked.

She shook her head once, slow and certain. "I've made peace with the risks. I'm ready."

"Consider me jealous," I murmured.

Her thumb brushed across my skin, and my whole body lit up beneath her touch.

"I guess, if I'm being honest...The only thing I'm nervous about," she said, her voice barely above a whisper, "is that if anything happens to us... I won't get to do this again." She tucked a strand of hair behind my ear. "Or this." She pressed a kiss to my cheek. "Or this." Her nose skimmed the column of my throat, and I let my head fall back, breath hitching.

"Or this," she added, as her fingers traced a slow path along the edge of my stomach, teasing the skin at the band of my pants.

Butterflies took flight low in my belly, wings brushing every nerve ending. I closed my eyes, anchored in her warmth, in the way she touched me like we still had forever.

Even if tomorrow said otherwise.

"Briar..." I whispered. "These tents don't lock."

"Then I guess we'd better hurry," she replied breathlessly as her hand dove down past the waistband and panties, her fingers instantly finding my eager center. I groaned at the first swipe of her fingers against my clit.

"Well, well, well, Hollis," she said, teasingly dancing a finger through my wetness without dipping into my core. "Are you ready for our next duet?" Her lips found mine just as her fingers slid into my pussy.

I cried out and her mouth drank it up.

Her thrusts were calculated, deliberate, and punishing. I felt my knees giving out beneath me as I clung to her shoulders for support. Her fingers played me like an instrument only she knew how to master and I was completely lost in the sensation of her.

"I need you," I whispered against her mouth.

"You have me," she answered, pressing her thumb against my clit which toppled me over the ledge and into a quick eruptive orgasm.

My hands dug into her shirt as I fought my body's urge to collapse. She held me around the waist as her fingers stilled within me, soaking up the last of my climax.

"More," I whispered, breathless, fingers curling around the waistband of her pants.

Briar glanced quickly toward the tent's entrance—just a

flicker of caution—then her eyes snapped back to mine, full of heat. Without a word, she guided us to the far side of the tent, slipping behind the makeshift table stacked with crates and maps.

She lowered me gently to the ground, the world narrowing to the two of us, hidden behind strategy and plans, hearts pounding louder than any war drum.

Then, with a look that could burn down empires, she slid her pants down, her eyes never leaving mine.

I followed her lead, slipping my borrowed clothes off my body until we were both bare below the belt. She pressed a hand against my shoulders and slowly led me to lay on my back. The soft, chilled ground comforted me against the raging heat of her touch.

She crawled over me slowly, deliberately, until her hands were braced on either side of my head, caging me in. Her eyes found mine, those deep, earthy brown eyes, the color of soil and warmth.

I reached up, brushing my fingers along the curve of her cheek, tracing the shape of her jaw, the warmth of her skin. Her dark hair fell in soft curtains around us, framing her face like something sacred. She looked down at me with a wonder that stole the breath from my lungs, like she couldn't believe I was real.

"You're the most beautiful woman I've ever seen," I whispered.

Her eyes shone, glassy with emotion, and then, with a teasing smirk, she said, "Clearly you've never looked in a mirror."

Then she lowered her core to press gently against my leg. The moment I felt her wet center slide along my sensitive skin, I felt a long satisfied groan tear from my throat.

"I want you to come all over me, Briar," I whispered, tangling my hands in her hair. She smiled down at me as she moved her hips. Slow at first, I felt her body trembling with each slide of her pussy against my skin. Her thigh pressed against my throbbing clit, still reeling from the last climax, but with every movement of her body, I felt my pleasure crest.

"Fuck," she breathed, her eyes falling shut.

"That's it, baby. Use me," I ordered.

Her eyes snapped open and she met my gaze. There was an inferno within them. Quickly, she pulled my leg up so that it rested on her shoulder, opening my core to her completely. This time when she slid her core against my body our clits met and both of us cried out at the sensation. She was done taking her time. She pistoned her hips eagerly and passionately, her fingers dug into my thigh as our slick centers slid against each other.

We exhaled in harmonized passion as our bodies danced to the music we made together. My head fell back and my back arched as my eyes fell closed.

I felt her hand cup my cheek and I opened my eyes to find her staring down at me. Her hips were moving slower, more languid. Savoring.

"Love really isn't a strong enough word for how I feel about you, Brexlyn Hollis," she whispered, pressing a kiss to my leg as her hips rocked against mine.

"Maybe you can write me a song," I replied back in breathy disjointed words as my second climax began cresting in my lower belly.

"Only if you sing for me baby," she said, picking up her pace. I felt my core tighten in anticipation. The pleasure building and building beneath my skin.

"Oh fuck, Briar.. I'm close..." I cried out.

"That's it, Hollis. Sing for me," she grunted as she slid against me. The friction, the love, the words, it was too much and I felt my orgasm crash into me drowning me in nothing but her.

And I fucking sang for her in a beautiful symphony of pleasure and love.

Her breath hitched and her body stilled above me as she found her release. We sat there, bodies joined, for a few more minutes as our breathing returned to normal. When she slid off of me, she smiled sheepishly as she handed me my pants.

A few minutes later, we were dressed again, clothes rumpled, hair messy, hearts still racing in that strange in-between space where adrenaline hadn't quite faded and reality hadn't fully returned. I shifted on the ground beside her, stretching out until we were lying on our backs, shoulder to shoulder, staring up at the inside of the tent. The canvas overhead was dim and still, lit only by the golden flicker of the waning sunlight filtering through the flaps of the tent, its glow softening the edges of the night.

We didn't speak for a while. Just breathed.

Eventually, I nudged her with my elbow and turned my head toward her. "So... when were you planning to tell me you're secretly a military genius?" I asked, teasing just enough to make her smile.

She chuckled, eyes still on the ceiling. "Genius is a stretch. More like... I'm good at strategy. Seeing how things fit. Edgar and Devrin did most of the heavy lifting."

"You're being modest," I said. "You're kind of miraculous, you know that, right?"

She turned her head then, met my gaze fully. No sarcasm, no deflection. "Thank you," she said, soft and honest.

Silence settled in again, heavier this time, more thoughtful. The kind that seeps into your bones when the future is close and terrifying.

"So... it all starts tomorrow?" I asked, already feeling the pressure creep back into my chest, the same tension she'd helped ease away minutes earlier.

"Technically tonight," she said, her voice quieter now.

"First wave goes in during the early hours, before sunrise. If they can clear the perimeter, jam the sensors, get us those blind spots..." She exhaled, dragging a hand across her face. "Then wave two will follow tomorrow morning. Then when wave three takes the guard towers...."

"We go in," I finished for her.

"Yeah," she nodded. "That's the goal. By this time tomorrow night, we'll either be standing inside that Show Center... or...."

"Or we will have failed," I finished again.

I swallowed hard, the weight of it settling in my chest like a stone. Twenty-four hours. One day. Just long enough to imagine everything that could go wrong.

She must've felt it, my spiral creeping in again, because she shifted, pressing her arm against mine more firmly, fingers brushing mine until I instinctively laced them together.

"Hey," she said gently. "Don't do that."

"Do what?"

"Worry yourself into the ground before anything's even happened." Her thumb moved across my hand in slow, steady strokes. "We've planned this. Edgar's been preparing for this for years. And whatever happens tomorrow... we face it together."

I looked at her again. Her face was calm, but not emotion-less. There was a flicker of fear in her eyes too, she just wore it differently. Braver than me. Or maybe just more practiced at hiding it.

"I really want to believe that," I admitted.

She squeezed my hand. "Me too," she whispered.

I didn't say anything after that. Just held her hand. Let the silence return.

Outside the tent, the wind shifted. Somewhere in the distance, I could hear laughter.

"We should go find the boys," Briar said, pushing herself

up with a soft grunt and brushing loose strands of hair from her face. Her voice was calm, but there was something else behind it, something heavier lingering under the lightness. "They're gonna want to spend as much time with you as possible before we go marching into the gates."

I nodded, but didn't move right away. The idea of spending time with my Wildguard, *all* of them, hit my brain like a spark to dry tinder. A wave of wicked, wildly inappropriate thoughts flashed through my mind before I could even attempt to shut them down.

Briar, ever the people-reader, caught the shift in my expression instantly. Her lips curved into a knowing smirk.

"You're picturing all of us at once, aren't you?" she added over her shoulder, casting me a sly wink.

My face went up in flames. "Briar," I hissed, scandalized and way too flustered to pretend otherwise.

She just laughed, a low, wicked sound that made my blood burn, and tossed a look at me like she already knew exactly what kind of chaos she'd stirred.

"Come on, let's go see if Edgar has a soundproof tent."

BEX

THE TENT WAS snug with all of us tucked inside. A soft hush hung in the air, broken only by the shuffle of cards and the occasional creak of canvas overhead. The space had been patched together with spare blankets, a few scattered pillows, and someone's old coat repurposed as a draft-stopper near the flap. Not much. But it was warm. And it was ours. For the night at least.

Ezra was stretched out on a bedroll near me, arms folded behind his head as he stared up at the tent's roof like he was memorizing it. Briar and Zaffir sat in the corner as they played a game of cards on an overturned crate, their playful rivalry was something so beautiful to see. It made my heart ache.

When we were together, I didn't care where we were. The blood, the war, the waiting, it didn't matter. As long as I had them. This little stitched-together family. That was enough. But how long would I have it....

Thorne ducked through the flap then, his boots kicking up cold air as he fastened the tent closed behind him.

"The first wave's getting into position," he said, his voice low.

The warmth in the tent wavered. My heart clenched. Just like that, the quiet bubble we'd built thinned, and reality came crashing through.

War was no longer on the horizon. It was here. And war meant blood. It meant loss. It meant someone I loved could be gone by tomorrow.

I looked at each of them. Ezra, silent beside me, Briar and Zaffir, stilling mid-game, Thorne, standing near the door, and the thought struck hard and sudden...

What if this was the last time we were all together?

I swallowed against the lump forming in my throat. "Thorne?" I whispered.

He turned to me instantly, the gentleness in his eyes cutting through the weight pressing on my chest. "Yes, love?"

I hesitated. The words were heavy, but they had to be said.

"What are the odds that all five of us make it out of this?"

The question landed like a thunderclap. Ezra stiffened beside me. Zaffir exhaled, slow and careful.

"Brexlyn..." Zaffir started gently.

"I'm okay," I said quickly. "Really. I know what this is. I know what it means. War doesn't give you guarantees. It just takes and takes and sometimes gives back something broken. And I know... we *all* know... that not all of us might make it through."

The silence that followed was painful. Raw. No one had the heart to lie. That was the kind of truth you couldn't bandage over.

Thorne crossed the tent and sank to his knees in front of me, taking my hands in his. His touch was warm, grounding, steady even though his voice shook slightly.

"I could give you the odds, but they don't matter," he said softly. "Because life isn't about numbers, or percentages. It's not about how long we last or how safe we play it. It's about what we do with the time we're given. What we fight for. Who we love."

Tears welled in my eyes and fell before I could stop them. He caught one with his thumb, brushing it away like it physically hurt him to see it there.

"I just..." My voice broke. "Tonight might be the last night we're all together like this."

"Maybe," he admitted, voice thick. "But if it is, then let's make it mean something. Let's not waste it being afraid of the end."

Ezra sat up beside me and reached for my hand. His fingers trembled slightly as they wrapped around mine. "If I get to spend the rest of my life with you, even if that's just the next twenty-four hours," he said, voice low and rough, "then I'll count myself lucky. I'm yours, Bex. Always. That's what matters to me."

I squeezed his hand tightly, afraid if I let go, any of this might slip through my fingers.

Briar stood and crossed to us, crouching behind me and resting her chin gently on my shoulder. "We didn't survive the Reclamation Run just to die now. I've gotta believe that means something," she murmured.

Zaffir joined us too, sitting on the floor by my side, his voice like a low ember. "I don't know what will happen after this. Praxis... the world... it'll be different. We'll be different. But no matter what it looks like, I want to be where you are."

I felt their hands on me. Each pressing their skin against mine in a show of comfort, of solidarity.

"For a long time..." I began, clearing my throat as emotion rose thick and unrelenting in my chest, "I thought I'd already had the only family I was ever going to get."

They all turned toward me, their eyes soft, quiet, waiting.

"I had Jax. And Ava. Her brother. And when my mother

died, it felt like that was it. As I got older, I told myself that family only shrinks. That eventually, one by one, people leave, or die, or just stop choosing you. And the circle only gets smaller."

I paused, blinking through the sting in my eyes. A memory rose, rushing back in unflinching detail thanks to my mind. Jax curled in on himself after one of his worst nights, his body shaking, my hands too small to do anything but hold him together. That morning, I truly believed I was going to lose him. Another person I loved, slipping through my fingers.

"I never thought I'd be lucky enough to grow my family again," I said, my voice breaking around the truth. "But I did. I got all of you."

Tears slid silently down my cheeks, but I didn't wipe them away. I wanted to feel them. I wanted to remember this.

I looked at each of them, letting my gaze settle for a moment. just long enough to drink in the miracle of their presence.

Ezra's green eyes met mine first. There was still steel in them, always would be. But now I could see through the cracks, where softness lived just beneath the surface. He let me see the version of him no one else did. That was his gift to me.

Then Zaffir. His golden eyes found mine like they always did, steady, gentle, grounding. He wasn't in his Praxis metallics anymore, and somehow that made his whole face seem brighter, freer. Like he'd stepped into the world as the person he was always meant to be. And he chose to be here. With us. With me.

Briar's honey-brown gaze caught mine next. And it hit me, again, how I'd never truly known what it was to be adored until she looked at me like that. Her eyes made promises, wordless, silent ones, that she would stand beside me in every storm.

And then there was Thorne. Mischief danced behind his

bright eyes, even now. He didn't have to say anything. Just one look, and my chest lightened. That was his magic. The way he turned grief into laughter, fear into flame.

My throat ached, my heart full to the point of bursting.

"This is my family," I whispered, voice barely audible over the pulse in my ears.

They were silent, but not because they didn't know what to say. Because they *felt* it. I could see it in their eyes.

I drew a breath that trembled at the edges. "For a long time, love has felt like a trap. Like the deeper I felt it, the more likely it was to disappear. My mother. Ava's brother. Jax... almost. It always felt like love meant eventual loss. And maybe it still does."

A sob caught in my throat, but I let it go. Let it crack me open.

"But being with you... loving you... being *yours*," I emphasized, reaching out to touch each of their hands. "It's taught me something. Love doesn't protect you from pain. But when it's real, when it's big enough, it helps you survive it. That's what you are to me. You're my survival."

Briar was the first to move.

She crossed the space between us without a word, cupping my face in both hands and pressing her lips to mine. The kiss was soft and deep, full of everything I couldn't say. Like she was breathing my pain in and exhaling back peace.

When she finally pulled away, Zaffir was there, his touch feather-light as he kissed me next, gentle and reverent, like he was handling something precious.

Thorne followed, lowering his mouth to the curve of my shoulder, pressing slow kisses along my clavicle, like he could anchor me to the present with each one.

A quiet moan escaped me as my head tilted back, and then Ezra was there too, leaning in, his mouth brushing mine even as Zaffir remained close. Our breaths mingled, our lips moved in time, all of it a slow surrender to something far deeper than desire.

Every kiss a promise. Every touch a vow.

Hands and mouths were everywhere. Zaffir and Ezra stole desperate kisses from my mouth, and each other, while Thorne dropped his head and began pressing his lips against my lower abdomen above my waist line. I felt Briar's hands slide along my back, crawling their way forward along my skin until her fingertips brushed against my hardened nipples. I gasped.

The sensations were overwhelming, beautiful...perfect.

"Hey Thorne," Zaffir whispered, his voice darkening on the edges into that dominant tone I loved so much.

"Yes?" Thorne replied from his place at my feet, his mouth and fingers toying with the skin above my waist band.

"If I need our girl to come for each of us at least two times, how many orgasms is that?" he asked, and I felt my core tighten at his words.

Thorne smiled up at me from his knees. His eyes flicked deviously from me to Zaffir. "Does she need to come for herself too?" he asked as his fingers played with the fastener of my pants. I was moments away from swimming his hands away and pulling my clothing away myself.

"Hmm, great question," Zaffir said, pressing a kiss to my lips. "What do you think, Brexlyn? Think you can show your Wildguard how you like to be touched?"

I moaned into his mouth and Briar's fingers pinched the hardened peak of my nipples from behind me. I leaned my head back onto her shoulder.

"Answer me, Brexlyn, or I'll make them stop," Zaffir ordered.

"Yes," I breathed.

"You heard the lady, Thorne," Zaffir said, smiling wickedly.

"Two for each of us, that's ten," Thorne whispered against my skin.

My eyes widened. "That's not possible," I replied, an edge of thrill and panic lacing my words.

Zaffir gripped my chin in his fingers and forced my eyes to his. "Did you forget that your Wildguard is known for rising to challenges?"

I shook my head, biting my lower lip with a smile.

"Thorne, take off her pants," Zaffir ordered, without ever pulling his eyes from me.

"Gladly," he replied. I could practically hear the smirk in his tone. A few moments later, his fingers hooked in my clothing, and pulled it down until the cool air brushed against my sensitive skin.

I felt Thorne's hands slowly traveling up my bare legs, leaving goosebumps in their wake. My core was wet and waiting, practically begging to be touched by my Wildguard. Ezra's mouth found my earlobe and his tongue and teeth took turns tasting my skin. Briar's fingers continued their gentle and sensual exploration of my hardened nipples, while Zaffir locked my eyes in place.

Thorne's fingers trailed along my thighs, then gently he pressed them open. My core was exposed to them, and I felt my body trembling with anticipation of Thorne's fingers working me. His fingers rose, gently tracing tempting lines along my inner thighs as his touch climbed toward my center. I moaned at the anticipation.

"Stop" Zaffir said, and with that one word, he commanded us all. Thorne and Briar's hands slipped away from my skin, Ezra's kisses ceased and I felt a whimper escape my mouth.

"Give us two, Brexlyn. Then you can have us," he promised in that dark, infuriatingly sexy tone. Then with a single kiss to my lips, he took a step back and his eyes trailed down my body toward my glistening center.

My other Wildguard sat around me, their bodies close enough for me to feel their presence, but not close enough to touch me, and my skin was desperate for them. I felt Briar shift so she could see me more clearly, her dark eyes hungry and warm.

One by one, they lowered their gazes to my core. And so I gave them the show they were asking for.

My fingers inched toward my center. Which was so needy and desperate, I knew it wouldn't take long to give them their first orgasm that they required of me. The first swipe of my fingers through my wet center elicited a moan from my mouth that was echoed by the others. Yeah. It wasn't going to take long at all.

I pressed my fingers onto my clit, applying the perfect pressure. I felt the climax cresting as my thighs shook. My breathing began to hitch, coming faster as I chased my orgasm. When it hit, I felt my body tense and then release, my fingers still on my center and I felt the pulsing of my climax rush through my skin.

"Fuck," Thorne whispered, licking his lips like a starving man looking at his next meal. I needed his mouth on me.

"Good girl," Zaffir praised.

"Very good," Ezra echoed, his lips hovering dangerously close, yet not close enough to my ear.

"One more, Brexlyn, then you get us," Zaffir promised. And I nodded, a pliant, desperate girl lost in sensation and desire.

I slid my fingers into my wet channel, and I could still feel my walls pulsating with my first orgasm. I could hear how wet I was. My own release coating my fingers. I let my head lull back as I pleasured myself. Feeling their eyes on my body, watching me as I made my body sing with lust, was like an aphrodisiac. Within a few minutes of feeling my fingers curl within my body, I felt another climax begin to crest.

"That's it, baby," Briar whispered.

"She's close," Thorne replied.

"That's our girl," Ezra praised.

Their words spurred me forward and I slid my free hand to my core, pressing onto my clit as my other hand slammed into my pussy.

"Coat those fingers Brexlyn," Zaffir ordered, and it was those words that set it off. My body convulsed around my fingers as my second orgasm slammed into me, hard and fast. I was breathing hard, my skin already shining with a thin sheen of sweat, and they hadn't even touched me yet.

I knew I was going to be ruined tonight. And I knew I was going to love every second of it.

"That was perfect, Brexlyn," Zaffir praised again and then he nodded to Thorne who crawled forward, pulled my hand from my center and drove his tongue into my still throbbing pussy. I cried out, my still sensitive body feeling every movement of his mouth on my skin, but then Ezra swallowed the sound by kissing me. I felt fingers return to my breasts. Delicate, gentle fingers. Briar.

I was in bliss. Pure. Perfect. Bliss. Thorne's tongue devoured me as Ezra and Briar worshiped my body with their hands and their mouths. I opened my eyes and found Zaffir watching the scene unfold in front of him with dark hungry eyes.

"How does she taste, Thorne?" Zaffir asked, his eyes never leaving mine.

"Like a fucking five course meal," he answered between swipes of his tongue in my center. I bucked my hips, pressing into him.

"Make her come," Zaffir replied.

"Aye Aye," Thorne responded before tossing each of my

thighs over his shoulders and pulling my center ever closer to his mouth. He closed his mouth around my sensitive bundle and sucked, the pressure built and made my whole body tense.

"Oh, fuck," I gasped as my third orgasm found me. I felt weak, and pliable, but I wanted more. I wanted everything they were willing to give me.

Thorne sat back, licking his lips. "Delicious," he said with a wink before sliding out from between my legs. Ezra took his place, pulling me off the crate and tossing me to the ground. Quickly, he ripped his pants down and freed his cock. It was thick, stretched and taut.

"I"m going to fuck you now, Bex," he said, lining up with my slick channel. I nodded, which got cut off by a scream as his cock filled me.

"You're fucking perfect," Ezra whispered. "You were made to squeeze my cock."

And the way my body held onto him, the way he pulled back and slammed into me, hitting me in just the right spot, made me really believe that was true.

Zaffir stepped closer, he had pulled his cock from his pants and was quietly stroking it. I watched him with what I can only describe as positively feral eyes.

Ezra's gaze drifted to him too. Both of us, drooling over his perfect body as our bodies joined.

"Ezra," Zaffir said, looking down at him. "Think you have the skillset to multitask?" He stepped closer bringing his hardened cock close to Ezra's face. His meaning was clear and I felt my core tighten around Ezra in anticipation for it.

"Oh fuck," Ezra cursed. "Our girl really likes that thought," he said, slamming into me with one quick hard thrust before slowing to a more casual pace.

"You want to watch Ezra take me down his throat, Brexlyn?" Zaffir asked, his eyes burning with need and power.

"God, yes," I replied.

"You heard our girl, open up," he said. Ezra met Zaffir's eyes, then his jaw fell open, his tongue jutting out. Ezra's cock pressed in and out of me as Zaffir lowered his onto his waiting tongue.

Then, with a quick and punishing pace, Zaffir slammed his dick into Ezra's mouth. All three of us groaned. I watched as Ezra welcomed Zaffir's thick cock down his throat, and with every thrust into his mouth, Ezra matched by slamming himself into my core. It was a sinful, erotic display and I had never felt so completely deprived of my surroundings and lost to feeling.

Briar leaned down, kissing my mouth, her tongue swirled with mine and I gripped her hair, holding her to me. She breathed into me. "God, your mouth," she whispered, smirking down at me.

"Wanna see what else it can do?" I whispered, meeting her gaze. She leaned down, took my bottom lip in between her teeth and bit. The tiny slice of pain only heightened everything around me. Briar pulled back, just enough to relieve herself of her pants. Then she was straddling my face and lowering her wet and glistening core to my mouth.

I couldn't see Zaffir fucking Ezra's throat anymore, but I could hear it. The grunts, the moans, the delicious wet sounds. And my core was tightening around Ezra's cock as another climax was building.

The first swipe of my tongue through Briar's pussy was like tasting something forbidden and perfect. And the sounds it pulled from her were downright delicious. I wrapped my hands around her hips, pulling her down until she was suffocating me with her core. I wanted to lose my senses to her. She slid her center across my mouth, riding my tongue like she too was lost in me.

I felt a mouth close over my hardened peaks, and with Ezra's cock in my pussy, and Zaffir's slamming down Ezra's throat, I knew it was Thorne. I released one hand's hold on Briar's waist to tangle it in Thorne's hair. Keeping his mouth on me as he licked and nipped.

I didn't know where I ended and where they began. I heard Zaffir groan as his climax found him, and that must have spurred Ezra on, because he was slamming into me with fervor now. Pulling yet another climax from me. I clenched around his cock, and he cursed, spilling himself inside of me. I moaned, and cried out, the sound muffled by Briar's pussy. I let my hand drift from Briar's waist to her clit and rolled beneath my touch as she bucked on my tongue. Her release found her, and her taste exploded on my tongue. Sweet and perfect. I drank her up, lapping at her release until she carefully rose from my face as Ezra slid his cock from my center. I instantly felt empty.

"Thorne," Zaffir said. Thorne looked up at him, without pulling his lips from my nipples. "Time to fuck our girl," he said. Finally, Thorne released my nipple with a pop, and climbed his way toward my legs. When he got there, he gripped and flipped me around until I was face down on the blankets. He pulled my hips up until I was on all fours and before I could even regain my bearings, he was slamming his cock into me.

"I could fucking live in your pussy, love," Thorne whispered through clenched teeth.

Briar pressed her lips to mine, tasting herself on my tongue. We both moaned into each other's mouths.

"I love you," she whispered against my lips.

"I love you," I replied back.

"Brexlyn," Zaffir said, kneeling in front of me. I glanced up at him, as my body shook from Thorne's relentless pace.

His fingers found my chin, forcing my gaze to meet his. I was panting, my whole body felt weak and alive.

"You look beautiful when you're falling apart for us," he

whispered. "I wish I could film you." My core tightened around Thorne at the thought.

"Oh shit," Thorne cursed.

"Hmm," Zaffir said. "You liked that?"

I nodded.

"Soon, baby," he promised.

I glanced down, seeing his cock twitching back to life after emptying down Ezra's throat. I licked my lips.

"Are you going to give me your mouth?" he asked, smirking at me. I nodded again, words completely lost to me as Thorne continued his pace.

"Open wide," he said, lining his cock up with my mouth. The moment the tip hit my tongue, I moaned around him. Then closed my lips around him, taking him as deep as I could manage in this position. Zaffir's hands cupped my cheeks, tender and loving as he let me set the pace.

"Holy shit," I heard Ezra whisper from beside me.

I'd lost count of how many times I'd come, but I knew they were just getting started with me, and that thought made my whole body shiver.

I felt someone run their fingers through my slickness around Thorne's cock, and slowly swirled their finger around my tiny tight hole.

"Yes," I cried around Zaffir's cock.

"She likes that, Ezra," Zaffir whispered.

"I know," he replied before sliding two fingers into me. Working in tandem with Thorne, the two brought me to yet another earth-shattering climax. I was sobbing with love and lust as Zaffir emptied himself down my throat, I swallowed eagerly, not willing to waste a drop.

Thorne groaned as he found his climax.

My body felt spent and tired, and when Thorne and Ezra pulled themselves from me. I fell forward onto my chest, focusing on breathing and forcing my heart rate to come down.

My body was coated with sweat, and my thighs were slick and sticky with my release and others.

"Beautiful," Zaffir praised, sitting down on the ground near my head, his chest rising and falling. Ezra and Thorne joined him. Sitting near my head. Their bodies, just as spent as mine.

I glanced at them, smiling weakly as my body came down from its continuous high.

"Where's Briar?" I asked, but my answer came in the form of two fingers sliding into my sensitive pussy. "Oh!" I gasped.

She kneeled over my body, pressing her chest to my back as she pinned me down. "Sorry, baby. You gave me an orgasm, but I didn't get one out of you yet," she whispered into my ear as she worked my core with her fingers. I felt her reposition herself between my legs, her hands working in tandem to draw me pleasure out.

As two fingers delicately hooked inside of me, swiping expertly against my most sensitive spot, she pressed two fingers against my clit. Her touch elicited a mixture of pain and pleasure from my overly sensitive bundle of nerves, and it was fucking euphoric. It didn't take long before my breathing ramped up again and my fingers were digging into the blankets in front of me.

I glanced up in front of me to see Zaffir, Ezra and Thorne watching my face with hungry, love-filled eyes. They watched me writhe beneath Briar's expert fingers like some would watch their favorite show.

Briar was working me, touching me in ways I had no idea I could be touched. I felt my body clenching her fingers, desperate for her. The pressure in my lower stomach built and built, becoming almost painfully full as she fucked me.

"Briar," I cried out. "Stop.. I'm... Oh my God," I

mumbled, pressing my face down into the blankets, but she didn't stop. In fact she pressed further, harder. Her fingers reached directly to the source of the building climax and practically ripped it from me.

As the climax hit me, I felt wetness spill from me in a tidal wave, and with each convulsion of my body, more wetness came too.

Briar's fingers stilled within me. And when I finally found my breath again, and my mind cleared from the pure and utter bliss of that full body orgasm, I glanced up to find my other Wildguard watching me with open mouths.

Embarrassment flooded me instantly, and I tried to sit up. But Briar leaned over my back and pressed a kiss to my cheek, then my neck, then my shoulder blade.

"Holy shit," Ezra whispered.

"That was the hottest thing I've ever seen, Brexlyn," Zaffir replied, his more dominant energy had slipped away.

"Damn, Briar," Thorne said with a low whistle. "How'd you do that?"

Briar pressed another kiss to my cheek. "I just understand women," she said and I could feel her smirk against my skin.

"I bet I can do that too," Thorne said moving toward me, but Zaffir put a hand on his shoulder and kept him back.

"Let our girl catch her breath, Thorne," he said, and I sent him a smile I hoped he could read as a thank you.

My body was spent and tired and as good as I felt, I knew I needed a moment to recover from the pleasure they'd just given me.

"Take the time you need, love," Thorne said, smiling at me.

"Yes, Brexlyn. Take a few minutes to breathe and recover. Because by my count..." His eyes darkened. "You still owe us four orgasms tonight. And I plan to collect."

I smiled up at him, at all of them, my Wildguard. My

heart. My impossible, beautiful miracle. Because in that moment, surrounded by their warmth, their hands, their eyes that saw all of me and loved me anyway, I knew with aching certainty that if this was our last night, if fate had already written the end, we would meet it like this. Together.

No regrets. No fear. Just us, in the quiet dark, choosing one another with everything we had left.

If I never got another sunrise, another kiss, another breath in their arms... this would be enough.

CHAPTER
TWENTY

ZAFFIR

I woke up with my back screaming and every muscle aching like I'd just sprinted through a battlefield barefoot. Which, in a way, we sort of had, only the battle had taken place in a cocoon of blankets, whispered promises, and desperate hands. And if I felt like this, I couldn't even begin to imagine how Brexlyn was holding up. By the time we'd drifted to sleep in the wee hours of the morning, we'd gotten our ten orgasms from her.

My mind drifted to our girl, and how beautifully, fiercely she had taken all of us. The way her body moved with each of ours, like she'd been made for us, for this. She gave herself to us like she knew it might be the last time, and we met her with everything we had.

I shifted slightly and glanced over.

She was fast asleep, tucked into Ezra's side, her head resting in the crook of his arm. My own body was curved around him from the other side, the three of us locked together like puzzle pieces. Briar was curled around Brexlyn's back, one hand still resting over her heart like she'd been keeping watch even in sleep. And down at the foot of the bedrolls, Thorne had somehow wedged himself between her legs, his head pillowed on her stomach, one arm thrown across her hip like he couldn't bear to let her go.

My chest swelled, painfully, sweetly, with a thudding heartbeat I couldn't ignore. I loved them. I loved Brexlyn with every fractured, stubborn piece of my soul. I loved Ezra, too, maybe differently, maybe quietly, but just as deeply. And Briar and Thorne... they were the kind of people who showed you what it meant to be loved with their actions.

What I felt when I looked at them wasn't the same kind of love, but it was real. It was family.

Carefully, I untangled myself from the pile of limbs and warmth, trying not to wake anyone. I slipped a shirt over my bare chest, someone's shirt, I didn't know whose, and padded quietly toward the tent's flap. My joints cracked in protest, but I welcomed the soreness. It was proof that last night had been real. That we'd carved out something good, something ours, before we ventured forth into the unknown.

We probably shouldn't have worn ourselves out like that with what was coming. But I didn't regret a second of it. We needed that night. We needed her.

And more than anything, we needed the reminder that we're still alive.

Today isn't promised. None of this is.

So we took it while we could. Held onto it with both hands.

The sun had just barely crested the horizon, washing the camp in a warm, amber glow that made the canvas tents shimmer like soft-lit lanterns. The stillness was surreal, like the world was holding its breath. I stood just outside the food tent, stacking a plate with dried meats, fruits, and a hunk of bread, my fingers moving on autopilot. The air smelled of dew and ash from the fires of last night.

I'd never been outside the gates of Praxis before. The

closest I'd ever come was filming the Wildguard as they returned bloodied and victorious from their first trial. Out here, everything felt... freer. Raw. Untamed. And terrifying in a way that made my heart beat faster.

Most of the camp had gone quiet. By now, the first two waves should've breached the gates. Should've started the chain reaction that would either free the Collectives, or bury us all beneath the rubble of what we tried to change.

A figure stepped up beside me. I turned and found Edgar standing there, his expression unreadable, his arms folded, posture straight as ever despite the early hour.

"Edgar," I greeted with a small nod.

His eyes scanned me, lingering just a second too long, and I caught the brief flicker of something hard in them—distrust. I didn't blame him. As far as anyone outside my little circle was concerned, I'd spent every day up until yesterday as the Praxis puppet. Even I would've been wary of me.

"How did the first waves fare last night?" I asked, trying not to let nerves slip into my voice.

He grabbed a strip of jerky from the serving tray and chewed on it slowly before answering. "According to plan."

Vague. Guarded. As expected.

"Has the third wave moved into position yet?" I tried again.

This time, he didn't even bother responding. He just looked at me, brows slightly furrowed, jaw tight.

I sighed, setting the plate down on the table. "You don't trust me, do you?"

He didn't answer right away. Then he gave a single shake of his head.

"You know what my Praxis-assigned cameraman said to me after my last trial?" he asked eventually, voice low and bitter.

I met his gaze and waited.

"When I came back bloodied but breathing...When I'd survived and so many others hadn't, he walked up to me, completely unfazed by the carnage, and said, 'Congratulations.'" He spat the word like it tasted foul. "Congratulations for making it out alive. For putting on a good show. For surviving long enough to give him some credit for being the one behind the lens."

My chest ached with the weight of his confession. How many times had I said the exact same thing to my Challengers?

"Congratulations for being the perfect puppet." He shook his head, a humorless laugh breaking in his throat. "It didn't even register how sick that was until later. At the time, I just nodded. I said 'thank you.' Like it was some kind of achievement I should be proud of."

I watched him quietly.

"Praxis has a way of warping our perception," I said, my voice low, edged with shame. " Growing up, we didn't see the Run for what it was. It was entertainment. It had drama, hero journeys, and competition. The Challengers from the Collectives weren't victims to us. They were stars. Celebrities. We idolized them. We bought into the illusion so hard we didn't question what it cost them to get there. Or to get back."

I swallowed, forcing the next words past the tightness in my throat. "We rooted for them, we memorized their names, we wore their merchandise. And the worst part is the whole time, we told ourselves we were doing something *good* for them. That we were giving them an opportunity, redemption, fame, a better life. That's what they drilled into us. That's what we believed."

I looked up at Edgar, his face unreadable, but watching me closely.

"I see it differently now. Praxis is a system that tells itself it's merciful, when all it's doing is feeding off the suffering it creates. And I was part of it." I shook my head slowly, trying to force the sting behind my eyes to calm. "I'm not proud of how long it took me to wake up. But I'm awake now."

I took a breath and kept going.

"You know what they teach us in school? That the Collectives were selfish. That they rebelled against unity, against preservation. They said Praxis had every right to cut them off, to strip their access, isolate them. Let them starve or die out. And when they didn't? When they created the Reclamation Run instead?" I gave a bitter laugh. "That was supposed to be a gift. A noble act."

My stomach churned even repeating it aloud. I spat the words, the lies I'd once parroted without question. "And I believed it. I swallowed every bit of it because why would the people who swore to protect us, lie to us?"

I paused. Let the silence settle between us.

"I hate that it took falling in love to see through it all. That it took her to show me the truth. But I'm grateful, too. Because once you see it, you can't unsee it. You can't go back."

Edgar stood quiet for a long moment. Then he stepped closer and clapped his calloused hand on my shoulder.

"I believed it too, kid," Edgar said after a long pause. His voice was rough, worn down by time and truth. "I ate it up. The fame, the applause, the way people looked at me like I was something bigger than I was. Like I mattered. It was intoxicating."

He ran a hand through his salt-and-pepper hair, fingers dragging like they were trying to scrub the memories from his scalp. "I let it define me. Let it convince me I was one of the lucky ones. Chosen. Important. But then, the moment that year was up, the moment I was no longer useful to them... Praxis tossed me aside like I'd never even existed." He exhaled, bitter and tired.

"That was when the shine started to fade. When the glitter and gold finally fell from my eyes."

I swallowed around the lump in my throat. "I think we can do that," I said, voice quiet but steady.

He looked at me, eyes narrowing with curiosity. "Do what?"

"Help them see. Shake the glitter and gold from their eyes too." I turned my gaze toward the horizon, where the gilded gates of Praxis caught the first light of morning. They gleamed like a beacon, like a lie made beautiful. "It's hard to imagine, I know. Especially after everything. But I don't think most of them are evil, Edgar. I don't think they're all complicit because they enjoy it. I think most of them are just... blinded by gold. Like I was."

He followed my gaze, eyes landing on the same golden barrier.

"I'd bet," I continued, "that behind those gates, there are people just like us. People who've been fed the same stories, taught the same twisted truths. People who've never had the chance, or the courage, to ask the right questions. But if we can show them... if we can make them see the cracks in the gold, maybe we won't have to fight them all. Maybe they'll choose to stand with us. Or at the very least, not stand in the way."

Edgar studied me for a long moment, the lines of his face carved deep with doubt and history. Then, slowly, a smile pulled at the corner of his mouth. It was a tired smile, but not without hope.

"You might be onto something, kid," he said. "Maybe it's not about breaking the system with force. Maybe it's about waking up the people inside it."

He clapped a hand on my shoulder again, firmer this time.

"And maybe you were born in the wrong place, but you ended up exactly where you needed to be."

The words hit me harder than I anticipated. I did feel like

somehow I'd found my home despite that not being a physical place. But rather a team.

"Yeah, I think I did."

"The first wave was a clean success," Edgar said, his voice low and even. "They managed to jam the surveillance systems completely, quiet as ghosts. Praxis didn't see a thing. And now we're in their com systems."

My stomach fluttered, a strange mix of nerves and awe.

"That gave wave two the cover they needed to breach the perimeter and get in close," he continued, scanning the horizon with sharp eyes. "Explosives were placed exactly where we planned. Right now, they're waiting for the shift change to blow it all sky high."

I nodded, my gaze pulled toward the distant, golden gates. They gleamed like always.

Edgar glanced at the watch strapped to his wrist, then up again. "Actually..." he muttered, "if everything's running on schedule, we should be seeing some smoke any minute now."

We both fell silent, watching.

"Wave three is on standby. The second we see that smoke, they'll move," he added. Then he sighed and shifted the weight of his gear. "I should get back to my unit."

I turned to face him, more grateful than I could say. "We'll be right behind you," I promised.

He held out his hand, rough and weathered. I took it in mine and gripped tight.

"Good luck, kid," he said, voice softer now.

"You too, old man," I replied with a grin, forcing lightness into my voice.

He snorted. "Watch it," he said, giving my shoulder a playful swat before jogging off, his silhouette cutting a steady line across the field.

I stood there for a moment, unmoving, letting the weight of what was coming settle over me.

With renewed focus, I turned back to the food I'd gathered, fruits, dried meat, anything to keep our strength up. We were going to need every ounce of energy we could find.

As I started toward the tent, plate in hand, a sound stopped me. Dull at first, then louder. A deep, distant boom.

I turned back just in time to see it.

Dark plumes of smoke unfurled like ribbons into the sky, thick, heavy, undeniable. Black columns rising in stark contrast against the brightening morning light. The gates of Praxis were burning.

Wave two had done their job.

A thrill of adrenaline surged through me. It was time.

I ran the last stretch to the tent, heart pounding, legs quick. I didn't hesitate to pull back the flap. My Wildguard was still tangled in sleep and blankets, peaceful in a way we might never be again.

But peace had to wait.

"Wake up," I said, urgency threading my voice. "It's starting."

CHAPTER
TWENTY-ONE

EZRA

"WAKE UP," Zaffir's voice broke through the haze of sleep, urgent but steady. "It's starting."

My eyes fluttered open, vision blurry and unfocused. I turned my head and found Bex beside me, her lashes fluttering as her gaze met mine. There was a moment where the world outside didn't exist. Just her. Just this.

I wrapped my arms tighter around her, pulling her close in an instinctive embrace, like I could shield her from what was coming. She tucked her face into the crook of my neck, warm and drowsy, but the tension was already building in the space between us.

Near Bex's feet, Thorne let out a groan, clearly not ready to surrender the comfort of sleep. "Ugh, five more minutes," he muttered, throwing an arm over his eyes like a petulant child.

Briar was up in an instant. She rolled smoothly to her feet with a catlike stretch, eyes sharp and clear.

"It's starting?" I asked Zaffir, still trying to piece reality together. The dreamlike fog in my brain made everything feel distant, like we had all the time in the world, when in truth, we had almost none.

"Wave two's explosives just went off," he confirmed, kneeling beside the bedroll to set down a plate piled with dried meat, fruit, and hard bread. "Wave three's moving in to take the guard towers now. If they can secure them and hold the line, we'll be up next."

Briar wasted no time, already plucking fruit from the plate like she was picking weapons off a rack. She tossed a red piece of fruit to Bex with a wink. Bex caught it easily, offering a half-asleep smile in return.

I sat up, rubbing my hands over my face before grabbing a piece of jerky and taking a bite. The salt and chewiness grounded me slightly, helping to sweep the remnants of sleep from my system.

"So... if they take the towers," I said around a mouthful, "that means it's our turn?"

"When," Bex corrected gently, her voice still husky with sleep but her resolve already shining through. She offered me a soft smile.

I reached out and let my hand trace slowly down her bare back, savoring the feel of her skin under my fingers. Goose-bumps followed in the wake of my touch. I liked that I could still do that to her.

"Yeah," I murmured, "when."

"I'd say we've got a few hours," Briar interjected, crouching to lace up her boots with military precision. "Long enough to eat, clean up, gear up, and breathe. Maybe."

She was fully awake now. Sharp. Focused. Like a general. Honestly, it was impressive. Maybe even a little intimidating.

I looked around at the group, Zaffir sitting beside us now, Thorne muttering something incoherent into the mound of blankets and Bex, still pressed against my side, taking slow careful bites of her fruit. My chest tightened.

We took turns washing up, and then suited up in borrowed clothes and light armor from the armory tent.

Briar took charge, naturally. She moved through the weapons racks with a soldier's ease, hands brushing over the familiar contours of guns and blades. She holstered a sleek pistol at her hip and filled her bag with extra rounds, every motion precise, practiced.

Thorne gravitated toward a bow and a quiver of arrows, his fingers testing the string's resistance with a quiet reverence. "I used to hunt with one of these back home," he said, a rare seriousness in his voice. "It's quiet. I like quiet."

Zaffir, sweet and slightly out of his element, eyed the racks like they might bite. In the end, he chose a pair of small daggers that he strapped to his belt with a shaky but determined hand. But his camera, his real weapon, remained slung over one shoulder, ready.

I stared at the firearms like they were some alien relics. I didn't know the first thing about shooting one, and I sure as hell didn't want to risk hurting someone on accident. But a pickaxe, blunt, heavy, straightforward, I could handle that. It had weight. It made sense.

Bex was just as uncertain. Her hand hovered over a pistol before pulling back like it had burned her. She eventually grabbed a couple of daggers and tucked them into the loops of her belt. Then she picked up a large rifle, her fingers fumbling slightly as she tried to understand it.

"I don't know how to use it," she said, eyes wide with something between nerves and resolve.

"Me either," I admitted, grabbing a rifle of my own.

I quickly emptied the magazine and cleared the chamber, then slung it across my back. She did the same, watching me carefully.

"They don't have to know it's not loaded," I whispered, brushing a kiss across her lips. "Might be enough to make someone hesitate. Buy you a few seconds."

Bex stood on her toes and kissed me back, harder, like it might be the last time. Like she didn't want to forget the feel of it.

A few hours later, we gathered at the base of the hill that overlooked the perimeter of Praxis. The sounds of fighting that had echoed through the morning—shouts, the sharp crack of gunfire, and the distant boom of explosions—had quieted into an eerie lull.

We hadn't seen any retreating forces, no signs of panic, which meant the second wave had likely succeeded. The guard towers were down. The gates were exposed. We were next.

Briar scanned the hilltop and the golden glint of the city beyond it, then turned to face us. Her eyes were sharp, her voice low but commanding.

"Stay close. Stay quiet. Be ready."

And with that, she led us forward.

The climb toward Praxis felt a lot different than the last time we made this trek.

The last time we'd taken these steps, during the transportation trial, it had been about proving our strength and endurance to a government who'd had us under their thumb. But this... this was something else entirely.

Now, when we crested that hill and saw the golden gates ahead, the smoke and destruction of Nexum weren't locked out, they were trapped inside. This time, Praxis wasn't the only place untouched by chaos.

It *was* the chaos.

The moment we crossed the barrier, the air turned thick with death. The smoke from the explosions hung heavy. Ash floated through the sky like dirty snow. The scent of gunpowder stung my nose, mingling with the coppery tang of blood that coated the streets.

I kept my arm around Bex's shoulders, grounding both of us. Her hand curled into the hem of my shirt, fingers gripping tight. We didn't say anything. We didn't need to. Just kept walking, stepping around bodies of Praxis guards and Runaways alike, wreckage, the aftermath of the fight that had already torn through this place. They'd stood on opposite sides of the line—one draped in gold, the other in ash—but now they lay the same. Silent. Still. Because in the end, no matter the uniform, no matter the cause, we all bleed red.

The silence was eerie. The initial battle was clearly settled. But that didn't mean it was safe. Didn't mean we could breathe easy.

The tension hadn't gone anywhere. It just shifted. Burrowed deeper.

It was too quiet now. And I knew better than to let my guard down. Not yet.

"The Show Center is this way," Zaffir whispered, pointing Briar down a relatively deserted road. The windows on the buildings were shut tight, silence permeated the air. It was a vicious juxtaposition from the lively effervescence that we'd witnessed only a few short weeks ago when we first arrived in this town.

The Runaways had taken the Guard Towers. We could still hear them, faintly. Rebel voices echoing through the empty streets.

Footsteps snapped our attention forward. I stepped in front of Bex, the others fell into place beside me, ready for a fight. But it was Edgar who came out of the shadows, and our relief was instant, but short-lived.

"Edgar," Briar called. She moved toward him, but stopped short, when she took in the sight of him. He looked... wrecked. Ash smeared across his face, blood dried and cracked along the side of his neck. He kept one hand pressed to his stomach, where more blood had bloomed and soaked through the fabric.

"You're hurt," Briar said.

He waved her off. "Still breathing, and that's more than I can say for a lot of us."

"The towers?" Thorne asked.

Edgar gave a slow nod. "We've got them. Guards that are cooperating are locked in the lower levels. Anyone else, incapacitated."

Bex flinched at the word.

"But we've got another problem," Edgar said.

"What now?" Briar asked.

"Citizens. From the west side. They're pushing back. Trying to take back the tower."

"Citizens?" Bex echoed.

"Armed?" Zaffir added, his voice softer than usual.

Edgar nodded. "Not like us. But enough to make it a fight. And our people are already stretched thin. We took hits getting in."

Briar swore under her breath and raked a hand through her hair. "What's the play?" she asked.

"We hold them back as long as we can," Edgar answered.

"How?" Bex pressed.

Briar and Thorne exchanged a look, silent and steady. "However we have to," Edgar said.

Zaffir looked like he might be sick. "What if they surrender?" His voice barely carried, but it cut straight through the tension.

"If they surrender," Briar said, her eyes locking with his, "they won't be harmed."

Edgar shook his head, jaw clenched. "But that's a big if. And we don't have long. If they keep pushing, we'll lose the west tower by morning. And everyone guarding it."

The silence that followed said what no one else could. If we lost the tower, we'd lose the advantage we'd only barely garnered... and then the war itself.

"That's where you come in," Edgar said, his gaze moving from Bex to Zaffir. "You need to get through to them. Show them the truth. Make them see who they're really protecting, and what it's costing."

He took a step closer. His voice dropped, steadier, heavier. "Make them see it," he said again.

Briar placed a hand on his shoulder, firm. "Good luck."

"You too," Edgar said, meeting each of our eyes before turning, limping his way back toward the towers.

We stood in silence for a breath. Then I spoke.

"We need to move."

Zaffir gave a small nod. "The Show Center is just ahead," he said, calm on the surface, but his voice had a distant edge to it, like he wasn't entirely here anymore.

And I couldn't blame him.

His mind was probably with the people at that western tower right now. People he'd grown up with. Neighbors. Classmates. Maybe even someone he used to love. People who'd lived under the same stories he once believed in. People who weren't soldiers, but were still picking up weapons to defend a lie they didn't even know was a lie.

This war wasn't easy on any of us. But for Zaffir, it had to cut deeper. He wasn't just fighting Praxis. He was fighting pieces of his past.

And if those citizens died out there, if they lost their lives defending the version of truth Praxis had spoon-fed them since birth, was it even really their fault?

I didn't know anymore.

All I knew was that if we didn't get this right—if Bex and Zaffir couldn't reach them in time—there'd be more blood on the streets by morning.

BEX

How are you supposed to feel when you realize you're living through history?

That thought echoed in my head as we approached the empty, quiet Show Center. Now nothing more than a hollow shell haunted by the lies it helped shape.

I couldn't stop thinking about how my name would be remembered in Nexum, long after this was over. Because one way or another, it *would* be remembered. The only question was how.

Would I be known as the Runaway who helped ignite the fire that finally burned Praxis to the ground? The one who helped drag the truth into the light and gave this fractured place a real chance at freedom?

Or would I go down as a failed rebel with too much heart and not enough foresight, a cautionary tale about what happens when you challenge a system built on blood and gold without enough force to back it up?

A reckless idealist. A tragic footnote.

I didn't feel heroic. I didn't feel brave.

I felt numb. Frightened.

But most of all, I felt angry.

Furious at the lies that raised me. Furious at the people still too blind or too scared to question them. Furious at the way Praxis turned pain into entertainment and called it justice. Furious that it had taken me this long to see it all clearly.

Zaffir led us around the back of the Show Center, staying close to the building's wall with cautious steps. From the outside, the place looked abandoned, lights out, no movement in the windows, not even a whisper of sound. But none of us were willing to assume safety.

"They've most likely pulled my access. Veritas saw me. So be ready to break the door down," Zaffir whispered.

When we reached the service entrance, Zaffir held up his credentials to the scanner. There was a tense second of silence before the light turned green with a soft click. The door unlocked.

We all froze.

Why hadn't they revoked his access?

That single question passed silently between us, an electric charge snapping through the air. Praxis was many things, but careless wasn't usually one of them. Which meant one thing.

She knew he would come back.

Zaffir's voice dropped to a whisper as he slowly reached for the handle. "We need to be ready for the possibility that this is a trap. If they know we're coming, they could be waiting."

We nodded. No questions.

Briar and Thorne immediately shifted into defense mode, weapons drawn and eyes sharp. Thorne knocked an arrow. Ezra and I moved our rifles to the front, even though we both knew they were empty. But appearances mattered, especially in a place built on illusions. Maybe if we looked armed, we'd buy ourselves a few precious seconds.

Seconds we'd need if this went sideways.

I tightened my grip around the cold metal and tried to steady my breathing. My fear was a physical thing now, curled in my chest like a fist, squeezing tight. But I couldn't let it win. I turned my head just enough to meet the eyes of the people beside me, my Wildguard, my family, and offered a silent exchange of love, of gratitude, of strength.

We had made it this far together.

And maybe, if we were lucky, this would be the place where it finally ended.

The door creaked open, and we slipped inside.

It was dark. Colder than I expected. The kind of cold that sinks into your teeth and makes your spine ache. The hallway ahead of us was narrow and stark white, but it didn't help. The darkness still clung to everything.

When the door shut behind us, it left only a faint red glow spilling from an emergency light above the exit sign. Our footsteps were too loud in the silence. Sharp. Each one cracked against the tile like a warning shot.

It felt empty. But certainly not safe. Not by any definition of the word.

The hallway spit us out into a wide-open chamber. A sunken pit sat at the center, wrapped in terminals and black metal tables. Screens hung from the ceiling above it. Thick cables ran across the floor in every direction, pulsing with quiet electricity.

To the right, a glass-walled room was packed with gear, cameras, headsets, and who knows what else.

And so far, we didn't see anyone else.

Briar and Thorne exchanged a silent look, then split off, sweeping the outer rooms. Zaffir and Ezra flanked me, close, steady, watchful. Their eyes kept moving, scanning every shadow like it might blink.

And me? I stood still. My pulse in my ears. The breath caught in my throat.

This place was supposed to be the heart of it all. And all I could think was, maybe hearts were made to break.

Zaffir crept forward, slow and deliberate, eyes locked on the cluster of terminals ahead. His fingers hovered just above the hard drive at his belt. If he could get to those terminals, if he could connect, it would all be there. Every minute of footage that had been erased. Every bloodied second of truth. The proof Praxis had spent nearly a century burying.

All he had to do was plug it in.

Behind him, Briar and Thorne moved with precision, scanning corners, checking blind spots, their bodies slipping into the roles they showed me so naturally in the Wilds. It had been weeks since then, but they looked exactly the same now, lean, alert, lethal.

I already thought their skills were impressive. Now, I thanked every star in the sky that they had them.

Zaffir was almost there. Just a few more steps.

I adjusted my grip on the useless rifle slung in my arms. My palms were slick with sweat, making it hard to tell if I was trembling or just melting into the floor. Ezra stood beside me, solid but tense, his breath loud and uneven in the quiet. I was glad to know that I wasn't alone in this sinking unnerved feeling.

The moment Zaffir's hand touched the console, the screen flared to life.

A soft *click* and the whole wall blinked awake, flooding the room with a harsh, sterile glow. It wasn't just the terminals either, but the wall of screens sparked on in a slow, deliberate hum, washing everything in cold, blue-white light.

I sucked in a breath through my teeth.

It felt like we'd just fired a flare into the sky.

No more shadows to hide in. No more cover of darkness.

Just five Runaways in a spotlight, standing in the belly of the beast.

I saw the moment Zaffir realized it too, his posture stiffened, just a fraction. But he didn't stop. He reached down, pulled the drive from his belt, and looked at us over his shoulder.

He offered us a quick nod. Then turned back to connect the drive to the waiting terminal.

That's when the shot rang out.

Time didn't stop, but it staggered. Everything lurched into slow motion. I heard the sharp crack of the bullet, the shattering of glass somewhere above, and then the echo bouncing off the walls in endless ricochet. Before I could even register where it came from, Ezra's body collided with mine, shielding me as we hit the ground in a tangled heap.

Briar shouted something, maybe my name, maybe a command, but it was swallowed by the chaos as she fired a return shot. My fingers scrambled for the daggers at my belt. Cold steel, warm grip. I clutched them like lifelines.

More glass rained down, and my heart kicked into overdrive. Boots hit the floor in all directions and Ezra shot up beside me, gripping his pickaxe like a man ready to stand against the world.

I turned my head, trying to orient myself and that's when I saw him.

Zaffir was on the ground, facedown. Blood was pooling beneath his outstretched hand, dark and steady. My stomach dropped, until his eyes found mine. He was alive. Hurting, but alive. Fury burned behind his pain.

Then the world snapped back to full speed.

I launched to my feet and bolted toward him, ducking low, dodging shadows, my only thought was *'get to Zaffir. Protect him.'*

At least ten, or maybe more, Praxis guards had stormed

the chamber. Their uniforms were scorched, torn, splattered in old and fresh blood. They looked like war torn ghosts of the people they used to be. So did we.

One of them rushed me. Ezra stepped between us like a wall of rage, driving the blunt end of his pickaxe into the man's gut. There was a sickening crunch, and the guard crumpled.

I didn't stop running. Zaffir was trying to get up, struggling. Another guard was bearing down on him fast. I didn't think, I just moved. I sprinted and dove, clearing Zaffir's body and slamming both daggers into the guard's chest plate. They didn't pierce deep enough to kill, but the hit was solid, jarring, and it knocked him off balance long enough for Thorne to send an arrow clean into his throat. The guard gurgled, then fell.

I looked up, just long enough to nod at Thorne. He was already turning, aiming at his next target.

I dropped beside Zaffir. His hand was a mess. Blood streamed from a hole torn straight through the center of his palm. He cradled it against his chest, breathing in short, shallow bursts.

"Zaffir," I whispered, my eyes scanning for the next threat.

Another guard was heading our way. I stood, putting myself between him and Zaffir. He didn't hesitate as he slammed the butt of his rifle straight into the side of my head.

Pain burst across my skull in a flash of white. I dropped to my knees, blinking through the haze as the guard stepped toward Zaffir, rifle raised.

I kicked out, sweeping his legs from under him. He hit the ground hard, and Zaffir, gods, even injured, pulled a dagger with his good hand and drove it into the exposed flesh of the guard's throat.

The man thrashed, screamed, then stilled.

I turned to Zaffir, and his gaze drifted past me, to the

terminal. To the hard drive lying there, shattered. One single perfect, precise shot had destroyed everything.

The footage. The truth. Gone.

That had been the plan all along. They wanted us to get to the Show Center. They wanted for us to feel a sense of security. Then they'd take out the evidence.

A pair of hands seized my shoulders from behind. I fought like hell, elbows, knees, head, but they were faster, stronger. Zaffir tried to push up, to help, but the pain knocked him back down again, screaming as he gripped his ruined hand.

I kicked wildly as the guard dragged me backward, twisting in their grip, heart pounding like a war drum.

My eyes scanned the room.

Briar and Thorne were backed into a corner, hands up, weapons dropped, with rifles pointed at their heads.

Ezra lay facedown, unmoving, his pickaxe just inches from his hand. A guard stood over him, pressing the muzzle of a rifle into the back of his neck.

Everyone's eyes found mine.

And I knew.

We had lost.

We were *so* close. We had the proof. We had the story. We had the moment. And Praxis took it all away with one bullet. History would never know the truth.

Unless we found another way to tell it.

"I admit," a voice rang out, crisp and cruel, echoing through the chamber. "I didn't think you'd be *quite* this stupid."

The words seemed to come from everywhere, and nowhere, all at once. Then, the sharp click of heels began to echo against the tile, rhythmic and unhurried. We all turned toward the sound, tension spiking.

Archon Evanora Veritas emerged from the shadows. She was wrapped in shimmering gold chiffon, the fabric whispering with every step. It clung to her frame like a goddess carved in bronze. Elegant, regal, and terrifying. Her hair fell in polished ringlets down her back, untouched by wind or war, making her look more like a vision than a person. More myth than mortal.

But when my gaze reached her eyes, I saw the cracks. The dark circles just barely hidden beneath perfect powder. The twitch in the corner of her mouth. Her gaze, sharper now, more alert, less sure. Like she'd been staring into the dark a little too long and had started to worry what might be staring back.

We had done that. We'd gotten to her. Even if we weren't able to finish this war. I could die knowing that we'd scared the unshakeable.

She smiled like a wolf. "The grid makes a wonderful hiding place," she purred, her voice honeyed and cruel. "Isn't that right, Mr. Stark?"

Her gaze sliced toward him where he lay slumped on the floor, his breathing ragged, his skin unnaturally pale. He was curled around the camera he'd brought with him. Protecting it like it might still be our salvation, if he got the chance. The blood was still flowing from his ruined hand, and his eyes were fluttering, losing their grip on consciousness. My throat clenched.

Tears burned hot in my eyes.

"Brexlyn Hollis," she said next, and the sound of my name in her mouth made me flinch. Her voice was velvet-laced poison. "Did you really think you were the first Challenger to try and fight back?"

I straightened, locking eyes with her as she approached, though the guard's grip on me tightened. She stopped just inches from me, her perfume, rose and something sharp beneath it, filling my nose like a choking sweetness.

"Did you think we didn't know about your little

Runaways?" she whispered, her smile growing as her finger traced a cold line down my cheek. I didn't move. I wouldn't give her the satisfaction. But her touch made my skin crawl.

"A century," she hissed, "a *century* of a system cannot be undone by a handful of desperate children and a single night. You think because you knocked on the gates, they'll fall down?" She laughed, low and gleeful. "You stupid, foolish girl."

She stepped back, turning to address the room, her voice rising like a sermon. "Did you really think all my guards were stationed at the towers? That I would be so careless? That even if you managed to subdue my armies, that my citizens wouldn't also stand against you?"

The pit in my stomach dropped straight through the floor.

Tears slipped from the corners of my eyes, hot and angry and helpless.

I felt the strength drain from my limbs. The hope. The fight. It all bled out of me like Zaffir's blood on the floor.

We were surrounded. Beaten. Outmaneuvered.

And Evanora Veritas had just reminded us that the monster we were fighting had multiple heads. And we'd miscounted.

"Why?" I asked. My voice cracked with exhaustion and fury, the weight of everything we'd lost pressing down on my chest. Zaffir bleeding on the ground. Ezra pressed to the floor. Briar and Thorne at gunpoint.

Veritas tilted her head at me like I was a puzzle she was bored of solving.

"'Why,' *what*, dear?" she asked lazily, lowering herself into a chair. She reclined, calm and unshaken like all of this was a performance and she already knew how the final act ended.

I took a shaky breath and stepped forward despite the guard's hand still tight on my arms.

"Why don't you listen?" I demanded. "When your people

are screaming that they're hurting? When they're telling you they're starving, that they're dying, that they're scared. You sit there in your golden palace while everything burns. Why?"

Her lips twitched, almost like a smile. But her eyes were cold. She didn't blink.

"You're in a position of power," I continued, voice rising. "You could change it. You could end the Reclamation Run. You could release the stockpiles. Feed the families. House the kids sleeping in alleyways. People trusted you. Believed in you. You were supposed to protect them."

She watched me silently, her fingers drumming against the armrest.

"You could make things better for everyone. So why don't you?"

The silence stretched.

Then she smiled. Slowly. Venomously.

"Oh, Brexlyn," she said, her voice syrupy sweet, "because fear is control."

I stared at her, not understanding. She leaned forward, her voice dropping into something almost intimate.

"If people are afraid, they obey. If they're desperate, they comply. Hunger makes them quiet. Sickness keeps them too weak to riot. A frightened citizen will do anything to survive... including turn on their neighbor."

She stood, now, moving toward me like a viper poised to attack. She stopped just inches from me. Her perfume was cloying and thick, sickly sweet.

"If my people were safe, if they were happy and full and free... then they wouldn't need me. Not really. And they certainly wouldn't tolerate a system like mine." Her smile sharpened. "So I make sure they're never quite comfortable enough to dream."

I felt the air leave my lungs.

"People like you," she said, "you believe in the lie that the system is broken. That it just needs to be fixed. But you're wrong. It isn't broken." Her voice was a whisper now, just for me. "It's working exactly the way it was designed."

She stepped back, sweeping her arms wide like a game show host presenting her prize.

"The Reclamation Run was never about distributing resources," Veritas said, her voice like honey laced with poison. "It's about ensuring the Collectives stay just weak enough to never rise." Her eyes gleamed with something unholy, selfish righteousness, the kind of moral certainty that only comes from someone who's convinced themselves they're the savior in a story they wrote. She took a step forward, palm rising to cup my cheek like a mother comforting a child. I flinched at the contact. Her skin was cold, too soft.

"I offered you a deal once," she said softly, as if we were the only two people in the room. "And you threw it away. Normally, I wouldn't repeat myself. But you, Brexlyn... you are something rare."

I twisted away from her touch, and her hand fell.

"So," she said, voice lowering to a whisper so intimate I could feel it coil through my ears like a snake, "Out of the goodness of my heart, I have another offer."

She smiled. I didn't.

"Go on camera. Address the Collectives. Tell them the rebellion was a mistake. Tell them Praxis was right all along. Call off the Runaways. Tell them you were misled, manipulated...deluded, even. Say it however you like... just say it. And I'll let you live."

The bile crawled up my throat.

"I can see the refusal in your eyes," she said, chuckling like this was some tedious chess match she was still winning. "So, let me sweeten the deal for you." She leaned in, her next words curling like smoke around my ear.

"If you do this, I'll let you choose who else can be spared. Your Wildguard... or your brother. Your choice, of course."

The room spun.

"I won't even make you pick right away," she added with a smirk, "though I imagine you already know."

My mind reeled.

Jax. My little brother. My blood. My lifeline. Still just a kid, tucked away with Ava for now, but dying every day. Praxis didn't need to kill him with a bullet, they were killing him with denial. Denial of treatment. Denial of care. Denial of life.

And my Wildguard, my found family. The people who bled for this cause, who followed me into every dark place, who believed in me when I didn't believe in myself. Ezra, still gasping beside me. Thorne and Briar, bruised and beaten, yet still standing with silent defiance. Zaffir, barely conscious, clutching his camera in his hands as he barely held his eyes open wide enough to watch.

Briar shook her head slowly. Thorne gave a slight, solemn nod. Ezra's eyes, so full of pain and love, locked onto mine like he could transfer strength through his stare. And Zaffir... his fingers twitching over his camera like even now, even bleeding out, he still hoped it would bring us salvation.

My heart shattered and rebuilt itself in the same breath.

I looked then, beyond my circle, to the guards. Praxis soldiers, worn and battered just like us. Just like the citizens they were trained to subdue. And I wondered how many of them had family. How many believed they were the heroes, just like we did. How many were hurting, too.

I looked back to Veritas.

She stood poised, expectant, so sure she had me. So sure that power and cruelty and a gilded smile could crack a girl like me.

But if she thought I would kneel to save myself, or choose

who lived and who died just to give her the power we'd taken from her, then she never really knew me at all.

I stared her down.

"Thomas Halden," I whispered.

Evanora's brow furrowed, a flicker of confusion breaking through her icy composure.

"Horizon. The very first casualty of the Reclamation Run. He died trying to win electricity for his Collective."

Her eyes hardened, but I saw the twitch in her jaw.

"Lira Voss," I said louder. "Steelheart. Refused to compete in your sadistic Medical Trial when you told her to operate on her own mother. She begged you for mercy. You handed her a scalpel. Then had your guards shoot her when she refused. Her mother died on the table anyway."

My voice echoed. Clear. Anchored. I stood taller as the names formed like armor around me. I remembered their faces, their stories, each one stitched into my memory with blood and fire.

"Junia Rhade. Oasis. Lost her eyesight during the fuel trial. But Praxis still forced her to compete in the next trial. She died within five minutes. You broadcast her screams."

Evanora opened her mouth to speak, to lie, maybe. But I didn't give her the space.

"Mirelle Dox. Canyon. She was pregnant when you left her to survive in the Wilds alone for a week. When she died your cameras zoomed in on her stomach."

Each name lit a fuse inside me. Each memory sharpened my rage.

"Be quiet," Veritas hissed, her voice low and dangerous.

But I didn't stop. Name after name. Dozens of them, from a century of death and lies.

"Cassian Roe. Ember. Figured out a shortcut in the transportation trial through some tunnels, so Praxis collapsed them on top of him."

More names. More death. More pain.

"Elin Wren. Ironclad. She burnt to death while singing your national anthem. You called it poetic," I spat. "Angus Ratch. Saltspire. His last words were 'I love you, mom.'"

"Shut up!" She screeched.

"Nial Torvich," I choked, my voice faltering just once. "Canyon. He killed himself after surviving your twisted game. His little sister still lights a candle for him every single morning." My heart cracked open wide at the thought of Ava and her pain.

I saw her flinch.

"Elise Fairchild. Nile Fulton. Dani and Victor Cale. Beron Goaler. Winnie Fetter. Franklin Shale. Dominic Shallow—"

I heard Briar and Thorne inhale sharply beside me. Dominic. The body they'd found on day one.

"Fenly Nots. Lark Harbor!" I screamed. And the pain and anguish in my voice was enough to silence the room.

"Enough!" she shrieked, and her palm flew across my face with a crack that rang louder than her scream.

The sting bloomed across my cheek, but I stood still, eyes locked on hers. The guards flinched. Their hands slackened on my arms. And in that silence, something shifted. The shape of power had changed. I felt it.

I raised my voice again, this time a weapon forged from truth.

"Every single person Praxis has killed in the name of Reclamation. Is it hard to hear their names, Archon?"

She looked at me now like she wanted to silence me for good. And I knew she would.

"You want me to lie," I said. "You want me to smile into a camera, tell the Collectives that I made a mistake? That Praxis is just and honorable."

I stepped forward. The guards didn't stop me.

"Well, here's the truth." I looked her in the eyes and saw something finally crack.

"You think offering me a choice between the people I love will break me. My brother, my guard, my family. You think mercy is something you get to ration."

I smiled. And it was genuine.

"But I won't choose between them. I won't give you the performance you want. I would rather burn beside them than build a world where you get to call that mercy."

She stumbled back a step. Just one. But enough.

And for the first time, through the glitter and the politics, the gowns and the bloodshed, Evanora Veritas looked completely, and totally, afraid.

"Kill them," Veritas hissed, her voice laced with venom. Sharp, cold, unyielding.

I froze. Every muscle in my body clenched, steeling itself for the inevitable.

This was it. The end.

I closed my eyes for the briefest moment, breathing in the last seconds before death. I waited for the deafening crack of gunfire, for the final shudder of breath to leave the bodies around me. I waited for my Wildguard, my family, to be torn from me in an instant. I waited to follow them, to meet my brother in whatever came after, to die with some kind of grace if not victory.

But the shots never came.

Silence swelled.

Veritas realized it just as I did.

"What are you waiting for, you idiots?" she barked, voice tightening with disbelief. "I said *kill them!*"

The guards shifted.

But not toward us.

In perfect synchrony, their rifles turned, clicking into place, now aimed at her.

Veritas's expression cracked like glass beneath a hammer. Her posture faltered, her eyes snapping wide, throat tightening around the panic that suddenly rushed in.

"No," she breathed, stepping back, her voice shrill. "What are you doing? Stop! I am your Archon!"

One of the guards behind me moved. Slow and deliberate. His hand rose to his helmet and unlatched it with a hiss. He lifted it from his head and revealed a face beneath the armor. Not cold or mechanical, but human. A young man with dark, sweat-matted hair, blood on his cheek, dirt in every line of his face. His gaze flicked to Veritas. Then to me.

He looked just like us.

"For the will of the people," he said, steady and clear.

A single breath escaped me, sharp and staggering. The air rushed in behind it, filled with more than oxygen. I met his eyes.

"We survive," I replied softly.

Veritas stumbled backward, her polished façade fracturing with every step.

"You don't know what you're doing," she spat. "There are Praxis loyalists in every corridor, in every district, in every Collective. You cannot reach them all. You may have rallied a few lost souls, but you'll never touch the system. We destroyed your precious little hard drive."

Her desperation was a storm now, unraveling every part of her once-untouchable composure.

"Yes, you did," said Zaffir, his voice raspy from pain.

Everyone turned. He was still on the floor, blood seeping through his shirt. Slowly, he pushed himself up, hands still wrapped around the camera he'd shielded with his body like it was the most sacred thing he'd ever held.

"You destroyed the drive," he repeated. "But we didn't need it."

His fingers shifted on the camera.

And there it was.

The blinking red light.

The same one that had haunted me. That had captured our every breath, every tear, every moment of suffering during the Run. The one that made me feel like I was being hunted. Dehumanized. Watched.

But now, now it meant something else entirely.

It meant *witnesses*. It meant *truth*.

Zaffir stood, shaking but unshaken. His face was pale, lips split, but his voice was certain.

"All I have to do is load this footage," he said, raising the camera ever so slightly. "And all of Nexum will see. See Praxis and you for exactly who you are and what you've done."

A breath rippled through the room. Even the air seemed to pause, listening.

Then Zaffir took his first step toward the terminal.

Veritas lunged forward like a predator cornered, voice shrill with panic.

"*NO!* I order you to stop!" She shoved past the last of her illusion of control, stumbling toward Zaffir. But the guard behind me moved faster, stepping cleanly into her path, blocking her with calm finality.

"You will not do this!" she shrieked, her voice cracking, hysteria breaking through her regal mask.

Zaffir didn't flinch. He kept walking.

Her eyes darted around the room, desperately searching for a loyalist, an ally to take back the power slipping through her fingers. "One of you! Do something! Stop him!"

But no one moved.

Not for her.

Then her wild eyes found me, and I knew what she was going to do before she did. She charged, hands grasping the rifle slung across my chest.

I didn't resist. I let her take it.

She yanked it free and spun on her heel, raising it with unsteady hands. The muzzle jumped from Zaffir to the guards and back again, her breath coming in short, furious bursts.

"Stop right now or I'll shoot!" she barked. But her voice lacked the weight it once carried. It wasn't power. It was fear.

Zaffir didn't stop. Step by step, he crossed the floor toward the terminal. The guards around the room raised their rifles, ready to take their shot.

I couldn't help the smile that tugged at my lips. A quiet, knowing thing.

"I said stop!" she shouted again, voice ragged, trembling. "I swear, I'll—"

She didn't get to finish.

Zaffir reached the terminal. Slowly, he raised the camera and brought it toward the port. Her finger squeezed the trigger.

Click.

Nothing.

No shot. No bullet. Just silence.

Because after all, Ezra was right. An empty rifle *could* buy us some time.

I turned to him where he sat propped up nearby, and he met my gaze with that familiar, cocky smirk.

The screens in the room flickered, then glowed to life. One by one, monitors and walls lit up, casting a cold white light across the chamber. And then the image appeared.

Veritas. A vicious wild smirk as she spoke.

"People like you," her voice echoed, smooth and deliberate, *"believe the system is broken. That it just needs to be fixed. But you're wrong. It isn't broken..."*

Her whisper was barely audible in the room, but the playback had captured it perfectly. A secret no longer.

"...It's working exactly the way it was designed."

"No..." she whispered again, her gaze locking on the screen

as if sheer will could undo what had already begun. The blood drained from her face. Her arms dropped, rifle hanging useless in her hands.

"Turn it off!" she screamed, whirling toward the guards. They didn't budge.

She spun in place, unraveling. "*The Reclamation Run was never about distributing resources,*" her recorded voice played again, dripping like poisoned honey. "*It's about control. About ensuring the Collectives stay just weak enough to never rise.*"

"If you don't stop that feed right now, I swear, I will have you all executed!" she snapped, but her voice held no power anymore, just desperation.

The guards closed in. Not threatening. Just final.

Her own words continued playing. The carefully curated lies of the regime, shattered by the truth she'd hidden for decades. Then mine. The names. The people who'd been used as pawns of Praxis. They echoed through the room, drowning out her outraged and wild cries.

Zaffir stepped back from the terminal, limping toward me. He reached out, wrapping his arms around my shoulders and pressing a kiss to my temple.

"You did it," I whispered, overcome.

"No, Brexlyn," he murmured back. "*You* did."

Ezra reached us next. He folded us both into his arms, pressing a kiss to my lips, then to Zaffir's forehead. A breath of warmth in the coldest room we'd ever stood in.

Behind us, Veritas thrashed in vain.

"Don't touch me! Don't touch me!" she screamed as the guards seized her arms. Her movements were frantic, animalistic, her grandeur crumbling.

I didn't look back. I didn't need to. She was no longer worth the effort.

A hand brushed the small of my back. I turned, and there was Briar. Her eyes burned with light and something gentler, deeper. She kissed me like she'd been waiting her whole life for it, like it was the last kiss either of us might ever get.

Then Thorne was there, folding me into his arms. His hands slid up my spine, grounding me. Anchoring me. Home.

And then...a single gunshot.

Sharp and final.

Silence swept through the room like wind through ash.

The Archon was dead.

And Praxis?

Praxis had finally fallen.

CHAPTER
TWENTY-THREE

THORNE

THE NEXT THREE days were some of the hardest we'd ever lived through. We had won but the silence that followed victory wasn't what I'd call peaceful. It was hollow and heavy. There was damage to assess, lives to mourn, entire systems to unravel and rebuild. And time, as always, was working against us. For three long, tense days, Nexum had no governing body. No leader. And without leadership, especially with a population fueled by years of grief and injustice, chaos was waiting at the door.

It was Edgar Soonwater who finally stepped forward, calm and measured, and suggested that a temporary governing council be formed. A body made up of former Challengers, those who had fought, survived, and earned the people's trust. People who had lived in the Collectives, not above them. People who knew what it meant to hunger, to hurt, to hope.

The Wildguard hadn't planned to be part of that. None of us wanted power. After all we'd fought to tear down, the idea of standing on a pedestal felt wrong. But there was a responsibility in victory, and we owed it to the people who had followed us, believed in us. We agreed to serve, only until a new system could be voted on.

No one ever really talks about what comes after the rebellion. The war stories always end with the villain's fall. But the truth is, the hardest part is what follows. What do you do when the goal you spent your entire life chasing has finally been reached? When there's no more fight, only the fragile pieces of what's left?

So we made decisions.

There will be an election. A fair one. For the first time, every Collective will have a voice in who leads them next. My guess is it'll be Edgar. He's good. Not perfect, but he acknowledges those flaws. He's kind. He listens. And maybe he'll call himself Archon. Or President. Or something entirely new.

Praxis will be renamed too. The word alone makes people flinch, and we want a future unburdened by that fear. A new name. A clean beginning. One step at a time.

And as for us...we've taken up residence in the Archon's old house for the time being. That grand white building with its sweeping pillars and polished marble halls. The one where I once stood, trembling in a borrowed suit, and looked up to see the person who would change my life forever.

So when I walked back into that place, into those echoing halls, once thick with the weight of Veritas' rule, I didn't feel fear. Or resentment. I smiled. Because I didn't see tyranny. I didn't see Praxis.

I saw Bex.

I stood on the balcony, arms resting against the railing, watching the city below exhale. The streets, once patrolled and silenced, now hummed with cautious movement. People were out, talking, rebuilding.

The sun was dipping low, casting the whole city in soft gold. It was beautiful in a way I wasn't ready for. Beautiful and overwhelming. My breath caught, and I closed my eyes against the sting in them.

I heard the footsteps before I felt her, light, steady, familiar. I didn't turn. I didn't have to. I knew my sister's presence anywhere.

"Ma would be really proud of you," Briar said softly, slipping her arm through mine. Her head found its place on my shoulder..

Her words cracked something open in me. I nodded, jaw tight, the lump in my throat too thick to speak around.

"We finished what she started," she murmured, her voice like a balm over a long-aching wound. "We were her legacy."

A broken breath escaped me. "I wish she could have seen it," I said, my voice fragile. "I wish she could have known it wasn't all for nothing."

Briar held me a little tighter. "I think she does," she said simply, lifting her gaze to the sky.

I followed her eyes, looking up through the soft fading light. I used to stare at the stars and wonder if my mother could see the same ones, if maybe, somehow, through all the distance and time and absence, we were connected by the same pieces of sky.

Now, that same sky stretched wide and whole above us. And I didn't have to wonder anymore. I knew.

"She's there, you know," Briar said. "She's in every step we take forward. Every law we rewrite. Every kid who grows up not afraid of the dark. Every person who gets the resources they deserve without dying for the privilege."

The lump in my throat swelled, but this time it was paired with a strange, quiet peace.

"She always said the stars could tell the future," I whispered. "Maybe this was what she saw."

Briar smiled gently. "Then she knew we'd win. Even when we didn't believe it ourselves."

The stars blinked into view one by one. I leaned into Briar and let the silence speak for us.

"There you two are," Bex's voice rang out across the balcony, warm and rich and so achingly familiar it still made my heart stutter. Briar and I turned at the same time, instinctively parting just enough for her to slide between us. She always fit there. Like that space had waited for her all along.

She nestled in, one arm around each of us. I pressed a kiss to her lips, soft and slow, while Briar leaned in to kiss her cheek. Bex laughed, a little breathless from the double affection, and I felt it vibrate through her chest into mine.

"Hey, love," I whispered, still close enough that my lips brushed hers.

"Hi," she murmured back, her voice smiling.

"Did you hear anything yet?" Briar asked, her voice low but tense as she stepped into the room.

Bex looked up from the screen in her hands, worry etched into the lines around her eyes. "Nothing," she said softly. As soon as we could, we sent a message to Ava. Told her to bring Jax here. "Still no reply."

"Bex," Briar whispered. Pressing a kiss to her lips.

"I know," Bex whispered, and the sound of her voice twisted something in my chest.

I wrapped my arms around her from behind. "Don't worry, love," I murmured against her temple, brushing a kiss there. "I'm sure they're okay. Things are... strange right now. Even with the railway open, there's barely any infrastructure. No real schedules. No idea who's actually running things. And who knows how far they had run to stay safe during the Reclamation. It's not exactly an easy trek."

She leaned into me, just enough that I could feel some of the tension ease from her shoulders. "They're probably already on their way," I added gently. "Probably stuck at some broken checkpoint or waiting on a repurposed cargo train that hasn't run on time in twenty years."

I believed it. I really did. But I still couldn't stop checking the door every time I passed it. Just in case.

"Thanks," she said after a long moment. She turned in my arms and kissed me softly, slow and grateful. "For always knowing what to say."

"I don't always," I admitted against her lips. "But I mean it. They'll be here. He'll be here."

Her eyes closed. Just for a moment. And I held her tighter, because we both needed to believe it.

"I came to tell you both that dinner's ready," she added, glancing at Briar.

I raised an eyebrow. "Did Edgar cook again?" I asked, already grimacing. "No offense, but the man's better with battle strategy than he is with garlic."

Briar laughed, and Bex smacked my shoulder with a huff of fake outrage.

"He tries," she said, but her tone betrayed her agreement.

"Tries to assassinate us with flavorless stew," I teased, and Briar snorted.

"I don't care if it's charcoal soup," Briar said, pushing off from the railing. "I'm starving."

She turned toward the door, leaving me and Bex in the glow of the fading sunlight. Bex made to follow, but I wrapped my arms around her waist and pulled her back against me.

"Me too," I whispered into her ear, letting the words drip with a different kind of hunger.

She shivered in my arms, and I felt her breath catch in that way that never stopped thrilling me. Her hands came up to rest over mine, lacing our fingers together across her stomach.

"You're insatiable," she said, leaning back into me with a grin I could feel in the curve of her spine.

I kissed the spot just beneath her ear. "Only for you."

"You go on ahead, Bry," I called after my sister, without pulling my eyes from the gorgeous creature before me. "I'm gonna have an appetizer."

"Didn't need to know that!" Briar called over her shoulder with a chuckle, while she slipped out of the room.

The instant the door clicked shut behind her, I didn't hesitate. My hands found Bex's waist, pulling her close until there was no space left between us. I pressed her back against the wall, my whole body leaning into hers, and my mouth crashed onto hers with a hunger that had been building for far too long.

This kiss was desperate, urgent, a need that refused to be tamed. We'd shared plenty of kisses over the past few days, but none like this. None where I could finally touch her fully, where every nerve ending sparked with the electricity of what I'd been holding back.

Her scent wrapped around me, heady and warm, pulling me deeper into the moment. I drank in her kiss like it was the only thing keeping me tethered, matching her every breath, every trembling moan that escaped between us. The world around us blurred until all that existed was the heat of her skin against mine, the wild rhythm of our hearts, and the fierce, aching desire to never let go.

"Thorne," she whispered breathily as I sank to my knees before her. Her hands latched onto my shoulders as I stripped her bare, exposing her glorious, glistening core to me. I licked my lips as I leaned forward.

The first swipe of my tongue had her arching against the wall. The next drew a curse from between her perfect lips. The third sent her hands tangling into my hair. By the time I slid one of my fingers into her wet heat, she was nearly there already. I sucked her clit into my mouth, rolling the bud along my tongue, relishing the way it made her body shake beneath my hold.

"Yes, Thorne," she cried. "I'm so close," she added. My perfect woman was going to come all over my tongue, then my dick, and she was going to scream the whole time. I was giddy just thinking about it.

Another thrust of my fingers into her had her orgasm ripping through her. Her walls clenched around my fingers and I tasted her release on my tongue as she drenched my face. She pushed at my head, desperate to get me away from her sensitive throbbing pussy. But I wasn't nearly finished. I never would be.

I stood and freed my hardened cock from my pants, and I was entering her before she'd even come down from the high of her first orgasm. She screamed out, and I grunted against the feel of her body still pulsing with pleasure around my cock.

"Thorne, oh fuck," she moaned and I caught the sound with my mouth. I kissed her, saying every word I never could with each brush of my tongue against hers, and each thrust of my cock within her. This was the vow I'd made to her, not with rings or ceremonies, yet, at least. But with every breath, every touch, every time I chose her again and again. This was the love that had carried us through fire and ash. I would never want for anything else. Never need for more than what she already gave me just by being here, by being mine.

"Tell me you love me," I demanded.

The world outside could crumble, could still shake beneath the aftershocks of Praxis's fall. Rebuilding might take lifetimes. Systems might falter. People might stumble. But in my arms was the only truth I needed, her.

Her steady heartbeat. Her lips pressed to mine. Her warm body around mine like a promise I would never take for granted.

As long as I had her, her laugh, her fire, her fierce and tender love, I could survive anything. Even the end of the world.

I felt my release crest and as I slammed into her one last time, I knew that this was what victory meant to me. This was the future I'd fought for.

The future I'd do anything to protect.

"I love you," she replied, giving me everything I ever needed.

CHAPTER
TWENTY-FOUR

BEX

It had been a week since Praxis fell, and every day without word from Ava or Jax was like another stone added to the weight already pressing on my chest. Each hour stretched endlessly, tight with the ache of not knowing. My Wildguard had been doing their best. Hovering close, filling the silence with warmth and laughter and sensual touches, trying to draw my mind away from the gnawing uncertainty. But nothing could erase the cold truth that every night I went to bed without knowing if they were safe.

I startled awake, breath ragged, sweat cooling on my skin like guilt. My heart thundered, desperate and wild, as if trying to punch its way out of my chest.

Then, hands. Soft, familiar hands finding mine in the dark, grounding me like always.

Briar.

She eased me back down with a touch that had always meant safety, her fingers combing gently through my hair.

"Another nightmare?" she asked, her voice hushed with sleep and concern.

I nodded, my body sinking into the mattress beside hers. "Yeah," I whispered. My voice felt raw. "It's been a week, Briar."

"I know," she said, stroking my cheek with a featherlight touch that somehow held me together.

"What if they're not okay?" I asked, the words escaping before I could stop them. I hated giving shape to that fear. Hated how it lived in the corners of my mind, just waiting to come to the light.

She didn't answer right away. Instead, she traced the edge of my jaw with her fingertip, letting the quiet settle.

Finally, she spoke. "I have to believe they're okay," she said, her voice steady but soft. "I can't imagine we fought our way through everything... just to lose them now."

I nodded, because I felt the same. Because if I didn't hold onto that belief, I would unravel.

She slid her hand over my heart, her palm flat and warm against my chest. "Do you feel them here?" she asked.

I closed my eyes, breathing into her touch. And I did. Always had. As if somewhere, deep inside me, invisible threads still tied us together.

"I do," I said.

"Then they're okay," she said, with a certainty I didn't have but wanted so desperately to borrow. "You'd know if they weren't. You'd feel the absence."

I swallowed hard, letting the silence settle again. Letting her belief wrap around me like a blanket.

"I want to believe that," I whispered.

She kissed the space just above my heart and rested her head against my shoulder. "Then hold onto it. Just a little longer."

We stayed curled together in the hush of the morning, our bodies twined, our breaths falling into rhythm like the quietest song. The soft orange light of dawn filtered in through the window, casting long golden stripes across the bed, warming our skin in patches. Time seemed to slow, just for us, in the stillness of that early hour.

"I love you, Briar," I whispered, my voice low, reverent.

She turned her head, her sleepy eyes finding mine, and I leaned in to kiss her. Her lips were warm and familiar, home. I lingered there, then pulled away just enough to speak again. "I have something for you," I said, the words brushing against her mouth.

Her brows lifted slightly in curiosity as I slipped out from beneath the covers, the chill of the air stark compared to the warmth we'd just shared. I padded across the floor and opened the closet, heart thudding a little faster. It had taken days to make it back to the cabin where we'd hidden during the Run. By some miracle, it had remained mostly untouched, one small pocket of peace spared from the chaos.

I reached inside and gently took hold of the neck of the guitar. My fingers curled around the worn wood, familiar and solid. I turned, cradling it like something sacred as I walked back toward her.

Briar had sat up, the sheets falling loose around her hips. Her bare shoulders caught the sunlight, and her hair spilled over her back like a curtain of ink. When she saw what I held, her lips parted in a soft gasp.

"You went and got the guitar?" she breathed, her voice trembling slightly as her eyes shimmered with sudden tears.

"Of course I did," I said, kneeling before her. "I couldn't bear the thought of a world without your music. I hope I never have to go a single day without hearing your voice again."

Her eyes met mine, wide and shining with so much love it almost undid me. She took the guitar from my hands with a tenderness so beautiful. She traced her fingers over the curves of the wood like she was memorizing it all over again, then carefully set it beside her on the bed.

Without a word, she reached for me, tugging gently until I climbed into her lap, straddling her. Her arms circled my waist and she tucked her face against my chest like she was trying to crawl into my heartbeat. I held her close, one hand stroking through the silky waves of her hair, the other curled around her back, anchoring us in this moment.

She tilted her head up slightly, her lips brushing my skin. "Your heartbeat," she whispered, "it's like the steady beat to my favorite song."

Then our lips met. And this kiss was anything but lazy. There was a fire behind it. A passion. A song. I wanted to sing with her forever.

She guided my body like it was an instrument she knew by heart, her hands firm on my hips, gathering the fabric of my nightdress until it was bunched around my waist. Slowly, deliberately, she drew my body closer to hers until I felt the warmth of her press against mine.

A gasp slipped from my lips as I sank into the rhythm she set, my core brushing against hers. "Briar...," I sighed, voice shaking as it fell into the space between us.

Her grip tightened, and she pulled me closer still, brushing her nose along my jaw as she spoke, breathless and low. "That's it, beautiful," she murmured, voice like velvet. "Just like that."

Each word ignited a spark deep within, every shift of her hands a reminder that she knew every part of me, where to guide, where to tease, how to draw out the ache until it shimmered between us. At that moment, nothing else existed. Not the world beyond these walls, not the weight we'd been carrying. Just this — her hands, her voice, and the slow, consuming song.

"Come for me," she demanded in a soft, delicious whisper. Her fingers dug into my hips as we picked up the pace, our bodies chasing the euphoric friction. I bucked against her with wild abandon, her pupils were blown as her own climax crested.

"Oh my god, Briar," I cried out as my orgasm slammed into me, she didn't let my body's convulsions slow our rhythm, her hands pulled my hips against her as she pressed up against me. I felt the heat of her core as she slid against me, and I felt mind numbingly weightless as she moved my body where she needed it.

As I sank down from the mountaintop of my climax, I felt Briar reach her own. Her gaze was fixed to mine, burning bright as a trail of curses tumbled from her lips. Her hands, still tight on my hips, stilled completely, yet the pressure remained. I pulled her closer, looping my arms around the curve of her neck as she buried her face in the warmth of my chest. Her breath was soft and hot against my skin, and I pressed a kiss to the top of her head, holding her as we came down together.

Time stretched languid and slow until our breathing settled, until the world felt quiet and whole. Our grip on each other softened, but we didn't move apart. Not yet. Not when every beat of her heart pressed against mine felt like its own music.

I smiled down at her, brushing my fingers through the tangled threads of her hair, tucking a loose strand behind the delicate curve of her ear. Her eyes rose to meet mine, and in that moment I was lost. Captured by the depth and warmth in those amber depths. I watched her as she watched me, and felt myself fill with a quiet, unshakable awe.

This was Briar. The brave one, the tender one. The one who carried songs like sparks in her chest. And in that still space between breaths, I felt the love settle in my bones.

Knock. Knock.

The rap at the door came only a second before it was

pushed open. Zaffir, Ezra, and Thorne spilled into the room. I was still tangled in the sheets with Briar when I yanked the comforter over both of us, and Briar launched a pillow across the room.

"Get out!" she yelled as Zaffir caught it midair, grinning.

Thorne slapped a hand over his own eyes and nearly bumped into Ezra's back as he came to a halt.

I giggled at the scene, brushing hair out of my eyes, until I noticed the expressions on their faces. The humor drained from my body instantly. Whatever this was, it was serious.

"What is it?" I said sharply, rising to my feet and pulling the comforter tighter around myself.

Zaffir stepped closer, a faint, disbelieving smile tugging at the corners of his mouth. "They're here," he said.

My breath caught in my throat. "They're... alive?"

He nodded, and suddenly it felt like the air had been ripped from the room. Tears blurred my vision, and before I could think, I was bolting toward the door.

Ezra's hands caught me mid-sprint. I spun on him, fiery and desperate. "What are you doing? Let me go!"

He met my stare, soft and knowing. "You might want to get dressed first," he said quietly, brushing a glance down at the thin nightdress I was wearing.

Heat rose to my cheeks, and I gave a quick, breathless laugh as I nodded. "Right," I said, brushing away the sting of impatient tears. I pulled a casual dress from a nearby chair and shrugged into it with shaking hands, my heart beating wildly.

Then I was moving, flying down the hallway, bare feet skimming across the floor. I could hear them behind me — the others falling in step — but all I could focus on was the sound of my own heartbeat thundering in my ears. The air felt charged. The world felt brighter, electric.

I rounded the final corner and flew down the stairs, my breath burning in my chest. And then I stopped.

There they were.

Alive. Here.

Jax was tired and pale, leaning heavily on Ava, but the moment his eyes met mine, a smile broke across his face like the rising sun. Without thinking, I was moving, running to him, dropping to my knees as soon as I was within reach. My arms wrapped around him, holding him as gently as I could as he sank down to hug me in return.

"Oh, Sprout," I whispered into the curve of his neck as the sob bubbled from my chest. "I missed you so much."

"Hey, Bex," he said, voice shaking but strong.

I pulled back just enough to really look at him, brushing the hair from his forehead as the tears streamed down my cheeks. Against every odd, every fear, every desperate prayer thrown to the stars... he was here.

I sank back on my heels and gripped his shoulders, scanning every inch of him like I could memorize this moment forever. "How are you?" I asked, voice shaking. "How do you feel?"

He shrugged out of my hold the way he always did when he felt like I was fussing too much, and a shy, boyish giggle bubbled from his chest. "I'm fine!" he squealed, grinning as if to prove it.

"Yeah," I breathed, brushing a hand lovingly through the messy strands of hair falling across his forehead. "Yeah, you are." My voice cracked, and I smiled down at him like I could bottle this moment, like it could carry us through every dark day we'd ever survived.

Then I looked up and met Ava's gaze.

My best friend. Her blonde hair was messy, streaked with dust and sweat, and she was leaning hard on the crutch at her side, exhausted from the long journey that brought them home. But she was here.

I rose to my feet, and she pulled me into her arms before I

could say a word. We sank into each other, the years of heart-break and terror and sacrifice pressing down, and somehow lifting, just for a moment.

"Thank you, Ava," I whispered into her shoulder. "Thank you for keeping my brother safe."

Her arms tightened around me until it felt like she'd never let go. "Thank you," she said hoarsely, voice shaking, "for avenging mine."

We stood like that for a long moment, wrapped in an embrace built from threads of pain and strength and remembrance. The loss of her brother would always be a part of us, a flame that refused to extinguish, but right now, for just this moment, it felt like a quiet ember. Not burning. Not suffocating. Just there, reminding us of how far we'd come.

I pulled back and smiled at her as she wiped tears from her eyes, brushing one from my own.

Behind me, I heard Jax shift, and when I glanced over my shoulder, I found him staring curiously at Zaffir.

"Who are you?" he asked, head tilted, voice soft and shy.

I smiled, brushing a hand over Jax's hair as I glanced toward Zaffir and the rest of the Wildguard.

"Sprout, this is Zaffir," I said, brushing a hand through Jax's hair as I introduced him. Zaffir sank down to one knee, resting on the balls of his feet until he was closer to Jax's level. The warm light from the windows caught the hint of emotion burning in his golden eyes as he offered Jax his hand.

For a moment, Jax just studied him. His wary gaze, sharp and assessing for a boy so young, flicked from Zaffir's hand to the rest of him, and then to me.

"Did you help Bex save the world?" he asked quietly, brushing a strand of hair from his own forehead.

My breath lodged in my throat, and I felt the sting of tears rising. My little boy thought I saved the world.

Zaffir smiled, soft and genuine, as if the question itself was an honor. "She didn't need my help," he said, voice low and confident, "but I'd do anything for her."

Jax watched him for a long moment, then gave a shy nod and placed his small hand in Zaffir's. The sight nearly undid me.

Ava spoke up then, brushing hair from her tired, sun-creased forehead. "You recognize Thorne and Briar from the screens, right, kiddo?"

Jax glanced over, blinking at the tall, serene man and the luminous woman beside him. "I like your songs," he said shyly to Briar.

Briar sank down until she was closer to him, smiling that warm, open smile that had brought strength to so many of us. "Then I'll teach you some," she promised, brushing a hand across his shoulder, and Jax beamed.

"And this is Ezra," I said, leaning closer to the man who was quietly holding the edges of the room, watchful and wary until now.

Jax crossed to him, craning his neck to look up, and offered the kind of bold, unfiltered statement only a child can make. "I like your name," he announced.

Ezra's deep chuckle rumbled from his chest as he sank down to Jax's level, brushing hair out of the boy's eyes. "Then you've got good taste, kid," he said, smiling.

"Come on," Thorne said, heading to lead Ava and Jax down the long hallway. "Let's get you settled, maybe a hot bath, some fresh clothes."

Jax glanced back over his shoulder, brushing hair from his eyes, a hint of worry tugging at the edges of his voice.

"Don't worry, Sprout," I promised softly, brushing my hand over his. "I'm not going anywhere."

He gave a shy smile and tightened his grip around mine before releasing it and following Ava and Thorne down the hall.

I watched until they disappeared, until the sound of their voices ebbed into silence. The world was still broken. The ruins of Praxis still smoldered in places. But for the first time in a long, long while, I had a big family. And that family was whole. We were together. We were here.

CHAPTER
TWENTY-FIVE

BEX

My nerves felt like frayed threads as we stood at the entryway of the medical building. The place was run down, bustling quietly with activity, and yet every sound felt muffled, every color too sharp. Jax and Ava had been back with us for two weeks now, and every second felt like borrowed time. Even that felt like too long to wait for this moment, after all the years of desperation and heartbreak. But things were still tense in the city, and resources weren't easy to secure right away, even as Edgar worked to redistribute them fairly.

I tightened my grip around Jax's hand, brushing my thumb over the small, faint scars that marked his skin. This was supposed to be a hopeful moment. But I felt rooted to the spot, unable to take a step, unable to breathe.

"Hey, love," Thorne said quietly, brushing a shoulder against mine. "You okay?"

I nodded, but the motion felt like a lie. My legs refused to move.

"Jaxy," Briar said softly, leaning down until she was eye

level with him, brushing hair from his forehead. "Why don't you and I go inside, get you signed in? Bex will be right behind us."

Jax didn't hesitate. He offered her that shy, crooked smile that I cherished and laced his hand with hers, disappearing through the door with Briar, whom he quickly took a liking too. He was just as desperate for a family as I was. And words couldn't explain the joy I felt knowing that my Wildguard could be that family for both of us.

I watched until the door swung shut behind them, swallowing hard as decades of fear bubbled to the surface. Suddenly, I was shaking. Suddenly, I felt like I was falling.

Thorne was the first to move, looping strong arms around my waist and hauling me tight against him. I sank into the solid warmth of him as Ezra pressed in close, brushing the line of my spine with the palm of his hand. Zaffir was right there too, brushing hair out of my eyes and tucking it behind my ear.

"What's wrong, Brexlyn?" Zaffir asked, voice low and soft, brushing the edge of my desperation.

"Are you alright?" Ezra asked quietly, brushing a kiss just below the angle of my jaw.

I pressed a shaking hand to my chest, forcing myself to draw breath when Zaffir's voice came low and commanding. "Breathe for us, baby."

I tried. The air came in ragged, felt like swallowing broken glass. But I kept going until it was deep enough to sting, until I felt the sting of tears burning my eyes.

"I'm sorry," I finally whispered, brushing the heels of my hands across my damp cheeks. "I should be over the moon right now. This is what we've been fighting for. This is why we kept going. But..."

"Love," Thorne said, brushing the side of my face with the

tips of his fingers. "You don't owe us an explanation. You don't owe an apology for being scared."

"What do you need?" Zaffir pressed, brushing a hand down the curve of my spine.

I shook my head, swallowing hard, looking from one to the next until my gaze landed on Ezra. "I don't know," I confessed, voice shaking. "I'm just... scared."

"You're scared," Ezra repeated quietly, brushing hair out of my eyes.

I met those deep green eyes and felt the weight of every unspoken thought settle between us.

Ezra pulled me closer, brushing a kiss to the side of my temple as he spoke. "That's what you're afraid of," he said, voice low, soft and sure. "That after all this fighting, after every second we've survived, after every night you refused to give up on him... you're afraid it's too late."

I nodded, leaning harder into him as the sting bubbled into quiet sobs. The three of them surrounded me, pressed close until the shaking ebbed and the terror gave way to something quieter, smaller.

Thorne pressed a kiss to the top of my head. "He's going to be okay, Brexlyn. Whatever happens, we're here. We're with you."

Zaffir framed my face with long, warm hands, brushing away a stray tear.

Ezra pressed closer from behind, resting a hand on my waist, brushing his nose along the shell of my ear as he spoke, low and soft. "That boy is here because you refused to give up on him."

I drew a breath then, deeper than the one before, brushing the sting of fresh tears from my lashes as I pressed into the circle of the people I loved. The world was still broken. The ruins of Praxis still haunted every corner of this city. But right here, pressed between the three men who refused to let me carry this weight alone, I felt my feet finding solid ground.

With my hands tangled with theirs and their support guiding me, we stepped across the threshold into the hospital.

"JAX!" I called, leaning out the door as I watched him and Thorne chasing after a scuffed old ball across the lawn. "You heard what the doctor said. You need to rest after treatments, remember?"

He didn't reply at first, focusing every ounce of concentration on aligning himself, wobbling for a moment before swinging a leg. The ball rolled forward, wobbly but strong, and Thorne let out an approving whoop as it bumped to a halt just shy of him.

"He also said 'controlled exercise' was important for rebuilding strength," Thorne called out, grinning like the proud big brother he was quickly becoming.

"Traitor," I sighed, unable to hide the smile tugging at the corners of my mouth as Jax looked back at me, brushing hair from his sweaty forehead, grinning like he wasn't in the constant pain I knew he felt.

Briar, perched nearby, offered a slow clap and a wink, as she shuffled closer to snag the ball.

The doctors weren't shy about how hard the years had been on Jax, how much damage had been done by going so long without the treatment he needed. The illness had progressed further than any of us would've hoped. But despite it all, they were hopeful. Hopeful that we could give him more years, more moments to laugh, to play, to tease, to just be a kid surrounded by people who cherished him.

How many more? They couldn't say. No one could. But it didn't matter. Whatever time he had left would be ours to fill with warmth, with belonging, with a love that refused to run out. Every breath he drew was a gift, and every single day we got to spend with him would always be enough.

Ava sank down beside me on the deck with a quiet sigh, brushing a hand over the wood beneath us as she watched my brother race across the yard as fast as he could. She set her crutches off to the side with a sigh. The sun was warm on our shoulders, and for a moment, the world felt like it was holding its breath just for us.

"You've made something really beautiful here, Bex," she said softly.

I smiled, brushing hair out of my eyes and looking at the scene in front of us. Jax chasing after a ball as Thorne and Briar egged him on, their laughter rising like music. "Yeah," I whispered. "But I never could've done it without you."

Ava glanced at me, puzzlement in her tired, strong gaze. So I turned to her and pressed my hand over hers. "Ava, you kept him safe. You protected him. You knew what was coming and refused to give Praxis the chance to use him against me. I couldn't have done any of this if Veritas had gotten to him first."

Ava offered a shy smile, brushing a strand of hair from her forehead. "I was a part of the Runaways for a long time," she said quietly, brushing a finger across the moth tattooed on the inside of her wrist. "After Nial died, I promised myself I'd do whatever I could to bring Praxis down. Whatever it cost."

I watched her, brushing my thumb over that same tattoo. "Why didn't you tell me?" The question came out soft, and I hoped she could hear the trust behind it.

Her voice was even softer when she spoke. "You always had more to lose than I did, Bex. You had Jax. I didn't want you to have to choose between standing with the resistance and keeping him safe. So I kept it to myself until you went and found it yourself."

She glanced out at Jax, laughing as Thorne scooped him up and spun him in a circle. The sound bubbled across the lawn, filling every crack and space where pain had lived for too long.

Ava smiled faintly and shrugged. "Then you met Thorne and Briar, and I knew. The Greys are kind of Runaway royalty. I saw the way you looked at them. They way they trusted you. And then I knew it...you were always going to fight. Always going to rise. It's who you are, Bex. The one who fights for those who can't. The one who finds a way."

She adjusted herself, brushing a hand down the thigh where her decades old injury still pained her. "I've believed in you since we were kids, Bex. And I've never been so proud to call someone my sister."

I pulled her into a tight hug, brushing my nose into the soft fabric of her shirt. "I love you, Ava," I whispered.

She gave a quiet chuckle as she stood, adjusting the crutch under her arm. "Yeah, yeah. Now, if you'll excuse me, I have an appointment to get fitted for a prosthetic."

I smiled, brushing a hand down her arm as she started off. "Congratulations, Ava. I'm so happy for you."

She glanced back with a wink. "Thank you, for making it a possibility."

As she walked away, I turned to watch the trio still playing in the yard. Jax, with that stubborn streak he got from too many days trying to run before he could walk, was chasing after the ball again.

"Careful, Jax!" I called out.

"I'm fine, Bex!" he yelled back, voice dripping with the kind of sass I'd only ever heard from a certain Grey twin.

"Yeah Bex, we're fine," Thorne teased.

I glanced at him, arching an eyebrow. He shrugged and offered a sheepish laugh. Whatever mischief was blooming between those two was going to be a force of nature.

I crossed my arms, shaking my head with a smile as Ezra came up beside me, looping an arm across my shoulders and brushing a kiss to the top of my head. "They're okay, beautiful," he promised quietly. "Look at him. He's laughing. He's playing. He's living."

I glanced at the trio one more time. Briar brushing grass from Jax's knees, Thorne tossing the ball in the air as he called for another round, and felt a wave of warmth settle deep within me.

"Yeah," I breathed, brushing my hand down the length of Ezra's arm. "I think you're right."

Then Zaffir was beside us, brushing a kiss to my cheek, looping an arm low around my waist. His long fingers brushed teasingly across Ezra's torso, earning him a narrowed gaze that sparked tension in Ezra's jaw. Zaffir only winked, brushing a whisper across the shell of my ear.

"I've got something I want to show you," he said, voice low and teasing.

I glanced out across the lawn to where Jax was shrieking with laughter as Briar stole the ball from under his nose.

"They'll be fine," Zaffir promised, brushing a kiss to the side of my neck. "Come with me."

Ezra fell into step beside us, brushing the length of my spine as we crossed the threshold and started down the long, echoing hallway.

"Where are you taking her?" Ezra called, brushing a hand down Zaffir's shoulder.

"By all means, come along," Zaffir replied with a crooked smirk, breaking into a slow jog as he pulled us down the corridors.

I followed, breathless, grinning as the sound of our footsteps melded together. No matter how long we spent in these towering halls, it never felt like a home. These walls still held too many echoes, too much pain, too much history.

I didn't know what home was anymore. I hoped we could find it someday. Or make a new one. But I did know that no matter where we ended up, as long as I had my Wildguard, then there would be happiness.

Zaffir pushed open one of the heavy double doors, and it gave a soft, tired groan. The room beyond was dark, nearly pitch black, except for a faint shimmer from the domed ceiling above. He pulled me inside, and as the door clicked shut, my eyes began to adjust. Slowly, the darkness revealed itself, a ceiling littered with stars. Not just a handful, but countless tiny lights, swirling and twinkling like a living masterpiece.

I drew in a breath, brushing a hand across my mouth. "What is this place?" I asked, voice soft and awestruck.

Ezra stepped closer, brushing the back of my hand as he tilted his head toward the dome. "It's called a planetarium," he said quietly, brushing a finger toward the giant lens that rose from the center of the room. "With this device, you can watch whole galaxies move. See the universe as it was meant to be seen."

Zaffir's hand tightened around mine, tugging me to the center where he'd laid a blanket out across the floor. A picnic basket waited for us, and as I sank down beside it, Ezra followed, brushing a hand across my knee.

"Just so you know," Zaffir said with a wink, "I was informed to tell you these sandwiches are courtesy of *Restaurante De La Grey*."

I smiled so hard it hurt as I sank down, brushing a hand across the blanket. Ezra sank down beside me, brushing a warm hand across my thigh.

"I don't even know what to say," I whispered, brushing a hand across my mouth as I looked between the two of them and then up at the stars.

"Then don't say anything yet," Zaffir said, brushing a knuckle down my jaw. "I have more to show you."

He rose, crossed to a nearby terminal, and pressed a few keys. Suddenly, a soft hum resonated through the room, and music floated down from hidden speakers. Gentle strings and soft piano surrounded us, filling the space until it felt like the stars themselves were singing.

"Close your eyes for a moment," Zaffir said quietly, brushing my hand as he sank down beside us. I did as he asked. "And when you open them... I want you to see yourself the way I always have."

I drew in a breath and opened my eyes.

The ceiling came alive. The stars winked out, replaced by a montage of moments, moments I hadn't even noticed he was capturing. My reflection winked down at me. At first, it was a shot of me from the night of the vote in Canyon, worried and brushing hair from my forehead. Then another, sitting on the train, tears streaking down as I spoke about my brother. Another as Nova's hands framed my face, brushing color across my skin. Another still, laughing openly, wildly. Moments when my jaw was set, when my chin rose and my voice refused to falter.

Each moment rolled across the dome like a whisper of who I was. Or who I had always wanted to be. They were pieces of a person he'd witnessed every step of the way. My breath hitched as the montage ended and the stars winked back to life, swirling and burning brighter than before.

For a moment, I didn't move. Couldn't speak. The sting of tears blurred the stars above. Then I turned sharply, launched myself into Zaffir's arms, and wrapped myself around him.

"Thank you," I breathed, pressing my forehead to his. "Thank you for seeing the real me...even when I couldn't't."

He sank into the embrace, brushing a hand down my spine until it came to rest low on my hip. Then he pulled back just enough for our eyes to find each other. Those golden irises shimmered in the starlight, soft and burning, and then he was kissing me, long and slow and deep, stealing the breath from my lungs.

A sound bubbled low in my chest as I opened for him, his tongue brushing the seam of my mouth until I yielded.

Beside us, I felt Ezra's hand glide down the line of my spine. Grounding, warm, certain. The stars basked us in shimmering light in a moment that felt as infinite as the galaxies sprawling across the dome.

"I have something for you too, beautiful," Ezra said quietly, brushing a hand down the curve of my spine. When I turned to him, I noticed the set of keys hanging from his long fingers, winking in the soft light. My breath caught as I looked from the keys to his smiling face.

"What..." I stammered, blinking down at them. "What is this?"

He pressed the keys into my palm and folded my fingers around them. "The keys to our cabin."

I gaped, brushing a thumb across the metal. "What do you mean?"

"I don't know if 'home' will ever look like it used to," Ezra said slowly, brushing hair from my cheek, "and after Kade died, 'home' stopped being Canyon for me. This place..." He waved loosely toward the room we were in. "This place was never going to be home. But you, Bex? You have always and will always be my home." His eyes flicked to Zaffir over my shoulder. "You both will."

Zaffir smiled then, brushing a hand along Ezra's jaw as Ezra glanced down at him. "And Thorne and Briar," Ezra added, brushing a finger under my chin, "and Ava. And Jax. You're my family. All of you. Whatever we build from here on out, it starts with that."

I pressed the keys to my chest, unable to find words as he went on. "I talked with Edgar. I told him we were happy to help him get the world back on its feet, but I also made it clear that we needed a place for ourselves. So he gave us the Challengers' village."

"The village?" I asked, voice rising as if I hadn't heard right.

"Every single cabin there is ours to fill, ours to make a home. There's one for Ava. One for Jax and you. And this one..." He tapped the second key resting in my palm. "This one is ours. The Wildguard. The place where we found each other, where we learned who we were to each other and what we could become. Where we learned to trust and forgive and laugh and live. The place where this family came from. This key is for us, Bex."

My fingers shook as I clenched both keys tight. The sting of tears blurred my vision until I was looking at him and Zaffir through a mist of emotion. Ezra smiled, brushing the pad of his thumb across my wet cheek.

"This is the home that matters now," he said softly. "This family is what matters now."

I surged forward before he could say another word, cupping his face in my hands and capturing his mouth with mine. It was a long, deep kiss, a kiss that spoke of belonging, of belonging nowhere except to one another.

My tongue sought out Ezra's, deepening the kiss as I felt the heat of his hands trail down the curve of my spine. Suddenly, Zaffir was pressed against my back, brushing a trail of slow, burning kisses along the side of my neck. I sighed into Ezra's mouth, surrendering to the warmth and weight of both of their bodies enveloping mine.

My hands roamed over Ezra's chest until I found the hem of his shirt, tugging it upward until it came free, exposing every hard line of his torso. Zaffir whistled low in my ear as the sight of him came fully into view, strong, broad, and beautiful.

I tilted my head back over my shoulder, finding Zaffir's

mouth and capturing it in a languid, burning kiss. Meanwhile, Ezra worked the straps of my tank top down from my shoulders, brushing calloused fingers across bare skin as he pulled it slowly down my arms, until I was bared to the room and the warmth of their gazes.

For a moment, we were suspended there, breathless and tangled together, hands and mouths finding every surface, every curve, every scar as we sank deeper into one another.

"Brexlyn," Zaffir's voice was a low, teasing whisper brushing against the shell of my ear, sending a shiver down my spine. "Did you enjoy Ezra's gift?"

I nodded, breathless, unable to piece together words as both of their hands roamed over my skin, leaving trails of fire in their wake.

"Then don't you think he deserves a proper thank you?" Zaffir purred.

I met those molten gold eyes, then glanced toward Ezra, who was leaning back on the ground now, legs slightly parted, pupils blown wide, every inch of him focused on us as we sank down to him. Together, Zaffir and I closed the space between us and Ezra like predators approaching a prize.

I hooked a finger into the band of Ezra's pants and drew them down slowly, teasing every inch of skin as I uncovered him, until he was bare before us. The sharp intake of his breath spoke louder than words.

Beside me, Zaffir sank closer, brushing a kiss across Ezra's hip as I drew my gaze up to Ezra's dark, smoldering eyes and smiled.

"Yeah," I said, brushing my palm across Ezra's thigh as I sank closer, brushing my lips just shy of where he needed them most, "I think he does."

I settled in between his spread legs and wrapped my fingers around his hard length. He exhaled sharply at the first brush of my hand against him. I began pumping, slowly, tauntingly and he was lost to the sensation. I dropped my mouth and took Ezra all the way to the base. My lips tightened around him, my tongue rubbing against the underside of his hard shaft as I drank him in.

"Oh fuck," Ezra groaned, his head falling back.

"God, you are beautiful on your knees," Zaffir said from behind me as I continued to bob on Ezra's cock. I felt his fingers dance along my thighs, drawing taunting circles closer and closer to my center. I wiggled my ass for him, hoping he'd get the point. Finally his fingers brushed against my core, finding me wet and ready of course. I always was for my Wildguard.

I was taking Ezra as deep as I could manage in my throat, while Zaffir teased my clit with his masterful fingers.

"You know," I said, releasing Ezra with a *pop*. "Ezra technically got you a house too," I teased with darkened eyes.

Zaffir met my gaze, removing his fingers and sliding them into his mouth for a taste of my arousal. His golden eyes glinted with delight and mischievousness.

"You're right, Brexlyn," he said, crawling on the blanket beside me, forcing Ezra to widen his legs to accommodate us both. Ezra watched us with wide eyes, and heaving breath.

Zaffir lowered his mouth to Ezra's hard shaft, and licked from base to tip.

"Fuck," Ezra cursed, his fingers knotting in the blanket beside him.

"Hmm," Zaffir said, licking his lips. "Delicious."

Then we both descended on Ezra's cock. Within moments we were both running our lips and tongue over him in perfect tandem. We licked and kissed each other on and around Ezra. He drove his hips so that his cock thrust between our mouths.

Ezra's hand tangled in my hair and pulled me off of his cock and dragged my lips to his. He drank the taste of us off his lips in our kiss. "I need to taste you," he demanded. Pulling me up his body until I was straddling his shoulders backwards, facing Zaffir. Zaffir still masterfully sucked and swallowed at Ezra, as Ezra pulled my hips down. He devoured my pussy like it was the only thing he had ever wanted to do, and I screamed out his name. Zaffir watched us with burning eyes as his tongue painted Ezra's cock.

I bucked my hips, unable to stop myself from chasing the climax that was building in my lower belly. Zaffir reached a hand up and pressed his skillful fingers back against my clit and the pressure was just enough to have me detonating onto Ezra's mouth. He drank up every ounce of my arousal with eager laps of his tongue.

I felt them maneuver me around so that I was now laying down on Ezra, my back against his chest. Zaffir didn't wait for me to catch my breath, he simply lined up and slammed his cock into my pulsing core.

"Zaffir!" I cried out, as he fucked me though the shock-waves of my orgasm as Ezra held me from below.

I felt his hands snaking around to where Zaffir and I were joined and gently prodding at my tight entrance. I groaned as he slid the first finger in, and then the second. By the time he stretched me with the third finger Zaffir and I were both panting and desperate for more.

"Get inside of her now, Ezra," Zaffir commanded through his tenuous composure. "I need to feel you both."

Ezra removed his fingers, and replaced them with the head of his cock. This new angle made his intrusion utterly delicious and beautifully painful. I gasped as he slowly sank into me, inch by glorious inch. Zaffir slowed to allow us both to feel the slow claiming. When Ezra was fully seated, the three of us breathed heavily together, our chests rising and falling in rhythm.

Zaffir's eyes met mine, then flicked toward Ezra.

"I love you both," he whispered.

My heart cracked wide open, all my love, all my happiness bleeding into this perfect moment.

"You know how I feel about both of you," I gasped, still lost in the sensations of both of them stretching me so perfectly.

"Yeah," Ezra said, a strained, but solemn sound. "I fucking love you both."

Then Zaffir slammed into me, making us both groan. He thrust his hips with a speed that perfectly lit a fire under my skin. Ezra began thrusting his hips below me in time and I felt the shimmering stars above us as if they were in my veins.

Zaffir pinched my clit as he thrust into me and I cried out. I chanted his name, Ezra's name, the sound blending with our breathing and moans. The chorus was too much to handle. The love flowing between us was everything I could ever have wanted. I came hard, clamping around them both even as they continued fucking me.

My body lit with a red hot inferno. My skin tingled as the orgasm ebbed and settled into my weary bones. Zaffir and Ezra didn't pause as they chased their own orgasms. When they finally came together, it was the most genuine relief.

The symphony of their groans of pleasure mixed with my sighs of pure bliss echoed through the room. And for a long moment, nobody spoke, nobody moved.

Finally, they slid out of me, leaving me feeling empty, but satisfied. I sank into the warmth of their bodies, surrounded by the soft rise and fall of breathing and the quiet hum of the planetarium's stars above. We lay tangled together on the blanket, a mess of limbs and warmth.

About twenty minutes later, the door whispered open and Thorne and Briar slipped inside.

"You three look like you had fun," Thorne teased, brushing a hand through my hair as he sank down on the blanket above my head, leaning back to watch the stars.

"Jax is passed out, sleeping soundly," Briar said quietly as she settled between my legs, resting her head on my thigh.

Each of the four of them had a hand resting on me somehow, a palm brushing my hip, a hand resting over mine, a weight pressed lovingly to my leg. All of them tethering themselves to me. All of them making sure I felt every heartbeat of our family.

I smiled down at Briar, brushing a strand of hair from her forehead, and glanced at the rest of them. Zaffir, Ezra, Thorne, and Briar. My Wildguard. My heart.

Around us, the stars winked and shimmered across the dome. Shining on us, the way Thorne's mother always promised it would. The world was still rebuilding. The battles weren't over. There would be new trials, new heartbreaks, new victories waiting in the years beyond. But right here, surrounded by these hands, these beating hearts, this unshakable warmth, I felt certain of one thing.

After years of ruin and loss, after heartbreak upon heartbreak, after fighting for every breath we drew, we had reclaimed the one thing that had been lost for so long.

Hope.

EPILOGUE

BEX

FIFTEEN YEARS Later

MY FINGERS BRUSHED the cool stone in front of me, tracing the etched date like a familiar scar. I let my hand linger, grounding myself as best I could whenever I came here. Then, slowly, I laid the bouquet at the base of the headstone. Wildflowers, his favorite.

"Hey, Jax," I whispered, my voice soft, barely more than a breath.

After the fall of Praxis, the world changed. It wasn't instant. Nothing that deep-rooted ever is. But the moment their walls crumbled and their lies were exposed, something real began to take hold. Resources stopped being handed out like prizes. Healthcare was no longer a privilege, it became a right. And when the system finally opened its doors to everyone, Jax walked through them.

The diagnosis had come too early. The care had come too

late. But even so, despite the years of neglect, the ignored symptoms, the way the system once deemed him not worth saving, he lived.

Eleven more years.

Eleven *beautiful*, miraculous, hard-won years.

Years where he laughed. Sang. Sat at the kitchen table every morning with a cup of too-hot tea and a crooked grin. Years filled with stories, stargazing, telling stories in the dark. Years where he truly *lived*, no longer just surviving in the shadow of a broken system.

And when he finally passed, it wasn't because Praxis let him slip through the cracks. It was because his body was ready. He was at peace. Surrounded by us. His family. His hand wrapped in mine, the sun low and golden in the sky.

Still... sometimes I wonder.

If we'd toppled Praxis earlier... If we'd won more trials sooner... Maybe he could've had more than sixteen years on this Earth. Maybe he could've had twenty. Maybe he could still be here with me now.

Praxis has been a distant memory for fifteen years, but its corruption... it still lingers. Still claims lives. It probably always will. You can't undo a century of destruction overnight. Healing takes time. Justice takes time.

But I've learned I can't live in the what-ifs anymore.

Every single year I got to spend with Jax was a gift. A miracle Praxis never meant for us to have. And I won't taint his memory by drowning it in bitterness.

I smiled as I looked down at the flowers, vibrant against the grey stone.

"I miss you so much. Thank you for holding on," I said. "For staying as long as you could. I hope you're still watching the stars somewhere."

And in the breeze that whispered through the grass, I almost heard him say, *I always am.*

"Jaxson is unruly as ever, taking after his uncle," I said with a soft laugh, brushing a bit of moss from the top of the stone. "I swear he gets more like you every single day. I wish you could have met him. You would've adored him."

Just as the words left my mouth, a familiar shriek pierced the stillness.

"Momma!"

I turned just in time to catch the blur of motion that was my four-year-old, as he barreled into my arms with full-force enthusiasm. I laughed, steadying myself as I wrapped him up in a hug.

"Hey there, sprout," I murmured, smiling at my wild, bright-eyed boy.

"Jaxson Kade! Momma said to stay over here!" came the exasperated call from a little ways off.

My oldest approached with the kind of composed exasperation only an older sibling could master. Her brown eyes were a mirror of Briar's, shimmering with intelligence and calm. Her dark brown curls bounced with each step, and her face was peppered with the freckles I used to count on one of her father's noses. At eight, she already walked like someone older than her years, steady, graceful, and sharp-eyed.

"Come on over, you two," I said, reaching out and pulling her close while settling both kids on my lap. Their warmth against me made the air feel a little less heavy. "Come say hi to your uncle."

"Hi, Uncle Jax," Fenly Lark said, lifting a hand to wave at the stone with a knowing, gentle smile.

"Hi!" Jaxson echoed brightly, bouncing a little where he sat.

"Do you think he can hear us?" She asked, her voice soft.

"Oh, I know he can," I replied, smoothing a hand through her curls.

"Really?" Jaxson twisted around in my arms to look up at me with wide, earnest eyes.

"Absolutely," I said with certainty.

"Okay." He slid off my lap, kneeling solemnly before the headstone. "Psst, Uncle Jax... can you tell Dada Ezra that he should let me have ice cream tonight?"

A bright, bubbling laugh escaped me just as I heard the steady crunch of approaching footsteps.

"You don't need to bribe your uncle to get ice cream, kiddo," Ezra said warmly, sweeping Jaxson up into his arms with ease. Jaxson shrieked in playful protest, kicking his feet as Ezra hoisted him into the air. "I told you all you needed to do was clean your room."

Ezra looked... older, yes, but time had only sharpened what made him captivating. His salt-and-pepper hair suited him so well, giving him a kind of steady presence. The creases around his eyes were more defined now, but they only made his smiles warmer, richer. I still remembered the first time I saw him, lit up on that stage, like an unobtainable mystery but this version of him, the father, the partner. This version was even more beautiful.

"He's right, you know," Zaffir said, strolling up with that casual swagger he never lost. He leaned down conspiratorially toward Jaxson, who was now hanging upside down in Ezra's arms. "You can just ask me. You know I can't say no to you."

His fiery red hair had softened into something more burnished now, a deeper copper threaded with strands of silver at the temples. His golden eyes, still as vivid as ever, had taken on a tender quality I didn't know I'd fallen in love with until long after we'd begun. Time had sanded away his sharp edges, but left behind the most brilliant shine.

"What your father is trying to say," Ezra added, shooting a faux-annoyed glance at Zaffir, "is that you can have ice cream when you finish cleaning your room."

"But Dada, no fair!" Jaxson pouted, dramatically flopping his head back.

"Yeah, Dada," Zaffir echoed with a matching pout. "No fair."

I snorted. "Dangerous duo," I muttered, just as Thorne dropped down beside me and Fenly promptly shifted into his lap like she belonged there, which, of course, she did.

Thorne wrapped his arms around her with practiced ease. His beard was fuller now, his strong build more weathered, but his presence, steady, grounding, and full of humor, was exactly the same. He wore time like he wore everything, with ease. Fenly curled into him like he was her personal fortress.

A soft hand settled on my shoulder and I turned to find Briar sinking down on my other side. She pressed her cheek against mine, her breath warm as she sighed. Her once dark brown hair was now streaked with glints of silver, and her eyes, still that endless brown, held decades of love in their depths. She was radiant in the way that only someone loved and loving can be. And somehow, I found myself more in love with them all now than I was even yesterday.

"Hey, Ma?" Fenly asked from Thorne's arms.

"Yeah, sweetie?" Briar responded, her voice low and melodic.

"Can you sing to us?"

I turned and smiled at her, my heart swelling. Thanks to Briar, music was as much a part of our home as laughter or breath. Our children had grown up in a house filled with melodies, songs at sunrise, lullabies at dusk. Just as Briar's father had sung to her, she now sang to them, passing that legacy on like a thread of light through all our lives.

Briar nodded and began to hum, the first few notes delicate and familiar. The kids leaned into us, and for a moment, there was only the music, the wind, and the feeling of family stitched together by time, memory, and love.

"I walk the path where the wild things grow,
Where the pine trees whisper and the rivers flow,
With each step, I feel the earth 'neath my feet,
In the woods, I find my heart's steady beat."

Briar's voice wrapped around us like sunlight filtered through leaves. That soft, familiar melody stirred something in my chest, the same way it had that night in the Wilds. The night she found me when I was bleeding and scared, and she sang this song as if it could hold us together. Maybe it had. Maybe it still did.

"In the woods I am, and the woods are me,
A part of the leaves and the sky so free.
The wind in my hair, the sun on my skin,
In the woods I'm where wild things begin."

I joined in, my voice instinctively finding hers. Years of 'singing lessons' with her, of harmonizing in kitchens and fields and bedrooms, of lullabies hummed in the quiet hush of bedtime, it had carved a rhythm into us. One that still beat strong.

Fenly's voice came next. Clear, innocent, and achingly sweet. She sang with her whole heart. I looked at her and saw everything we'd fought for, everything we nearly lost. Her brown eyes sparkled with the same fierce light I saw in myself. That same softness that came from strength.

"No walls to bind me, no roads to pave,
Just ancient roots and a soul to save."

Fenly nestled herself between Thorne's arms as she sang. He held her like she was made of something precious. He looked at her the way he used to look at me after a trial. With awe, and a little disbelief that we were still standing. He was the one who reminded me that joy was just as strong as armor. That hope wasn't naive, it was necessary. He taught me to laugh, when I wanted to cry.

"I dance with the shadows, I sing with the rain,

In the woods, I'm free from sorrow and pain."

I looked at Briar then, her voice still rising and falling like waves. Her hair had streaks of white now, her freckles deeper from years under open skies. And still, she was the most beautiful thing I'd ever seen. Every line on her face held our story. Every laugh, every fight, every kiss that reminded us that we had survived. She saved me when I didn't think I was worth saving. She taught me to fight for myself, not just for others.

"So let the world turn, let the seasons fly,
I'll stay where the mountains kiss the sky."

Ezra stepped closer, Jaxson bouncing in his arms, giggling as Ezra spun him gently. His salt-and-pepper hair was tousled, his posture still strong. He taught me that we were more than the labels placed on us. That I didn't have to be perfect to be loved. That who we were becoming was just as important as who we'd been.

For I walk the path where wild things grow,
And in the woods, I've found my soul."

Zaffir's gaze found mine, and for a moment, everything else faded. His golden eyes caught the light just right, still burning with that quiet fire I first saw the day we met. But now, there was something deeper behind them. Time. Trust. Truth. He taught me how to loosen my grip on certainty, how to surrender to the unknown without losing myself. How to evolve, to stay curious, to never settle for the world as it is just because it's familiar. With him, I learned that growth is not a destination, it's a choice you make every single day.

"With moss as my carpet and stars as my guide,
I walk with the moon always at my side."

We were older now. Time had wrapped itself around us slowly, like ivy creeping up old stone, softening the cracks without erasing them. The sharp edges we once carried, carved by fear, by control, by the constant, bone-deep need to survive, hadn't disappeared. They still existed in the quiet moments, in the shadows of our memories, in the way we sometimes star-tled at loud noises or held our breath at bad news. But they didn't cut like they used to.

Those edges had dulled with every year that passed, soft-ened by laughter, by healing, by love. But still, on some days, they flared. Old pain doesn't vanish. It waits. It pulses beneath the skin like a phantom limb, reminding us of who we were and how far we'd come. A sound, a smell, a moment too much like the past could bring it back. We carried our scars in invis-ible places. We always would.

And yet, we were not broken. Just weathered. Smoothed by time, bonded by shared history.

But the love between us? It only deepened. Rooted. Like the Wilds themselves. Built from a thousand moments, battles and belly laughs, late nights and long silences, grief and grace, holding on and letting go. And through it all, we remained. Still singing. Still choosing each other. Still standing.

I looked at each of them—my Wildguard. My loves. My life.

And I felt it, deep in my bones. *This* was what we bled for. *This* was what we built.

This was everything.

"No need for a map, no need to know—
I'm home in the place where the wild things grow."

www.ingramcontent.com/pod-product-compliance
Lightning Source LLC
Chambersburg PA
CBHW070639180626
46817CB00006B/2167